Loughshinny

Kathi —

Thank you so
much for the support.
It's appreciated
more than you know.
Enjoy!

M Nimes

LOUGHSHINNY

A Novel

Michael C. Nunes

iUniverse, Inc.
New York Lincoln Shanghai

Loughshinny

iUniverse books may be ordered through booksellers or by contacting:

iUniverse
2021 Pine Lake Road, Suite 100
Lincoln, NE 68512
www.iuniverse.com
1-800-Authors (1-800-288-4677)

Because of the dynamic nature of the Internet, any Web addresses or links contained in this book may have changed since publication and may no longer be valid.

This is a work of fiction. All of the characters, names, incidents, organizations, and dialogue in this novel are either the products of the author's imagination or are used fictitiously.

ISBN: 978-0-595-46796-9 (pbk)
ISBN: 978-0-595-91086-1 (ebk)

Printed in the United States of America

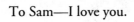

To Sam—I love you.

BOOK 1

CHAPTER 1

In North County Dublin, south of the town of Skerries, there lies a small fishing village named Loughshinny, and within that village there lived a man of twenty-two named Patrick Quinn. Patrick was a good and kind man who cared deeply for his God, his family, and his fellow man. This was a very special day for him, for it was the day he was to graduate from DCU, Dublin City University, with a Bachelor's Degree in Business Administration.

Patrick was very excited—more so than he had anticipated—as were his parents, Brian and Moira. They were very proud of him to say the least. He was the first in the family to go on to college, and to be graduating with honors only added to their pride.

Everyone in the entire Quinn and Meehan families was going to be at the commencement except Veronica Meehan, Moira's mother, who had died the previous February. Patrick had held out hope during that last year of her life, wishing that she would be here to celebrate this day with him, but sadly it was not to be. However, he knew that in a special sort of way her presence would be felt there anyhow.

The graduation was set to begin at one o'clock, which was two hours away. With the ride there taking approximately twenty-five minutes, they were left with only an hour and a half to get ready—not all that long in the Quinn household. Everyone, however, rose to the occasion, including Paul, Patrick's fourteen-year-old brother, and Sinead, his nine-year-old sister.

"Do I look all right?" Patrick asked, stepping from his room, dressed in his new graduation outfit: a pair of blue, pleated slacks, a white cotton dress shirt, and a solid crimson tie.

"All right? Why ya look better than all right, ya look wonderful! Doesn't he?" Moira said, smiling, as she looked to her husband.

"Ah, that he does," Brian confirmed proudly. "All the girls will be chasin' after ya."

Patrick stood only five foot seven, but handsome he was. He had jet-black hair cut short, an athletic build, and fine features that broke easily into a ready smile. He, in fact, resembled his father, while his two younger siblings had inherited their mother's red hair, fair skin, and freckles.

"Are ya sure?" he asked once again.

"Aye, of course, we're sure. And another thing I'm sure of is that if we don't get goin' pretty soon we're gonna be late," his mother returned hastily. With that said, the five soon loaded into their 1982 gold Renault and drove off. Upon arrival, they were greeted outside by the whole of their clan. Everyone wished Patrick luck as he hurried off to join his classmates. During the ceremony, he, along with fifty-two other students, received a special award for outstanding academic achievements.

When the graduation ended, all thirty-six of his family member headed back to the Quinn household, where most of the relatives hoped the real celebration would be; they were not disappointed, for Moira and Brian had planned this day for months. There were biscuits, sandwiches, and pates that Moira had labored preparing the night before, and pies and other desserts that every aunt and female cousin had contributed. Finally, of course, there was drink—and much of it— including quite a bit of fine Irish whisky.

"I'd like to make a toast," bellowed a large man who had just come from the kitchen and was now making his way to the middle of the living room. It was Moses Quinn, Brian's oldest brother and childhood mate, who had traveled the world over and who now owned a small chain of furniture stores located out of Skerries. He stood well over six-feet tall, had a long, flowing white beard, and did indeed greatly resemble his Biblical namesake. "Excuse me, people," he said once more, "I'd like to make a toast." Everyone quieted down.

"I toast to you, Paddy. We are all very proud of you.

> 'May your future be bright
> And your days filled with joy.
> And if ya marry and father
> A wee girl or wee boy,
>
> Always keep smilin'
> As ya are on this day.

Now let's hear it for Paddy,
Hip, hip, hurray!'"

With this, Moses animatedly raised his glass while everyone chuckled and followed suit.

No sooner was the toast completed, than from the back of the room a voice shouted, "That was pretty good, Moses, but I think I can better ya." The voice belonged to Patrick's cousin, Shane McCabe, from up north in Drogheda. "Are ya ready?" he asked.

"Sure, lad. Take your best shot."

"Okay, here I go: 'Here's a recommendation to you, Paddy,
for a happy, long life.
Make lots of money,
And never, ever get yourself a wife!'"

Now even more laughter permeated the dwelling, especially from the male contingent.

"I didn't find that particularly amusing," Maggie, Shane's wife, said with a glare. "I guess we all know where you'll be sleeping tonight." Once again, everyone burst into laughter—everyone, that is, except Shane, who for the rest of the party could continually be heard whispering that it had only been a joke.

Patrick soon began making the rounds, talking with all his relatives and thanking them for coming.

"So, Patrick, have ya decided where you're going to look for work yet?" his aunt Catherine asked from her seat on the couch as she sipped at her tea. Catherine was one of Moira's younger sisters and Patrick's favorite aunt. He loved her because she was kind and gentle and reminded him of his grandmother, both in appearance and habit. While his mother was boisterous and at times rather opinionated, Katie, as she was known to everyone, was quiet and reserved, also like his grandmother.

"Not yet, Katie," he answered.

Moses, who was close by at the time, came over. "I hear there's lots of work out west, around Mayo and Sligo," he said. "I've got some friends out in that part of the country. I could talk with a couple of them if ya'd like. One owns an office furniture supply company. Pidgeon's his name. He's a fine bloke."

"What?" Patrick simpered. "Pidgeon?"

"Yeah, Harold Pidgeon. He's a Brit, but I don't hold that against him," Moses said, chuckling. "We did a lot of traveling together back in the sixties, and besides he owes me a favor or two. Plus, I'm also friends with a chap out in Galway who owns a large hotel there, and he's thinkin' about possibly opening a second. I'm sure he could always use a young business wiz to help him out."

"Thanks, Moses, but I'm not a wiz."

"Maybe not yet," Moses retorted. "Boy, you're too modest. Ya have to learn to accept some praise when it comes your way because, God knows, it doesn't come often."

"We kind of hoped he would look for work in Dublin or, at least, the vicinity. There's gotta be tons of jobs around," Moira said, walking over with Brian.

"Yeah, it's up to him wherever he wants to work. And we'll be behind him whatever his choice, but we would like to see ya remain close," Brian seconded as he looked at his son and smiled. "Have ya given it much thought yet?"

"Much thought yet?" Moses grumbled. "He's been goin' to school for the past four years. For Christ's sake, the lad's got his degree. I would hope by now he'd have at least some idea of where he'd like to work. Isn't that right, Paddy? Come on, lad, speak up and tell us what's on your mind."

This was exactly what Patrick had feared would happen. He was cornered, with no way of escape. He thought for a moment, and then decided to go ahead and say what he had secretly been planning for the past two years. "Well, I have been thinkin' about it quite a bit, Da, and ya know … it's not as though Ireland's the job capital of the world." Finally, he had gotten the idea out of his head and into the arena. Now whatever happened, happened. All conversation in the immediate area ceased. All eyes and ears were focused on him, and he was nervous as hell. Nevertheless, he composed himself and continued. "The thought crossed my mind about possibly looking for work outside the country."

"Ah, I knew this was gonna happen!" Moira cried.

"And where, pray tell, are you plannin' on goin'?" Moses demanded.

"Please God, don't let him say England! No son of mine is gonna work in England."

"Well, I was thinking about possibly goin' to the States, and Boston in particular."

"The States? And Boston in particular? Ya don't even know anyone there."

"That's not true, Ma. I've got two friends that live in Boston."

"What two friends? I've never heard ya mention anything about friends living in Boston."

"Yeah, well, maybe I haven't. I don't know. But they're over there living and working, and that's the truth. And they're having one hell of a good time too."

"So, who are they?"

"Ya don't know 'em, Ma. They're just a couple of lads that I went to school with, Kevin and Phil. They graduated last year."

"Kevin and Phil who?"

"Kevin Flynn and Phil Doyle."

"Where are they from?"

"Uh, Jesus, Ma!" Patrick groaned. "Kevin's from Lusk and Phil's from Balbriggan."

"Ah, feck off!" Moses growled. "Don't ever say the word 'Balbriggan' around me. Damn near almost lost me life there once. Got mugged by a couple of hooligans, and one of them cracked me over the head with God-knows-what. The bastards stole fifty quid from me when I was out cold."

"Well, Phil's not like that, Moses. And besides, I've been corresponding with them regularly for the past year, and they say the opportunities over there are unreal. That I'd practically be guaranteed a job in the first week, and a good-paying one at that. I mean, it's worth a shot. Besides, I don't want to be confined to Ireland my entire life. It would only be for a short time anyway, maybe a year or two. Ya know, just to get some experience. And then I can come back here and get a really good job. Besides, I really do want to see America."

"Confined to Ireland?" Brian repeated. "Ireland's a fine country, Paddy. It's the land you were born and reared in. Ya shouldn't turn your back on her like this, ya know. You ever think that maybe that's the reason it's not the job capital of the world. Too many bright, young minds leave her because the salaries aren't as high as they are in some other countries. But we're moving in the right direction. I can see it. I mean, look at all the computer and technology firms that are …"

"But I don't have my degree in computers or technology, Da. It's in business."

"Well, what do ya think all those companies are. They're businesses, aren't they? And there's tons of 'em too. Yes, we're definitely movin' in the right direction. You just have to give it a little time, that's all. And besides, son, remember—money's not the only thing in the world."

"It's a ridiculous idea, Patrick. And I'm ashamed of you for even thinking it. Leave Ireland and go to America. Now I've heard it all!" Moses added in disgust.

Since the onslaught began, Catherine had remained silent, but she now felt it time to speak in her nephew's behalf. "No, now *I've* heard it all!" she professed with authority, catching everyone by surprise. "Ridiculous? Ridiculous by whose standards? By yours, Moira? Or by yours, Moses? Why, it sounds like a grand idea to me. Let the boy follow his heart, wherever it may lead him, even if it is to Boston. Besides, Boston's supposed to be a lovely city, and everyone in this room knows it as well as I do, even if ya don't want to admit it."

"Not you too," Moira exclaimed, her face wearing a sickened expression. "And what if he doesn't find work? And what if it ain't as lovely as you've heard and he gets hurt or even killed, huh? No, Patrick, I don't think it's a good idea."

"You're goddamn right it's not! Listen to what I say, lad, and listen good." Moses was vehement. "This is the land of your ancestors and your family and your friends. Leave it and you're leavin' your very self."

"Well, if it's so important to you that he stays, why don't ya just offer him a job at one of your stores then," Catherine said.

"I will. You're goddamn right I will! I'm planning on opening a new one in Kinsale soon, probably in the next six months. I'll make you the store's manager. I'll pay ya well too. Better than you'll get over there, I can guarantee ya that."

"Thanks, Moses, but I really do wanna go, if only for a short time. Just to see what it's like, ya know."

"Well, I've been, and I can tell you what it's like."

"Thanks, but … I've been thinkin' about it for a long time now and my mind's pretty well made up. I've even had my passport made."

By this time, Patrick's entire family was gathered around him, and each member was either a study in sadness or envy. An uncomfortable silence enveloped the room before Brian finally said, "We'll talk about this later, all right?"

"Yeah, all right, Da."

"Now come on, this is supposed to be a celebration. Let's all enjoy ourselves," Brian proclaimed, forcing a smile. The party soon resumed but with considerably less festivity. After about two hours, the relatives slowly began to trickle out. Upon leaving, each congratulated Patrick, but each also told him to weigh his decision carefully. When everyone was finally gone, Patrick went back into the living room and looked at both of his parents as they sat silently on the couch. They were so deep in thought that they didn't even hear him walk in.

"I just wanna thank you guys for everything. I really enjoyed the party."

Upon hearing this, Moira looked up at her child and though despondent smiled genuinely and said, "Congratulations on your big day, Paddy. I'm very proud of you. We both are."

"Thanks, Ma. I appreciate it." He then paused for a moment. "All right, well, um … I'm pretty tired. I guess I'm gonna get goin' to bed."

"Yeah, okay, son. Goodnight," Brian answered, also smiling.

"Goodnight."

Patrick headed up the stairs to his room, and when she heard the door shut Moira lowered her head onto Brian's shoulder and began to cry softly. "My little boy wants to go to another country."

"He's not a little boy anymore, Moira. He's a man now."

"He's still my little boy. I'm afraid, Brian. What are we gonna do?"

"What can we do? He's got it in his heart. We have to let him go and be behind him all the way, or else he'll never forgive us. Besides, Boston is supposed to be a nice town."

"I know, but I'm still gonna be afraid."

"And I too! But every person has to experience and learn for themselves, or else they'll never grow. And like he said, it isn't gonna be permanent. Just for a short time, to get some experience."

"Can't he get experience here?"

"I think his mind's pretty well set, Moira. He's a smart lad. He knows what he's doin'. Now come on, stop it, will ya. You're gonna make yourself sick worrying like this. Come on, let's go to bed."

She sighed. "All right." The two rose and ascended the stairs. It had been a long, emotional day, and both were exhausted.

CHAPTER 2

▼

The following morning Patrick awoke early but stayed in bed contemplating things. He wondered if Moses was right about it being a ridiculous idea. Moreover, he thought about what his father had said about turning his back on his country, and about how money wasn't the only value in life. Personally, he didn't feel as though he was denying his heritage; he just wanted to see America. As for the money aspect, that had absolutely no bearing on his decision. No, he just wanted the opportunity to land a decent-paying position with a good company, and as far as he was concerned, there just weren't too many of those in Ireland.

Mainly, however, he kept thinking about his mother, and how she would probably be constantly worrying about him. He loved her more than anything, but as of late she had been driving him to distraction with her crying and mood swings. Nevertheless, he understood her reactions and tried to be as sympathetic as possible. It had been a very trying year for her: she had lost her mother whom she loved deeply, she was going through menopause, and to top it all off, she had just recently been diagnosed with type 2 diabetes.

Patrick was deep in thought, when he suddenly heard footsteps crashing down the stairs. It was Sinead and Paul. They shared a bedroom, and, being the early riser that she was, Sinead would always jump on top of her brother to wake him. It was a product of her nature combined with her age. Paul never took too kindly to this, though, and the steady thundering of footsteps now heard resolutely throughout the house was a telltale sign to all that Paul was on a mission to pummel her. Everyone including Patrick rushed to her assistance.

"I'm gonna kill ya, you slapper. You're dead!" Paul shouted with fury as he pursued the girl frantically around the dining room table.

"Help!" she screamed, trying to evade her brother's lunges, but, alas, it was no use. He had just pounced on her when Brian luckily came upon the scene.

"Now stop it, both of you! And behave yourselves. And Paul, don't ever let me hear you call your sister a slapper ever again. Ya hear? She's just messin'. But you, you're older, and you know better. Try acting your age once in a while, will ya?"

"Ah, Dad, why do you always take her side, huh? She's the instigator. I'm just mindin' me own business, dreamin' away, and then she always has to jump on me. Now is that right?"

Brian placed his hand on his son's shoulder and looked him straight in the eyes. "Listen," he said, "you're almost a man now. Don't let trivial things like that bother ya. You should be protecting and watching out for her, not beatin' her to a pulp."

Paul thought for a second and agreed.

In the meantime, Moira had begun breakfast. As the bacon sizzled in the frying pan, everyone converged at the table. At first, no one spoke. Brian finally broke the silence. "So, Patrick, tell us. When do you plan on goin' to the States?"

Patrick looked up, nonplussed.

"Yes, there'll be much work to do to get you ready," Moira added.

Patrick couldn't believe what he was hearing. One minute they were pleading with him not to go, and now they were helping him chart his course. "Why the sudden change of heart?" he asked.

"Listen, son—if this is what you want, then we're behind ya 100%," Brian replied.

"Really?"

His mother sighed. "Yes, really. I guess we are. I don't know. Ya just have to promise us something, that's all."

"Anything," he conceded with haste.

"Jus' promise us that you'll look after yourself and call home often, all right? That's all we're askin'."

"I promise. I will."

"Yeah, I love ya, bro. And I'll miss ya. But Christ, finally I'll have me own room!" Paul interjected, causing everyone to laugh.

"You'll have your own room until Patrick comes home," Moira corrected as she looked at her eldest son with pride.

"Yeah, don't get too comfortable."

"Where's Paddy goin'?" asked Sinead, who by now appeared somewhat confused.

"Your brother's goin' to work for awhile in the United States," Brian answered.

Sinead, upon hearing this, began crying and said that she didn't want for him to leave. However, she finally accepted the idea when Patrick promised that he would send her back a big present.

The next couple of months were extremely busy ones for Patrick and his entire family. On the day his parents gave him their approval, it was Saturday, October 27, and he planned on leaving for the States sometime during the upcoming spring. In the interim, he had to call Kevin and Phil to let them know that, yes, he was indeed coming. He also had to apply for and receive his green card, and other pertinent documents needed for an extended stay in the United States. Finally, he purchased his plane ticket through Aer Lingus.

On hearing the price of the airfare, Moses offered to pay half, and, even though Patrick and his parents graciously declined, Moses' stubbornness prevailed. Ultimately, he ended up paying for the entire fare, which wasn't at all necessary since Patrick had worked his weekends for the past five years at a nearby farm in Rush and had managed to save a little over two thousand pounds. In the end, though, Moses always seemed to get his way somehow.

The month before Patrick left, there were many parties held for him. There was the one thrown by all the lads at his cousin Jimmy's house. Another, with all his relatives, took place at the posh Windmill restaurant in Skerries. And yet a third and more intimate one was reserved for his immediate family, along with Catherine and Moses, on the eve of his departure.

The anticipated day, June 20, finally dawned. Everyone, including Moses and Catherine, packed into the Renault for the ride to Dublin International Airport. Patrick was scheduled for an 11:57 a.m. departure. He would fly into Shannon and be held over until one-thirty that afternoon, at which time he would board a second plane that would touch down in Boston's Logan Airport five hours later and transport him from a land of myth and legend to one of reality, where a man's dreams could be realized through determination and hard work. Or so he thought.

They arrived at the Aer Lingus terminal shortly after ten. Everyone was emotional. Moses, characteristically, broke the silence. "Come here, lad, and give your ol' uncle a hug." Patrick obeyed enthusiastically.

Sinead, by this time, was sobbing uncontrollably. "Now come on, don't cry. Remember what we agreed upon?" Patrick said, kneeling down beside her. "Remember, you promised you were going to be a big girl, and I promised I was gonna send ya home something grand."

After a few moments she controlled her blubbering. "Make sure you don't forget, okay?" she whimpered, causing everyone to smile.

"I promise. I won't," Patrick whispered as he got to his feet and kissed the top of her head. Then, looking in his brother's direction, he smirked. "And you, ya punk. Stop beatin' the shite out of her, ya hear?"

"Yes, sir," Paul said mockingly, walking over. However, the hug he gave him was anything but mocking. It was sincere and heart wrenching and caused a sort of emotional chain reaction that filtered through the rest of the family members as they said their goodbyes.

Saddest of all was Moira's, whose face trembled as she tried to contain her tears—but it was all in vain. They came streaming down as she grabbed her child in her arms. "Oh, I'm gonna miss you so much!"

"Come on, Ma. Don't cry," Patrick pleaded. "I'll be all right. I'll call ya as soon as I land. I promise."

"You'd better."

"I will. I promise."

"Boarding is now beginning for Flight 137 to Shannon," a monotone voice announced over the intercom.

"You'd better get goin'." Brian nodded as he came up and placed his hand on his wife's shoulder.

Patrick grabbed his luggage and hurried through customs. When he was about one hundred yards away and on the verge of vanishing from sight down the long, steel corridor, he turned and waved one last time. Everyone waved back. Contented, Patrick proceeded to board his flight and to begin a new and what he hoped would be a truly memorable time in his promising, young life.

CHAPTER 3

▼

The trip across the Atlantic was a smooth one, and Patrick touched down in Logan at exactly one-thirty. As he exited the plane and entered the terminal, a feeling of ambivalence unexpectedly came upon him. He was very excited, on the one hand, but at the same time, very nervous.

What the hell am I doing? he thought as he went to collect his luggage. Upon arrival, he maneuvered his way through the mass of people and soon stood but a foot away from the conveyor belt that somewhere held his baggage. It took close to twenty minutes for the luggage to start coming around, and when Patrick finally spotted his second piece, he hurried over and scooped it up.

With that task out of the way, he now began looking around for his friends. In fact, the entire time he had been waiting for his suitcases to appear, he would, at intervals, look up and try to see if he could catch sight of them, but never with any luck. As he trudged through the terminal in search of them, he soon grew weary and took a seat. *They said they'd be here at half-past. Where the feck are they?* he grumbled to himself. About fifteen minutes passed, with still no sign of them, when from his left side a voice suddenly said, "Hello." Patrick responded by returning the sentiment to an elderly woman who was now sitting beside him.

"Oh, you're Irish. How pleasant! I'm Irish also. And I've still got my brogue after all these years," the woman chortled. "So, what part of the country are ya from? No, no, let me guess. Dublin, right?"

"Yeah, well, sort of," Patrick replied somewhat hesitantly. "I'm from Loughshinny. It's a small village outside of Skerries."

"Oh, yes—Skerries. I was there many years ago when I was a wee girl. It's a very beautiful place, isn't it?"

"Yeah, Skerries is lovely, all right."

"I myself was born in County Carlow. Carlow Town, to be precise. Don't remember it much now, though. I came to Boston with my family when I was thirteen. My father brought us over in search of the great "American Dream" but didn't have much luck in findin' it. Mind you, it was during the Depression. It was a bad time for everyone. He bounced around from job to job until he finally landed a decent-paying one with the Post Office," the old woman said, her mind beginning to drift. She sat silent for a few moments before saying, "How rude of me. My name's Bridget Murphy. And what's yours, if you don't mind me askin'?"

"No, I don't mind. It's Patrick, Patrick Quinn."

"Nice to meet you, Patrick," the old woman replied, smiling. By this time, he was wondering two things: why in the hell she initiated the conversation in the first place. And, secondly, when were his two friends going to come and rescue him from it.

"So, is there any particular reason you've come to Boston? Or are ya just doing a bit of travelin'?"

"No, I've come here to work."

"Good luck in findin' it!" she exclaimed. "Nah, I shouldn't say that. There are a lot of jobs here, I guess. But just not too many good ones, unless, that is, you're college educated. Are you?"

"Aye, I am. I have a degree in business from DCU."

"DCU? What's that?"

"Dublin City University. It's a newer school. The name's newer anyway. It used to be the NIHE."

"The NIHE?"

"Yeah, the National Institute of Higher Education."

"Sorry, but I've never heard of it before. Is it any good?"

"Why, yes. It has a very good reputation," Patrick replied defensively, which somewhat surprised him, since he was not a defensive person. "Besides, my two friends, Kevin and Phil, the two lads that I'm gonna be staying with, came over last year, and they both found good jobs, so I'm really not too worried. I just have to put enough applications out there, that's all. And hopefully, one will get me what I'm lookin' for."

"Well, I hope you get your wish, young man."

"Yeah, me too," Patrick chuckled. "Besides, I'm not too finicky. I'll take any decent offer I get. I just wanted to come over and get some experience, that's all. I'm not plannin' on relocating permanently."

"That's exactly what my father said many years ago," the old woman replied despondently.

"Well, these are different times, ma'am. When your family came over, it was probably on a ship or a freighter, right?"

"That's correct."

"Well, nowadays we fly. It's relatively cheap and takes absolutely no time whatsoever. What took you probably a week, if not longer, took me only five hours. And if for some reason I do happen to run into a bit of bad luck, it wouldn't be some great odyssey to get back home. Besides, I'm a very optimistic person, and, like I said, I'm not gonna be too picky. I just wanna work hard and try to save as much money as I possibly can for when I go back. It's not like I wanna be rich or anything."

"Then you're a goddamn fool!" a voice unexpectedly cried from behind. It was Phil. He and Kevin had arrived a few minutes earlier but had remained silent, just listening to the conversation.

Patrick immediately recognized the voice and jumped to his feet.

"Ya bastard!" Phil said, beaming, as he came up and shook his friend's hand. "How the hell ya doin'?"

"Good, thanks!" Patrick exclaimed, looking up. Phil was a tall, lanky man of six-two, with dirty-blond hair, cut short, dark, piercing eyes, and a slight under bite. Over all, though, he was a very good-looking man, and a fun bloke to be around because of his personality. At one moment he could be serious, and the next, the world's biggest joker. He was highly intelligent, a fact he was well aware of, and a great debater; and because of these attributes, could outwit most men in conversation, just as the great Voltaire once could. It was also because of these qualities that Patrick and he had almost come to fisticuffs during Patrick's freshman year over some long-forgotten topic. Throughout the years, however, the two of them had grown quite fond of one another and had become rather good friends.

"Hey, lad, good to see ya," Kevin said excitedly, by this time also shaking hands with Patrick. Kevin was Phil's exact opposite: short—standing only five-foot-four—and kind of on the husky side, with bright orange hair and hundreds of freckles. He was always cheery and despised any type of verbal confrontation. However, if any disagreement ever did come to fists—beware!—for he was strong and rugged from all the years spent laboring on his parents' farm. It was actually his idea in the first place that Phil and he, and the following year, Patrick, all move to Boston. His main reason for wanting to come was to get away from the humdrum daily existence of farm life. Of the two men, Patrick was most fond of Kevin, for he was truly a nice person. And because of this, he was even happier to see him.

"Thanks, it's good to see you too."

"Well, then, with all of that crap thankfully out of the way, I'd say we best be goin'. Come on, lads," Phil said jokingly as he threw his arms around the necks of both men. Patrick picked up his bags, and the three men started walking away, when he suddenly remembered the old woman. Turning back around, he asked, "Is it Miss or Mrs.?"

"It's Miss."

"Well, then, Miss Murphy, it's been a pleasure talkin' with ya. You take care of yourself, all right."

"Aye. And you also," she replied. "May God bless you, young man, and I hope things work out well for you."

"Thanks," Patrick returned with a smile as he and his two companions turned and started off once more. When they were about thirty yards away, and out of hearing distance, Phil asked, "Who the feck was that?"

"Just some old lady."

"How the hell'd ya meet her?"

"I don't know. I was just sittin' there waiting for you guys and she just started talkin' to me."

"Christ," Kevin muttered, "and she never stopped, did she?"

"You're tellin' me!"

The three men began laughing as they exited the Aer Lingus terminal and were just about to hail a taxi, when Patrick suddenly remembered the promise he had made to his mother. "Hey, lads, hold up for a second, all right? I have to call home just to let the family know that I've arrived safely."

"From here?" Phil asked incredulously. "Whadya mad? It'll cost you a fortune! Just wait and call from the house."

"No, I gave me word that I'd call as soon as I landed. Don't worry. It'll only take a second."

"All right, fine."

They walked to the nearest payphone. After placing his luggage on the ground, Patrick pulled his Telecom Eireann calling card from his wallet and punched in the numbers, but soon learned, that for whatever reason, it wasn't working.

"Bollox!" he growled in frustration.

"Relax, will ya," Kevin said, chuckling, as he went into his pocket and came out with a handful of change. "This should be enough."

"Thanks, Kev. I'll pay ya back, I promise."

"Ah, don't worry about it."

"Feck off, Kevin! Don't make me feel like a pauper. I told ya I'll pay you back, and that's what I'll do."

"All right, fine! Don't get all in a tizzy over it, for Christ's sake! If ya wanna pay me back, that's fine with me. But just to let you know beforehand, I charge interest, 10% to be exact."

"Jesus—ten percent? I guess I should've just kept my mouth shut, huh?"

"Aye, ya should've. But you wouldn't be you if ya did."

After dropping in quarter after quarter, the phone finally began to ring. However, instead of a second, the call turned into a ten minute ordeal in which both men had to get on the line, introduce themselves, and reassure Moira that everything was going to be fine. And it would have gone on even longer had Brian not told her to stop her fussing and leave them be. Patrick promised that he'd phone again soon, but before ending the call, Moira requested that both Kevin and Phil be put on the line once more, so she could give them each her blessing.

"Christ, I'm sorry about that. I didn't think that was gonna happen."

"Ah, don't worry about it. Our folks acted the same way when we came over," Kevin answered. "It's nothin'."

"Nothin' maybe to you, but it embarrassed the hell out of me!"

"Listen, Patrick. Ya should've seen my folks. They were whimpering like babies, even my dad, and he's a bruiser."

After apologizing once more, Patrick hailed a taxi, and the three men headed to W. Fourth Street in South Boston.

CHAPTER 4

▼

Amid a host of wisecracks and cheers, the taxi suddenly began to slow. It came to a complete stop in front of a white, dilapidated two-story house. As Phil and Patrick got out the left passenger's side door, Kevin stuck a ten-dollar bill through the opening in the partitioned plexi-glass divider, and told the driver to keep the remaining $1.40 for his tip.

"It's not much, but we call it home, at least for now, anyways," Kevin said.

"Ah, I'm sure it's not that bad."

"But it is!" Phil exclaimed. "Wait till ya see the inside! But the rent's dead cheap and the neighbors are all pretty sound, so I guess that makes up for it in a way. Plus, there's even a house up the street where five girls from Tipperary live. They're cool. They come over all the time and party with us."

"Oh, really?"

"Yeah, you'll meet 'em soon enough. They're always over," Kevin acknowledged as they walked up the front steps.

Upon entering the house, Patrick could see right away that Phil wasn't exaggerating: the paper was peeling from the walls, the paint was of a nauseating shade of aqua, and the ceiling was stained from what appeared to be years of tobacco smoke.

Patrick's jaw dropped.

"See, I told you it was crap."

"But it's clean, and that's the main thing," Kevin affirmed. "Now come on, let's sit down." He and Patrick walked over and took a seat on a large orange sofa, while Phil plopped down on a bright pink chaise.

"Well, at least the colors are coordinated," Patrick said jokingly, which caused the three to begin laughing. They talked about old times for a while, until Phil finally asked, "Hey, whadya say about goin' into town tonight and havin' some fun?"

"Nah, not tonight," Patrick answered, "I'm too tired."

"Well at least let's go up the street for a pint. There's this really cool pub called the Blackthorn. It's almost like the ones back home. Come on, you'll enjoy it."

"Nah, I don't feel like it, Phil. I told ya, I'm dead tired."

"Come on, just for one pint! I'll introduce ya to all the lads."

"Quit buggin' him, Phil! He said no! The lad just flew over three thousand miles. He's exhausted," Kevin interjected on his friend's behalf. "Oh, I remember when we came over, you slept for nearly two days straight. Ya didn't even get your arse out of bed! Remember?"

"Yeah, yeah, all right! I remember."

"Just let me get a good night's sleep, and I promise, tomorrow I'll go into the city centre with ya."

"They don't call it the city centre over here. Ya jus' say 'downtown'."

"All right then … tomorrow I'll go downtown with ya!"

"All right, fine. I give ya me permission to stay here tonight. But tomorrow … be ready for some real excitement. I've got a full day planned."

"Like what?"

"I'm not gonna tell ya! If I did then it wouldn't be a surprise, now would it? No, you'll just have to wait and see. But at this moment I'm feeling rather dry, so I think I'm gonna go have meself a few. Do you wanna come, Kev?"

"Nice host you are!" Kevin shot back, amazed that Phil wouldn't stay at home this evening and help their friend get situated. "No, I don't wanna go!"

"You don't mind, do ya, Paddy?" Phil asked as he edged his way toward the door.

"No, of course not. Go enjoy yourself. Like I said, I'm tired. I'll probably be sleeping soon, anyways."

"Well, if that's the case, then I hear the pub callin' me name. Get a good night's sleep, lad, so you'll be well rested and ready for tomorrow. I mean that. And that goes for you, too," Phil said, smirking in Kevin's direction, as he turned and headed out.

"The bastard!"

"Ah, don't worry about it," Patrick said. He then paused for a moment. "Hey, um … by the way, what does he have planned for tomorrow?"

"I don't have the slightest clue!"

The two men talked for another twenty minutes or so until Patrick finally let out a big yawn. "Jesus, I'm tired. You don't mind if I get goin' to bed now, do ya?"

"No, of course not. Why would I mind? Believe me, I know how you feel," Kevin admitted, getting to his feet. "Come on, I'll show ya your room." After picking up both of Patrick's suitcases, he then led him up the stairs to a room at the far left end of the hallway.

"Well, here it is. The sheets are clean, just washed them myself yesterday. The bathroom's just to your right. Um … I guess that's basically about it. If ya need anything else, just let me know, all right?"

"Yeah, all right, Kev. Thanks"

"Well, I guess I'll get out of here and let you get goin'." Kevin smiled as he turned and walked out into the hallway. He stood there for a second, motionless, before saying, "Just to let you know, Paddy, I'm really happy you're here."

"Me, too."

"Okay, well—goodnight."

"Goodnight."

Now alone, Patrick turned around and liked what he saw. Sure, it was small, but compared to the rest of the house, or at least the parts he had seen so far, it was nice. There was a twin-size maple cannonball bed jutting out from the west wall and adjacent to it, a small maple dresser. Directly in front of the east window, the only window in the room, was a flimsy-looking table and chair set. And on the floor, nearly covering its entirety, was a brand new white rug (with price tag still attached). Overall, he was very impressed.

After closing the door and examining his new room a little more closely, Patrick collapsed onto his bed and began staring at the ceiling, thinking about the eventful day. Yes, it had surely been exciting. Soon, exhaustion overtook him and he fell into a deep sleep.

CHAPTER 5

▼

A bright ray of sunlight filtered through the windowpane and Patrick slowly began to awaken. He lay there for a moment, disoriented, staring at the strange wall, until he finally remembered where he was. Then, looking over at his alarm clock, saw that it was 2:10 in the afternoon.

"Ah, bollox!" he grumbled, throwing off his sheet. He walked over and picked it up but soon found that it wasn't ticking. For all the trouble Kevin had gone through to make him feel at home, the least he could have done was wind the damn clock! Relieved, he dressed and then headed to the bathroom.

While he was washing his hands, he suddenly heard a loud bang, followed by what sounded to be yelling. He quickly finished what he was doing and made his way downstairs. Upon arriving in the kitchen, Patrick learned two things. First, it was only 7:52 in the morning. And secondly, the origin of the noise: for there on the floor was a large iron skillet, and all around it lay six fried, or more correctly stated, six mangled eggs.

"Good morning," Patrick said, yawning. Startled, both men spun around and saw their friend standing in the doorway, rubbing his eyes. "Good morning," they replied, then immediately resumed their argument.

"Butter fingers! That's what you are!" Kevin barked, shaking his head in disgust.

"Hey, I said I was sorry, didn't I? It was an accident!" Phil conceded from his knees as he began sopping up the eggs with a large handful of paper towels.

"Accident my arse! I saw ya over there flingin' 'em around like you were Julia Child or something, so don't lie! Now we don't have a goddamn thing to eat. I hope you're happy?"

"Overjoyed!"

"Aaahh, just sit down, you, and drink your goddamn tea!" Kevin growled, and then looking in Patrick's direction, asked him how he wanted his.

"No, thanks. I'm grand."

"Ya sure?"

"Positive. Well, ya know what, on second thought, I could go for some juice if ya have any."

"How's orange?"

"Yeah, that's fine."

"All right." After pouring the juice and handing it to Patrick, Kevin sat down and began looking through the morning's edition of the *Boston Globe*.

As he sat there, quietly sipping at his juice, a thought crept into Patrick's head. Actually, the idea had come upon him the previous day but he was reluctant to express it. Very casually, he picked up the classifieds. "I wonder if there's any good job openings in the paper today."

"Yeah, I wonder," Kevin reiterated, catching him by surprise. He looked over but Kevin just sat there, glaring intently at whatever story he was now reading.

A few uncomfortable minutes passed in silence before Patrick asked, "So, by the way, where are you guys workin' now?" It wasn't as subtle as he had hoped, but it would have to do.

Kevin began to laugh. "Why don't you tell him, Phil," he said, finally looking up.

"Currently, I'm unemployed. I was a sales clerk at Macy's, but I got canned about a month ago. It was a grand job. I really enjoyed it, and I never had any problems until that day," Phil stated solemnly as he began to retell the story. "I was working in the men's clothing department and I saw this older woman lookin' around, so I went over and asked her if she needed any help. Well, she was a Brit, and when she realized I was Irish, she just freaked. She started sayin' how the Irish are all bastards, and how her son was killed a few years before in some IRA bombing or something. Well, I told her, ya know, that I was sorry for her loss and that I didn't agree with the IRA's tactics, but *no*, that didn't matter to her! She kept on sayin' how we're all scum, not fit to live, the whole lot of us. Then she even began hittin' me with her purse! Well, by that time I just lost it. I told her that the English had brought it on themselves, and that she was in the wrong town if she didn't like Irish. Well, that just added to her fire, and let me tell ya … the bitch had fire! Then she told me to go to hell, so I responded by saying, 'well, ma'm, I wasn't plannin' on goin' to England anytime soon.' Well, that was the straw that broke the camel's back. She started goin' ballistic on me, screaming this and that. Christ, she was embarrassing the hell out of me. So I just flat out told her to feck off. Well, I turn around, and sure enough, there's the store's manager. She fired me right on the spot and then went over and tried calming the woman," Phil recalled glumly, shifting in his seat, and then paused for a moment before looking at Kevin and saying, "Hey, I'm sorry her son was killed. Believe me, I really am. But I wasn't gonna just stand around and take all that punishment, and for something that I didn't even do."

Kevin put his head down.

"Well, I haven't worked since that day. I have been looking, though, believe me. But luck," he chuckled, "she hasn't been on me side. I did get an offer last week from the Burger King up the street, and I almost took it, but I thought to myself, ya know, for God's sake, I went to college for four years. I'm not gonna work for minimum wage flippin' hamburgers."

"Well, at least flippin' hamburgers would help pay the rent and put some food in the freezer," Kevin murmured.

Phil didn't answer.

"Christ, I'm sorry. I didn't know," Patrick said, leaning back in his chair, taking in everything that was now being said. Well, that would explain why Kevin hadn't been his typical, happy-go-lucky self since his arrival.

No words were exchanged for a good five minutes until Kevin finally said, "I'm workin' at one of the Sovereign Banks downtown as a teller. It's a good job, and the money's decent, but not good enough to pay rent, buy food, and live off of without any help, and for so long a time. Christ, the way things are goin' now, I get my check and it's gone right away. I've even started dippin' into the emergency money my parents gave me."

"Yeah, I know ya have, Kev, and I'm sorry. I swear to God, when I find work, I'll pay ya back, every red cent."

Kevin didn't respond.

After yet another long silence, Patrick asked, "Hey, Phil. What did ya mean last night when ya said to be ready for some real excitement?" But before Phil could answer, there was a loud knock on the door which startled the three of them.

"Come in, it's open!" Phil shouted. The door immediately flew back and in walked the most beautiful creature Patrick had ever laid his eyes upon. It was Tara O'Malley, one of the Tipperary five. She stood about five foot four and had long, wavy black hair, porcelain white skin, green piercing eyes, and a glorious full figure.

"So, is this the one you've been ramblin' about for the past couple of months?" she inquired, taking a seat directly across from Patrick.

"Aye, it is," Phil answered. "Tara, I'd like for you to meet our good friend, Patrick Quinn."

"Nice to meet you, Patrick Quinn," the young woman said, smirking, as she extended her hand.

"Right, um, it's … it's nice to meet you, too," Patrick uttered, just barely, as he shook her hand. The three of them began laughing, for it was quite evident the cause of Patrick's sudden, almost comical behavior.

"Can he speak in complete sentences?"

"I think so? Can't ya, Patrick?" Phil gibed, on the verge of exploding into laughter once again. Patrick tried to compose himself but to no avail. Some unseen force had taken control of his brain, and it just wasn't working properly. "Yes, um … yes I can."

"Well, I guess that answers that question!" she chuckled.

Patrick put his head down in embarrassment.

"Well, I've gotta get goin'. I just came over to see him … and I'm glad I did," Tara said as she got to her feet, causing Patrick to blush. As she was heading out the door, she stopped abruptly and, looking back at Phil, asked, "Is it still on for tonight?"

"Of course it is."

"Then we'll see you later. And to you, Patrick Quinn—goodbye. It was nice meeting you."

"Yeah, bye, Tara. It was nice … it was nice meetin' you, also," Patrick replied, but she was already gone.

"A little tongue-tied, aren't we?" Phil asked jokingly.

"Ah, leave him be," Kevin said, coming to his friend's defense.

"Oh, Jesus! What the hell just happened?" Patrick cried. "I mean, I'm no Casanova, I know that. But I thought I was relatively sound with the ladies. Christ, I must've looked like a complete arse. Did I?"

"Yeah, ya did, sort of," Phil acknowledged, ever honest.

"Ugh! Now she's gonna think I'm an ejit."

"A gobshite's more like it."

"Ah, don't worry about it. The way it looked to me was that she was into ya," Kevin said, picking up his newspaper once more.

"Really? You think so?"

"I just said I did, didn't I?"

"Yeah, now come to think of it, I saw it, too. Paddy's got a girlfriend," Phil said tauntingly. "Paddy's got a girlfriend."

"Ah, leave it alone, you!" Patrick shot back, grinning, as they all began to laugh. A few moments passed before he finally remembered their conversation. "Now, getting back to what we were talkin' about before we were so rudely interrupted. What are we doin' today?"

"Ah, that's right! Today's the big day!" Phil exclaimed, springing from his seat. "Go get dressed, lads. We're goin' out."

"I'm not going anywhere today," Kevin responded. "I've got my laundry to do."

"Ah, the laundry can wait."

"No it can't, Phil. Christ, ya should've seen the shirt I had to wear on Thursday. It was filthy. No, no, I'm doing it today."

"Do it tomorrow."

"Are ya deaf, man? Didn't ya hear me? I said I'm doin' it today, and that's that. Besides, you know I like to have my Sundays free to relax."

Phil groaned. "You know something, Kevin? You're unbelievable."

"Unbelievable? What's so unbelievable about that?"

"Come with me for a second, all right, will ya?"

"Where?"

"For Christ's sake! In the living room, Kevin. Please, just for a second," Phil entreated as he motioned for him to follow.

"For cryin' out loud! All right, fine!"

The two men marched off and began talking. Patrick could only hear fragments of the conversation, phrases such as, "Why didn't you tell me?" and "Where did ya get the money for that?" But since the conversation apparently wasn't meant for his ears, he tried not to eavesdrop. They spoke for a good five minutes until there was a brief lull, followed immediately by the sound of feet trampling up the stairs.

What the hell's goin' on now? Patrick was thinking when the kitchen door suddenly flew open and in walked Phil. He came up to Patrick and smiled. "Go get ready, lad. We've got places to go and things to see." Patrick did as he was instructed, and when all three were finally ready, they left the house and headed up to W. Broadway.

The first thing on the agenda, quite understandably, was breakfast. They walked to the nearest Burger King and feasted on bacon, egg, and cheese biscuits and hash browns. By the time they left, it was close to eleven-thirty. "Jeez, Phil, you were right," Patrick said once they got outside, "that was pretty exciting.

Especially the part when they called out me order number and I ran up there as fast as I could. Let me tell ya, that stimulated the hell out of me."

"Ah, that was just the beginning, lad. There's more to come."

"Will ya just tell me where we're goin', for Christ's sake," Patrick retorted, now starting to get a little perturbed with the whole conspiracy thing.

"You'll find out soon enough."

"All right, fine. I'll play along."

"Oh, I know you will. You don't have much of a choice, now do ya?"

"I guess not."

"Then you're a very fine guesser."

They continued walking for another thirty minutes or so, chitchatting the entire time about how so-and-so was doing back home in Eire, when they turned a corner and came upon a crowd of people walking and running every which way. Some of them appeared even almost delirious. "Where the feck'd ya bring me?" Patrick asked as he evaded a young boy who had just nearly run into him.

"Welcome to Fenway Park," Phil replied, throwing his arms in the air, "home of the Boston Red Sox!"

"The Boston Red Sox?"

"Yeah, Paddy—we're goin' to a baseball game!" Kevin blurted out, no longer able to contain his enthusiasm, for this was his first game, also.

"Brilliant!" Patrick grinned, looking back and forth between the two men. As they were heading towards the ticket counter, he asked, "What's the price of a baseball game ticket anyway?"

"That's a good question. I don't know. But don't worry about it, though, it's on me," Phil replied. "My parents sent me five-hundred dollars last week to help carry me over until I find myself another job."

"No, ya need that! Besides, I've got me own money with me."

"I said, I've got it," Phil answered, reassuringly, as he threw his arm around Patrick's neck. When it finally came their turn, he walked up to the window and said proudly to the man selling the tickets, "Give me the three best seats ya have."

"All that's left are the bleachers."

"Brilliant! Then we'll take the three best bleachers ya have."

"That'll be thirty-six dollars, please," the man rejoined, pounding away at the keyboard. Phil handed him two twenties, and as he awaited the tickets and his change, he whispered to Kevin, "That's not bad, thirty-six dollars. A lot cheaper than I thought it was gonna be."

"Yeah, me too."

Upon receiving them, he handed a ticket to each of his mates, and they entered the park. Since this was also Phil's first game, he had no idea where the bleachers were, let alone, what they were, so he walked over to one of the many vendors and asked for directions. A young woman who was selling beer from a Budweiser stand provided him with the information. While he was there, he ordered three beers, gave one to each of the lads, and they then headed in the direction pointed out by the Bud lady. They soon found the appropriate gate, and as they ascended the ramp, a glorious sight came upon them—the green grass of Fenway! For a split-second they felt as though they were back home in the lush countryside. However, the awe soon wore off and they realized that, instead of a field or pasture, the scene more closely resembled a jungle, for there were screams and wails coming from every direction.

Phil immediately walked over to one of the many ushers and questioned him as to the whereabouts of their seats. The man asked to see one of their ticket stubs, and after a brief examination, pointed up and said, "Twelve rows up. See on the stairs, the numbers? Just go to the set of steps that say twelve and they're to your right. Seats 15, 16, and 17."

Phil thanked him and they headed up to the appropriate row and found their seats easily enough, though it was far from the type of seating he had imagined when he so haughtily purchased them. However, he didn't let on, but instead tried to convey the impression that these were the exact three seats he had intended to buy from the outset. "Isn't this great?" he exclaimed, surveying their surroundings.

"Oh, yeah, just wonderful!" Kevin snickered.

Patrick, who was sitting in the middle, whispered, "Jesus, this place is worse than Croke. Look at that," and pointed to a man six rows below who currently had his shirt off. He must have weighed in excess of three hundred pounds, with a back that was completely covered with hair that appeared to be at least an inch thick. This, coupled with the fact that he was perspiring heavily, made for one truly disgusting sight. But as the event commenced, it turned out to be a rather pleasant experience. The people sitting around them were all amicable enough, and the game proved to be an exciting one in which the Sox scratched and clawed their way back to an eleventh inning victory over the Cleveland Indians, by a score of 7–6. As they were leaving, Phil asked them if they had enjoyed themselves. Both men replied wholeheartedly, "Yes," and thanked him for bringing them.

"Now didn't that beat washin' your clothes?"

Kevin chuckled. "Yeah, it was great craic, all right. I'll give you that."

The three began the trek back to Southie, but four beers, combined with the walk there, was just too much for Phil. After a few minutes, he grumbled, "Ah, what the hell," and hailed a taxi. The whole ride back all three were giddy.

"Yeah, Phil, you were right. It was pretty exciting. Thanks again," Patrick acknowledged, stretching his back.

"That wasn't the excitement I was talking about," Phil answered, causing both men to do a double take.

"Now what are ya babblin' about?" Kevin asked.

"Just wait and see. You'll find out soon enough."

Patrick and Kevin both sat back and tried to imagine what was going to happen next. No sooner had they begun contemplating than the taxi pulled up in front of their house and they got their answer: hanging from the front porch was a large plastic banner which read, "Welcome to America, Patrick!"

"Where'd that come from?" Patrick questioned, looking first at Phil and then to Kevin. "That wasn't there when we left."

Kevin sighed. "Don't ask me. I know as much as you do."

"Well, come on lads. Make haste. I have to take a mean piss," Phil said as he opened the door and asked the driver how much they owed.

"Nine sixty," the man replied.

"Here's a ten. Keep the change."

After some terse remark, the driver sped off.

The three men slowly ascended the steps, the entire time glancing back and forth at one another and the sign overhead. Upon entering, they were immediately greeted with a loud chorus of "Surprise!" And surprised they were. Everyone, that is, except Phil, who had planned the whole thing in the first place. There had to have been at least fifty people there, including Tara and the rest of the Tipperary girls. Also in attendance were Barry Dempsey, Victor Kasimov, and the rest of Phil's old friends from Macy's and even some of Kevin's co-workers from the bank. Having known absolutely nothing about it, he appeared to be even more surprised than Patrick. All in all, it was a typical Phil production.

CHAPTER 6

▼

"Now this, this is the big surprise I was talkin' about," Phil shouted over all the voices as he nudged his way between the two men, threw an arm around both their necks, and pulled them in close. "Take a look around ya, lads," he whispered. "We've got women and drink and good friends. What more could a man ask for?"

"How about an explanation!" Kevin exclaimed as he gazed quickly about the room. "When the hell'd ya come up with this?"

"As soon as I heard Paddy was coming, my mind went to work. I said to meself, *What would be a great way to break the lad in? Why, I've got it. How about a party?* It may sound elementary in hindsight, but believe me, at the time, it was a rather daunting task."

"Oh, I'm sure it was."

"Yeah, Phil, absolutely brilliant. Did it come to you in some dream or revelation?" Patrick quipped.

"Will ya listen to that? I try to show the lad a good time and this is how he repays me."

"I'm jus' messin' with ya," Patrick said, beaming, as he threw his arm around Phil's neck and gave him a hearty shake. "I appreciate it, but I'm just a little nervous, that's all. Look at 'em. They're all smilin' at me, and I don't know a single goddamn one of them," he whispered out of the corner of his mouth.

"Well, come on. I'll introduce ya to everyone," Phil replied as he motioned for Patrick to follow. They walked forward a few steps when Phil abruptly grabbed Patrick by the shirtsleeve and walked him back over to where Kevin was still standing. He paused for a split-second before inquiring, "Hey, you're not mad at me, are ya?"

"Mad? Mad about what?" Kevin asked.

"I don't know. Settin' this whole thing up without consultin' you first."

""Hey, now that ya mention it, that's a good point. I probably should be sore, shouldn't I?"

"No, seriously. Are you?"

"Of course not. A little surprised. Well, make that a lot surprised. But not mad. I think it's a brilliant idea."

"Good. I just wanted to check," Phil replied contently as he turned and began guiding Patrick toward the mass of people. Ten minutes later, when all the introductions had been completed, Phil came close and whispered, "Now ya know everyone, especially Tara. I'm gonna slip away for a while, all right? I think her friend Sandra's got the hots for me. Let's see if me intuitions are correct."

Patrick chuckled. "Good luck."

"Aye, and to you too. Why don't you go chat it up with Tara. Who knows? Maybe, if ya play your cards right, you'll get some tail."

"Yeah, right! I doubt it."

"Hey, ya never know," Phil said, shrugging his shoulders. He then walked over to where Sandra was standing, and they began talking.

Now alone, Patrick began looking around for Kevin, but he was nowhere to be seen. The music was blaring by this point, and most people had gathered into small groups. Some had even begun dancing, and everyone was drinking. Everything was perfect.

Patrick soon made his way into the kitchen and grabbed a can of Heineken from the refrigerator. As he stood there, sipping at it, he suddenly began mulling over what Phil had said about striking up a conversation with Tara. After a short deliberation, he decided that, yes, he would, but he also thought it prudent to have a drink or two beforehand to loosen him up. And before he knew it, there he was, sitting on the sofa, relaxed (his third beer in hand), scoping out the scene. Within moments, over walked Tara and Maureen Stapleton, another of the Tipperary girls.

"So, Patrick Quinn, are you enjoying the party so far?" Tara asked as the two of them plopped down beside him.

"Yeah, so far it's been brilliant."

"So ya can talk in complete sentences, huh?" she said, grinning, as she gave him a soft slap on the leg. "I'm just messin' with ya. You know that, right?"

"Yeah, I know you are, Tara."

"Good." She then paused for a moment. "You've met Maureen, right?"

"Yeah, well—sort of. We said hello a few minutes ago in passing."

"Yeah, but it was a weak introduction, though. Don't ya think?" Maureen responded. "Let's do it properly this time." With this she stood, extended her hand, and said, "Hello, Patrick Quinn. My name is Maureen Stapleton. It's very nice to meet you."

Patrick, who had also gotten to his feet by this point, replied, "No, Maureen, the pleasure's all mine."

"Now, that's more like it," Tara exclaimed. "And you've met the rest of the girls?"

"Yeah, well, in the same sort of way that I met Maureen."

"Well, if we're gonna be neighbors, then you should be introduced properly," she said, and then called over to her friends. One by one, each came up and said hello once more. While he was shaking each of their hands, he thought to himself how cute they all were, not that this really surprised him. Patrick had always felt that along with the Italians, the women of Ireland were the most beautiful. However, there usually had to be at least one in every group who looked like the 'Missing Link.' Not the case here. Yet while they were all attractive, there was something about Tara that made her especially alluring, something he couldn't finger, but something that nonetheless captured his attention. Throughout the entire evening, Patrick and Tara talked. They even danced a few times. It was evident to anyone who came upon them that they were attracted to one another.

It was close to eleven by the time Phil and Kevin finally reappeared. Both were loaded. "Where in the hell have you two been?" Patrick inquired upon seeing them.

"Minglin'," they replied simultaneously. At this, the two men looked at each other and began laughing uncontrollably. After a few moments and much struggle, they controlled their laughter and took seats at opposite ends of the sofa. "So, did you shag her yet?" Phil no sooner questioned, sipping at his drink.

Patrick shot him a glare. "Nice thing to ask!" he snapped, half disgusted, half embarrassed.

"You know me, guys. I'm just messin' with ya."

"Ah, we do, ya pig. And I know one person who won't be doin' any shaggin' tonight!" Tara retorted.

Phil began laughing. "You may wanna speak with Sandra before you start talkin' like that. I wasn't the aggressor. Besides, I'm a very charming man. No woman in her right mind would pass up the opportunity to be seen in my presence."

"Well, if Sandra was smoochin' with you, then the only state of mind she's in is a state of confusion!"

"Hey, I take exception to that."

"Take it any way ya want, but it's true! She must be delusional by now."

"I don't know if I'd call it delusional. Crazed, maybe. Me God, ya should've seen her. She was like a mad woman. I nearly had to fight her off with a stick."

"Ooh, you're such a liar!"

"Relax, I'm only slaggin'. We were just up in me room, hanging out, all right. So don't tell her I was talkin' like that. She'd probably give me an arse whippin'."

"You're right about that."

"Well, I can see when I'm not wanted," Phil said, suddenly getting to his feet.

"Then you're very observant."

Phil didn't respond but merely looked at her, shook his head, and walked off while muttering something under his breath.

The entire time the two had been going at it, Kevin had remained silent. Patrick thought it strange until he realized he had since passed out. They tried reviving him, but to no avail. He was out cold. Even with the blaring of the music and the laughter and shouting of the revelers, he still didn't budge. So they lifted his legs up onto the sofa and put a couple of pillows under his head. If he was going to be out for the rest of the night, then the least they could do was make him comfortable. When they had finished tending to him, Tara asked Patrick if she could see his room.

"Sure," he replied. They walked up the stairs, and he gave her a tour of his small yet attractively furnished bedroom. She said it looked wonderful and that his friends had gone through a lot of trouble to make it look this nice.

By this point, it was close to midnight, and the party was starting to get a little out of hand. Everyone was drunk, and the neighbors had taken all they could. The police soon arrived and began ushering people out. It was a good half hour before they disbanded all the partygoers and restored order to the place. The whole time, Phil had tried to get the three officers to join in on the celebration, telling them that their superior wouldn't miss them for a couple of hours. Seeing, however, that his efforts were falling on deaf ears, he soon gave up and helped the police disperse the crowd.

By the time the officers finally left, only four people remained: the three residents and Tara O'Malley. They spoke for a short time, about all that occurred, before Tara said she had to get going. She was happy when Patrick offered to accompany her home. At first, both were silent. "So, Patrick Quinn, is it how you imagined it so far?" she asked shortly.

"Come on, Tara, stop that, will ya. Patrick or Paddy will do just fine."

"I'm just messin' with ya. All right, I promise. I won't call you that anymore," she assured, chuckling. "Well, has it?"

"Has it been what?"

"You know, how you pictured it to be."

"I don't know. I guess in some ways it has. Like, take for instance, the sky-scrapers. I'd never really seen one before yesterday. They're a lot bigger up close, but they're basically how I imagined them. I guess the major difference would have to be the houses. Everything over here's made of wood. I mean, I haven't seen a single brick or stone one since I arrived. I find that to be kind of strange. The lads even showed me one today that was like two hundred and something years old. Ya wouldn't think a house made from wood would be able to survive, let alone look as good as it did, after so long a time." Before Patrick had finished speaking, they were back at her house. After walking up the stairs and taking a seat on a rosewood bench that was to the left of the front door, Patrick asked her if it had been much different from what she had envisioned.

"Yes!" she replied quickly. "I always pictured it to be much larger. But mind you, I've never been out of Boston, though. Whenever I thought of the States, ever since I was a wee girl, I always pictured it to be this huge place, and Boston definitely isn't huge. Someday, though, possibly even this summer, me and a couple of the girls are plannin' on goin' on a few excursions. You know, to see it from 'sea to shining sea,'" she said with a grin.

"Oh, really? Where ya plannin' on goin'?"

"We really haven't decided yet. Maybe New York City. Possibly even Niagara Falls. I heard it's supposed to be lovely, especially at night. Did you know that after it turns dark out, they have lights of all different colors illuminating it?"

"No, I didn't know that."

"Yeah, they say it's wonderful. A friend of ours, Adrian Little, he went there sometime last summer and said it was like the greatest thing he'd ever seen. I also wanna go to San Francisco, but that's probably not gonna be for awhile, though. Yeah, I think out of all the places, San Francisco would have to be tops on the list."

"Oh, really? Why's that?"

"Well, my older sister, Maeve, she's traveled all over the world. For about five years that was all she did, moving from one continent to another, takin' on odd jobs as she went just to survive. She's been everywhere. Istanbul. Buenos Aires. Shanghai. Calcutta. Christ, she's even been to Timbuktu. And out of all the places, she said she liked San Francisco the best. She called it the 'perfect city', if there is such a thing. But like I said, that's not gonna be for awhile, though. We're definitely gonna try and hit one of the others this summer, hopefully Niagara Falls. Maybe you'd like to come along."

"Yeah, I wouldn't mind seein' it, all right. But I'm really not gonna have much time to do any travelin'."

"Oh, really? Why's that?"

"Work. That's the reason I'm over here."

"Well, having good work ethics is an admirable trait, Patrick, but you also have to have some fun, too. Remember—work to live, not the other way around."

Both just sat there silently for a moment, staring at one another. Each had had their fill of cheer, but drink wasn't the cause of what happened next. Before they knew it, they began kissing. At first innocently and then, after a while, more passionately. It went on for a short time, until Tara unexpectedly broke away and shot to her feet.

"Patrick Quinn! For God's sake, whadya think you're doin'?"

"Um, I didn't mean...."

Tara burst into laughter. "I'm only messin' with ya!" she cried as she sat down once more beside him and put her arm around his neck.

"Christ, Tara, don't do that to me. I thought you were serious."

"I know ya did. You should've seen the look on your face. It was hilarious."

Patrick sat motionless, trying to regain his composure. After a few moments, he too began to laugh. By this time, it was close to one in the morning and both were exhausted. Tara, who had since risen, looked down at him and said, "It's late. I really should be goin' in."

"Yeah, I know," Patrick conceded, also getting to his feet. He went up to her and they began kissing once again—this time even more excitedly than before—when she suddenly whispered, "What will the neighbors think?"

"Right." He looked around to see if anyone was watching.

"Jesus Christ, Patrick. I'm only kiddin'. Ya know something, if you're gonna be hangin' out with me and the girls, you're gonna have to learn how to take a joke," Tara asserted as she went into her pocket and pulled out her keys. As she was opening the door, she asked, "Do you want me to come by the house tomorrow?"

"You mean today?"

"You know what I'm talkin' about."

"Yeah, sure. I'd like that."

"Very well, then. I guess I'll see you today, Patrick Quinn!"

"I told ya ..." he began, but before he could utter another word she closed the door.

As he walked home that chilly, early summer night, he began thinking once more about how wise it had been to have had that first drink. Had he been uptight when they first began speaking, he quite possibly could have said something inappropriate or asinine, and then most likely would've sought refuge for the rest of the night in the confines of his room. Fortunately, that had not been the case. No, the night had gone perfectly! After arriving home, he soon fell contently to sleep.

CHAPTER 7

▼

The brilliant, early morning sunshine shone through the windowpane and reflected its glorious light within. It lit up the small room with a quiet but majestic feel.

At first, Patrick, who lay hidden thoroughly beneath his sheet, shook as though he was convulsing, but soon emerged and propped himself up. He immediately sank back down, for he was in a really bad way from all the drinking he had done the night before. "Ugh," he moaned, pressing at his temples. Seeing that this wasn't having the desired effect, he turned and looked over at his alarm clock, which now showed it to be six-thirty, the correct time he knew since he had wound it the previous morning. Realizing that it would be in his best interest, Patrick shortly fell back asleep. This decision turned out to be a sound one, for when he woke again three hours later, he felt better. Not good, mind you, only better.

He then headed downstairs to see how the lads were doing. He didn't have to wait long for his answer: for there in the kitchen, upon the floor itself, lay Phil sound asleep.

Patrick entered the room as quietly as possible, and was heading towards the sink to get a drink of water, when Phil unexpectedly sprang to his feet. "Good morning," he said, grinning, to his startled friend.

"Ya bastard! You did that on purpose, didn't ya?"

"Yeah, I had to."

"No, ya didn't! Christ, I nearly dropped a load in me draws. And you probably find that amusing, don't ya?"

"Yeah, well … sort of. No, no, you're right. I'm sorry. Let's start over, okay? Good morning."

"It's not that good. I feel like shite," Patrick muttered, sinking down at the table and laying his head upon it.

"Ah, that's right. I almost forgot. If ya have more than three you're in bits the next morning."

Patrick didn't reply.

"Now me, I can drink a fish under the table and still feel fine the next day."

Still no response.

Seeing that he wasn't in a joking mood, Phil finally eased up and asked him if he wanted some aspirins. Patrick lifted his head, and was just about to accept, when he unexpectedly bolted from his chair and began throwing up in the sink.

"Jesus! Are you all right?" Phil cried, rising to his feet.

Patrick didn't answer. When at last he finished, and had just begun to clean himself up, a loud bang was suddenly heard in the living room. "What the hell was that?" he asked.

"Whadya think?" Phil said jeeringly. "Go take a look." Patrick did and what he found was Kevin lying on the floor, face down.

"Rise and shine!" Phil shouted, making his way into the room.

Kevin lifted his head from off the floor and moaned in a sickly voice, "You're goin' to hell," as he tried to gain sight of his antagonizer. No sooner had he done so than he rolled over onto his back and began throwing up violently. Up in the air it flew, and down upon his face it fell.

"Christ almighty!" Phil howled as Patrick and he rushed over. Each grabbed hold of an arm and lifted him to his feet, all the while trying not to get any on themselves. After swaying in place for a moment, Kevin then fell back onto the sofa. He sat silent, waiting for his equilibrium to return, before finally looking up at Phil and asking, "Could you get me some aspirins and some orange juice in one of the large plastic glasses?" Phil hurried off without saying a word.

Upon receiving the pills, Kevin took them and the juice down in one large gulp. He then, once more, tried getting to his feet but stumbled in the process. Luckily, his friends caught him. When he was at last steadied, he looked back and forth between the two of them. "I'm gonna go take a shower now," he said, pulling himself from their grip and staggering up the stairs. When he was finally out of sight, the two men began cleaning up. Upon finishing, both washed up and took seats at the kitchen table.

"Do you want anything to eat?" Phil questioned.

"I thought there wasn't anything."

"There is now. I went shoppin' this morning."

"This mornin'? Whadya talkin' about?"

"Yeah, I went to the store at around eight."

"I nearly ended up havin' a heart attack just so you could take the piss out of me, huh?" Patrick sneered, finally realizing that the earlier episode had been all just a set-up. "I don't know about you sometimes."

"Yeah, well … sometimes I don't know about meself, either," Phil said with a smirk, getting to his feet. "Ya sure you don't want anything?"

"No, but I could go for some tea if that's all right?"

"Sure, your wish is my command," Phil replied as he walked over to the sink and began filling the teapot. After putting it on the burner, he whipped back around and proclaimed, "I'm gonna make meself the breakfast of all breakfasts!" and then proceeded to do just that. He made pancakes in one skillet, and a mountain of scrambled eggs in another; in yet a third, he cooked up bacon and some breakfast sausage. Well, no sooner was the food ready than in the room stumbled Kevin.

"Are we feelin' a little better now?" Phil asked tauntingly.

"No, and it's all your fault. You and your brilliant ideas," Kevin murmured, sinking down at the table.

"And he blames it on me! I wasn't the one who poured a fifth of vodka down your throat. You did that all on your own, big guy," Phil retorted as he placed a tea bag in each of the three cups and filled them with the steaming, hot water. After bringing them over, one at a time, he then proceeded to dish the food onto four separate plates and carried them over also.

"Ya know what, on second thought, I think I will have a wee bit to eat," Patrick said after examining the tasty-looking bounty.

Phil nodded as he walked back over to the cupboard and took out three large plates. After handing one to each of the men, he then sat down and they began to eat.

"Is there a church anywhere around here?" Patrick questioned suddenly.

"You've gotta be kiddin'?" Phil snickered. "You're in bits and church is what you think about?"

"Yeah, well … it's Sunday."

On hearing this, Phil began to chuckle.

"Why, you don't go to church anymore?"

"Hell, no! I haven't been in probably close to three years now."

"Oh, I didn't know that."

"Yeah, besides … it's just a big scam, anyways. Ya go and listen to someone preach about God, someone who doesn't even know Him. Ya sit there for the longest time listening to stories that most likely never happened, and then they even expect you to give money. No thanks. That's not how I intend to spend my Sunday mornings, but to answer your question, yes, there are a few Catholic churches in the neighborhood."

"So you don't even believe in God at all?"

"Listen, Patrick. Every man is entitled to his own opinions and beliefs, but let's be realistic. There's no such thing as a God. We're here in this world because of a natural process called evolution, and that's the only reason. We live our lives and then we die. And that's all there is to it."

"Hey, Phil, why don't you keep your atheist feckin' opinions to yourself!" Kevin snarled.

"Look who's talkin'! I've lived with you for over a year now, and I've never seen your arse go to church once! So don't be a hypocrite, all right?"

There was a brief silence. "Yeah, Phil, you're right. It has been a long time since I've gone, but that doesn't mean I don't believe in God. I just haven't had the time. And I know that that's not a good reason, but it's the reason, nonetheless. I do believe in God!"

"That's a bunch of crap, Kevin, and you're just sayin' it because Paddy's here. You spend your Sundays, your 'free time,'" Phil scoffed, "lying on the sofa watching TV or at the girls' house playin' some stupid board game. I know. I've seen ya. So don't preach to me about bein' a good Catholic boy, because you're not! And you know it just as well as I do."

"Think what ya want, Phil. I really don't care. But you know something, I think from now on I'll make the time," Kevin asserted as he sank back in his chair, drained. He still felt horrible, but as he argued with Phil, he battled through the discomfort of his hangover. However, the feeling of nausea soon became too great. At that moment, there wasn't a single thing Phil could have said that would have made him resume the debate. He sat completely still for a few minutes before saying, "Hey, Patrick. Why don't ya go get ready and we'll go to church together. I think it's about time I started goin' again, anyways." Then, pushing away his plate, he left the room.

"Oh, and you're welcome for the food," Phil called after him, but he was already gone.

"Thanks, Phil," Patrick said despondently, for he felt entirely responsible for the argument.

"Hey, no problem. And I was serious about what I said before about every man havin' the right to his own beliefs, and I'm sorry for tryin' to push mine off on you. Kevin was right. I should've kept them to myself."

"Ah, don't worry about it. Nothin' you could say could change how I feel. Besides, it's not like I haven't heard it all before," Patrick acknowledged. He then left the room and took a shower. When he had finished, Kevin and he walked up the street to St. Augustine's.

The mass that morning was an especially long one, and that, coupled with the way he felt, caused Kevin to wonder if it had been a wise choice to renew his faith on this of all days. "I don't remember it bein' so long," he said as they trudged back home. "My God, I thought it was never gonna end. Up. Down. Up. Down. Christ, at one point, I actually thought I was gonna throw up all over that little kid in front of us. That would've been nice, huh?"

"Yeah, it was pretty long, all right."

"Hey, wait up!" a voice unexpectedly shouted from behind. It was Tara. The men stopped and waited for her to catch up. "You both look like shite," she exclaimed, nudging her way between the two of them.

Kevin moaned. "And we feel like it, too."

"Well, why'd ya have to drink so much?"

"At the time, I didn't think I had."

"Well ya did. And I know because I personally had to help lay you down on the sofa after ya passed out. My God, you should've seen yourself, droolin' all over like you were some poor, simple creature."

"No suh!"

"Wasn't he, Patrick?"

"Aye, Kevin. It's true. First ya staggered into the room from God knows where, and ya tripped. Then you came over to where we were sitting and ya fell onto the sofa, and not long after that ya passed out. The whole time, too, you were foamin' at the mouth like some rabid dog. And I'll even tell ya something else if you promise not to get mad."

"What?"

"No. Ya have to promise first."

"Okay, okay, I promise!"

"Well … before ya passed out, you were ramblin'."

"Ramblin'? Ramblin' about what?"

"Should I tell him, Tara?"

"Yeah, he definitely should know. I mean, I would if it had been me."

"Yeah, I guess you're right. I would, too." Patrick hesitated. "Well, for a time there, you were talkin' pretty crazy."

"I was?"

Patrick frowned. "Yes, Kevin, you were. Ya thought you were some Viking warrior that had been lost at sea, and you were tryin' to get back home to find your long lost wife and son. You even went by a different name. Ah, what did ya call yourself? I can't remember now. Do you recall what your man's name was?"

"Vaguely," Tara returned, squinting. "Wasn't it something like Thurik or Murik? No, no! Now I remember! It was Burik, Burik the Great."

"Are you serious?"

"Aye! Ya had everyone in stitches. You were even goin' around askin' all the girls if she was your wife."

Kevin lowered his head. They walked for a short time in silence before Tara finally began laughing.

"What's so funny?"

"We're only messin' with ya!"

Kevin scowled. "What? Why'd ya—don't do that. That's not funny. Christ, ya had me goin' there for awhile."

"I know we did. Ya should've seen your face. It was beet red," she giggled.

"And you weren't droolin', either," Patrick reassured him. "Ya just sat down on the sofa and fell asleep."

"But if I may say so, I do feel ya had a little more than you could handle," Tara advised, finally starting to regain her composure.

"Yeah, I guess you're right. I mean … I woke up this morning not from my alarm clock's ringing, but from a shower of me own vomit."

"No suh?"

"I'm serious."

"Oh, you poor thing!" Tara said, rubbing his back, but the image of it was just too much for her and she began laughing once again. "That's terrible!" she cried.

"It's not funny! It was that damn vodka. I swear to God, I'm never touching it again. No, sir—beer is the only thing these lips will be seein' for a long time."

"That's what they all say."

"That's what who all says?"

"The alkies."

"I'm not an alcoholic!"

She winked. "Oh, I know you're not. You're just a social drinker, right?"

"That's right, I am!"

"Don't worry, your secret's safe with me."

Kevin, with a look of indignation on his face, decided to end the conversation right then and there. Without another word, he picked up his pace until he was a good twenty yards in front. By the time they got back it was half-past twelve. A few of the other girls soon came over, and the rest of the day was spent watching TV and talking. Everyone had a good time except Phil, who was up in his room sulking from all the abuse he had taken at the hands of Kevin. And even though Kevin had gone up there numerous times and apologized, Phil never set one foot from his room the entire evening.

CHAPTER 8

▼

The next morning, Monday, June 23rd, Patrick awoke to a refreshing breeze that gently wafted through his room. He lay there for a short time, basking in this tranquility, until the sensation slowly began to subside. When it had completely passed, he hopped out of bed and headed downstairs. Soon Kevin, and a few minutes later, Phil, joined him.

At first, all three were quiet. Phil finally broke the silence. "Very well, I accept your apology. But jus' make sure it doesn't happen again, all right?"

"He accepts me apology. Oh, thank God! Because I don't think I could've made it through the day with that hangin' over me head," Kevin jested in an exaggerated brogue, which in turn brought a smile to all their lips. "So, what's on the agenda for today, lads?" he soon asked, getting up to make some tea.

"Well, I was thinkin', today seems as fine a day as any to start looking for work, wouldn't ya say?" Patrick replied, looking back at him. "Any suggestions?"

"Jeez, not off hand. Ya just have to go and look. Just go downtown and apply at each and every place ya pass. Hit the banks and the department stores, and, oh, there's this street in Backbay, Newbury Street, with a ton of little shops on it. That's probably where you should go first. But to be honest with you, Paddy, I really don't know. They're out there, all right. But the thing is, ya just have to go and find 'em, because, God knows, they're not gonna come looking for you."

"Yeah, I know."

"Did ya check yesterday's classifieds?"

"Yeah, but there really wasn't too much pertaining to business. And the ones that they did have all specified that they wanted someone with a Master's. And unfortunately, that's something that I don't have."

"Well then, you're just gonna have to do it the way we did when we came over. Remember?" Kevin said, glancing over at Phil. "Ya just go and look, and hope for the best. And if the best doesn't come along then you take the second best, or the third, or even the fourth, but ya take it nonetheless. Because you're a stranger in a strange land and you can't afford to be choosy. Your survival depends on it. Plus, don't forget … ya have a college degree. It's not like you're some idiot off the street. To be honest with ya, Paddy, I really don't think you'll have much of a problem findin' something."

"Anything at your Sovereign?"

"If there was, don't you think I would've already had Phil workin' there by now? No, Sovereign's a good company. The people stay. I was really lucky to land that job."

"What time do ya have to be at work for?" Phil asked suddenly through a big yawn.

"Nine. Why?"

"I'll tell you what. You guys get ready. I'll go into town with ya, Paddy, and we'll look for work together. They'd have to be crazy not to hire two charmin' blokes such as ourselves."

Patrick smiled. "Yeah? All right, sounds good to me."

"I must be hearing things. Get me the Q-Tips, Paddy! Quick!" Kevin shouted as he jumped to his feet. "I thought I just heard him say that he was gonna look for a job."

"Hey—remember what you promised."

"I do, but through my astonishment I just merely forgot. I'm sorry."

"Oh, he's such a funny guy, isn't he?"

By eight-twenty, all three were dressed and out the door. They headed up to Broadway and caught the bus downtown. By the time they arrived, it was close to quarter-of.

"Good luck, lads," Kevin said as he sped off. They watched him as he weaved his way through the mass of pedestrians until he was finally out of sight.

"So, which way do you wanna head?" Phil asked casually as he examined a voluptuous brunette in her mid-thirties who was standing nearby, waiting for the bus.

"You're askin' me? How the hell should I know! You're the one who knows this city."

"Well, if me intuitions are correct, and mind you, they always are, then our best shot would probably lie in the financial district."

"Well then, the financial district it is. Lead the way."

The two men headed to the agreed-upon destination and began their search for employment. Over the course of the next five hours, each filled out numerous applications for jobs ranging anywhere from stockbrokers to secretaries, but as the day continued, both still found themselves unemployed. As they left the Liberty Mutual building, after filling out a six-page application/life history for a position selling insurance, both were exhausted.

"Christ, me hand hurts!" Phil cried, rubbing his ailing extremity.

"Mine, too. I don't think it's ever been this sore in all me life."

The two men stood silent for a few moments, each tending to his own healing process, until Patrick finally asked, "Well, how do ya think we fared so far?"

"Pretty well I'd say. I think we made rather good impressions with most of 'em. Well, and then ya have Charles Schwab! I'd bet me reputation that we won't be hearing from them anytime soon."

"And I wonder why!"

"Well, what was I supposed to do? Can you imagine the audacity of tellin' someone that they sound like a feckin' leprechaun!"

"Yeah, it was a rude thing to say, all right. But ya still didn't have to call him a prick."

"But he was!"

"But still! Whadya gonna do? Tell everyone who comments on our accent to feck off?"

Phil sighed. "Yeah, I guess you're right." He then paused for a moment. "I should've just kicked his arse. That's what I should've done."

"Aah, what am I gonna do with you?" Patrick replied, a slight grin playing over his lips.

They had once again just begun walking, when a great idea suddenly popped into Phil's head. Very noticeably, he began to lick his lips. Patrick caught sight of him doing this out of the corner of his eye but didn't let on, for he knew exactly where it would lead them. However, it was to no avail, for Phil knew he was watching and soon asked, "Are ya feelin' dry in the mouth?"

"No, not really. Why?"

"Christ, I'm thirsty. Thirsty as hell. Whadya say we go for a pint?"

"No, come on, let's not. You know very well that if we stop, that one pint's gonna turn into four or five, and then there goes the day."

"No, come on, I promise. Just one."

"Well, if you're so thirsty, why don't ya just buy some minerals or water?"

"Come on, Paddy, you should know better than anyone that nothin' quenches your thirst more on a hot summer's day than a nice cold beer. It's a fact."

"Bull! Water does the job a whole lot better, and now that's a fact."

"Please!" Phil implored, clenching his hands as in prayer and bringing them up to his lips. "Just one pint! I give you me word."

"You promise?"

"I swear."

"All right, fine," Patrick muttered, but knew full well that their day of job searching had come to an end, and only agreed because he too felt like having a sip. He wasn't wrong. They entered the nearest watering hole a little after two o'clock and didn't leave until close to five that afternoon. During that span, they consumed six pints apiece, so, by the time they finally did leave, both were pretty well lit up.

As they staggered along Bolyston Street that unseasonably humid June afternoon, Patrick told Phil he was a man of his word. Phil thanked him graciously for the compliment. They walked aimlessly for a few minutes until Phil finally hailed them a taxi, but before he got in, he broadcast loud enough for all to hear: "My name's Phil Doyle and I'm a Mick. I just wanna let everyone know that Charles Schwab sucks the big one." Some of the onlookers laughed, but most appeared to be offended. "That's all I wanted to say. Carry on," he motioned as he got in and slammed the door.

By the time they arrived back in Southie it was close to five-thirty. As they turned onto F Street and approached the girls' house, they saw that all five were out on the porch, drinking. The sight of the two men stumbling along caused the girls to break into laughter.

"Why don't ya come on up and rest your weary bones," hollered Joanne Neary, Sandra's younger sister.

"All right," Phil answered, "but just don't beg us to stay too long."

"Oh, don't worry. We won't," Tara gibed as she picked up two small bottles and handed one to each of them.

"What's this?" Phil asked, squinting, as he tried unsuccessfully to focus on the bottle's label.

"Lyncheburg Lemonade. Just try it, it's lovely," Sandra asserted from across the porch. She then paused for a moment before adding, "Oh, yeah, and what's this I hear about you and me smoochin' around the other night?"

"Hey, I thought you said you weren't gonna say anything? I told ya I was only kiddin', didn't I?" Phil grumbled, looking over at Tara.

"Relax! I told her you were. She just thought it would be good craic to confront ya with it. So there!"

"Oh," Phil uttered as he took a large gulp and lay back on the porch, fully extended.

"Yeah, she wasn't offended. Actually, she was kind of overjoyed when she heard," a voice said unexpectedly from behind. It was Heather Driscoll, the least personable of the five. She had loose lips and didn't like to work, and on more than one occasion the girls had even discussed the idea of asking her to leave. Tara, though, had always given her the benefit of the doubt. "Where's she gonna go?" she would always ask, and the response she received was always the same: "Who cares!"

Sandra glared at her. "Be quiet you!"

"Well, it's true, isn't it?"

However, before Sandra had a chance to respond, Phil got to his feet and with a large smirk, said, "Well, of course, it's true. And it's not just her, either. I can see it in all of you. Even you, Tara. And you, too, Maureen. Ya don't have to admit it, but it's there, all right."

"I wouldn't bet on it if I was you," Tara retorted, "because the only look you've ever seen from these eyes is a look of sympathy."

"Go ahead, deny your feelings all you want, but it's just not workin'. I can see right through you."

"My God, you're pitiful!"

"I have to apologize for my friend here. He's had a wee bit too much to drink," Patrick explained as he walked over to where Phil now stood. "Come on, let's get goin'."

"No, come on. I was only slaggin'. I don't wanna go. Besides, I could go for another of these Limeburg Lemonades."

"Lyncheburg!" Tara corrected as she grabbed another bottle from a large blue Coleman cooler.

"You're such a saint, Tara. You know that? I don't know how you find it in yourself to be so nice to such a despicable creature as myself."

"It's not easy, let me tell ya," she acknowledged with a smile. "Now you behave yourself, lad. Ya hear?"

"I will," Phil answered dejectedly, appearing almost embarrassed by his behavior. Such self-awareness on his part was, in fact, a rare thing.

With all the hostilities having subsided, everyone soon began to relax and have a good time. Before they knew it, Kevin stomped up the stairs. "So, how'd the job search go?" he inquired, taking a seat on the top step.

"Excellent!" Phil replied. "I'd say that by the end of the week we'll both be employed."

"Hey, that's great! Where'd ya go?"

"All over! Christ, I'd have to say we probably applied at close to fifty different places. But I'd say we probably have the best shot of being hired by a company named Charles Schwab. We really made one hell of an impression with the interviewer." At this, both Patrick and he burst into laughter.

"What's so funny?" Kevin asked, a perplexed look on his face. Phil then proceeded to tell everyone, word for word, exactly what had transpired at the Charles Schwab building.

"You're bad," Sandra said, giggling, at the story's completion.

"Yeah? Well, then, why don't ya come on over here and sit down next to my bad self and I'll tell ya some more stories about me day."

Much to everyone's amusement, Sandra got up and walked over.

"See, I told ya she's got the hots for you!" Heather blurted out maliciously.

"Hush, you!" Sandra snarled. "Why don't you get the hell out of here! Or better yet, why don't ya go for a nice, long swim in the Charles, and if we're all lucky, maybe some big fish will come up and swallow you whole. God knows, no one will miss you."

"Feck you!"

Sandra jumped to her feet and a fight was about to ensue, when everyone came between them.

"Heather!" Tara cried as they struggled to hold back the enraged woman. "What's your problem?"

"That little bitch over there's my problem!" she screamed, glaring in Sandra's direction.

"Maybe the girls were right when they said you should leave."

"Oh, really? You think I should leave? You all want me to move out? Then fine, I'll go!"

"No! We don't want for you to leave, just act a little nicer, that's all. Is that too much to ask?"

"Get your hands off me, all of you!" Heather shrieked, trying to break free. Upon being released, she ran into the house, crying.

"Why does she always have to make such a scene? She can't ever get along with anyone," Tara said as she leaned against the railing and covered her face with her hands. "To be honest with ya, I'm surprised she's still alive with some of the things I've heard her say. I really am." Standing there beside her, Patrick could see that the whole incident had had a really bad effect on her. Her hands were trembling, and she had a sickened look on her face. Both were silent for a few moments until Tara finally asked, "You don't smoke, do ya, Pat?"

"No, why?"

"Christ. Eight people and no one has a goddamn cigarette!"

"I didn't know you smoked."

"I don't, well at least not anymore. I used to. But God, I could really go for one now, though."

"Do you want me to go to the store and buy you a pack?"

"Yeah. Just let me run upstairs and get some money and I'll go with ya."

She hurried up and grabbed a handful of change from off her dresser, and then the two of them walked up the street where she purchased a pack of Marlboro Lights. After packing and opening the box, she took one out and just gazed at it. She hesitated for a split-second before putting it between her lips and lighting it from a book of matches she had gotten from the store's clerk. "Haven't had a fag in over a year now," she said as they walked back across the street and sat down on a green wooden bench. Both were silent.

"Do you feel better now?" Patrick asked only after she had taken her last drag and flicked the butt out into the street.

"I don't know. I just don't understand why she can't get along with the others?"

"Some people are just like that, Tara. And it doesn't matter how nice you are to them. It's just their nature. I don't know about Heather, if she's that way, I mean. I haven't had the opportunity to get to know her that well. But there was this lad I knew back in Loughshinny, Brendan, and he was the exact same way. His parents did everything for him, and I mean everything, but he would constantly be doing things to hurt them. On purpose, I think. Plus, he was really bright. Smart as a whip. He could've really done something meaningful with his life, ya know. But he never graduated. He dropped out and went to work on some fishing boat. He ended up drownin' at sea during this really bad storm a few years back. They said he fell overboard, but I don't believe it. They threw him out. I'd bet my life on it."

"Oh, the poor thing! That has to be one of the worst ways to die. That and by fire. I don't know which would be worse. Probably drownin'. Yeah, drownin' would definitely have to be worse," Tara said as she got to her feet and lit another cigarette. "Did they ever find his body?"

"No, they never did."

"Oh, his poor family."

"Yeah, and what's even worse, he was an only child. It destroyed them, especially his mother. You should see her. I mean, she used to be the most sociable woman in all Loughshinny. Always had a smile on her face. Now she walks around with this blank stare, like a dead woman. It's really very sad."

"Did you know him well?"

Patrick nodded. "Yeah, we were best mates growing up. But we had sort of a fallin' out. Or, at least, that's what I'd guess you'd call it." They had just begun walking back when he said, "Tara, can I ask you something?"

"Yeah, sure. What is it?"

"And you promise you won't get mad or laugh?"

"I promise."

"Well, ever since the party the other night, um ... well, I know we were both pretty loaded, and people do and say things when they're drunk, but I've been thinkin' quite a bit about what happened between us. I guess what I'm askin' is if you've been thinkin' about it, too? Or is it just some stupid idea I've got in my head? Remember—you said you weren't gonna laugh."

"I remember," she replied and then hesitated for a moment before saying, "Yes, Patrick. I have been thinkin' about you quite a bit."

"You have?"

"Yes. I mean ... I like you, Patrick. I do. You're cute and you seem like a really nice guy."

Patrick stopped dead in his tracks. He didn't know what would come from telling his feelings, but he certainly hadn't expected this. "Jeez, ya caught me off guard with that, Tara," he muttered, staring intently at the ground. "I don't know what to say."

"Well, you're gonna have to figure that one out on your own. I can't help ya anymore than I've already done. A girl tells you she's interested and attracted to you, there's only a few things ya can say."

"Well, I know what I wanna say. But I'm afraid I may not get the response I'm lookin' for."

"Well, all I can tell ya is to go with your feelings. You've followed them this far and you're still breathin'."

Patrick took in a deep breath, and then let it out. Then, without stopping to get another, blurted, "Tara, would you like to go out with me?" He stood back, eyes partially closed, as he nervously awaited her response.

"Why, yes, Patrick, I would love to be your girlfriend."

"You would?"

"Yes, I would."

He smiled and gave her a tender kiss on the lips. "You won't be sorry."

"I better not be! You'd better be considerate and sweet and respectful."

"I swear. I'll be all those things and more."

"Good! Well, with all the formalities out of the way, now let's get down to the important stuff. Whadya gonna get me to celebrate the occasion? A watch or a gold necklace? Or maybe some pearls? Well, which one is it gonna be, huh?"

"I don't know? Which one would you like the most?"

"Jesus Christ, Patrick! I'm only messin' with ya!" Tara exclaimed, giving him a soft tap on the arm. "My God, lad—you're too serious. Do me a favor, will ya?"

"Yeah, sure. What?"

"Laugh. Just once, please. I just wanna make sure you can do it."

"Hah, hah! Very funny. See, I can do it."

"Just wanted to make sure, that's all. If I'm gonna date ya, then you're gonna have to laugh, and laugh at everything. No, no, let me rephrase that. I don't want a stiff, but I also don't want a clown, either. Just be yourself, Patrick, and I'm sure things will work out just fine."

As they walked back, hand in hand, Patrick could tell this was the girl he had waited for his entire life. She was beautiful and kind, and what more could a guy ask for? Arriving back at her house, the two saw that the throng had long since disbanded. He followed her up onto the porch, and she opened her arms to him, her lips ready. They kissed. "Goodnight, Patrick," she soon whispered as she turned and opened the door.

"Goodnight."

It was only after she went inside and he began walking away that it finally hit him—Tara O'Malley was his girlfriend! He ran home as fast as he could. Upon entering, he found both Phil and Kevin in the front parlor, watching the news. "Hey, lads!" he whooped.

"Hey, where the hell have you been?" Kevin inquired, turning off the television. "You were there when the scuffle broke out, and the next thing we knew, you were gone."

"Yeah, well, I went to the store with Tara to buy some fags."

"Some fags?" Phil murmured from the chaise. "I didn't know she smoked."

"She doesn't. At least not anymore, anyway. She said she quit about a year ago, but with all the commotion I guess she just felt like havin' one. So I walked with her to the store to buy a pack, and it was a good thing that I did!"

"Why? What happened?" Kevin questioned, concerned if there had been any trouble along the way.

Patrick beamed. "Guess what?"

"Well, come on, spit it out!" Phil grumbled, starting to get a little vexed from all the secrecy.

"All right, all right, listen. I asked Tara out and she said yes. Isn't that great?"

"Hey, that's wonderful! I'm happy for ya," Kevin answered cheerfully. "Tara's a great girl. She'll make an honest man out of you. Not to imply that you're not one already."

"And guess what from over here," Phil interjected. "I asked Sandra out, and she said yes, also."

"Hey, congratulations!" Patrick returned, smiling.

"Well, it looks like the two of us are all set for the summer. Now we just have to find ol' carrot head, here, someone."

"What did ya call me? Carrot head? The last person who uttered those words is lying at the bottom of the Liffey this very moment."

"Ooh, look at me hands, they're tremblin'," Phil shot back mockingly.

"Yeah, whatever! Anyway, I can get someone myself. I don't need you two hooligans scouring the streets for me. Besides, I've already got my eye on some-one."

"Really? Well, why don't ya tell us the name of this poor creature so we can go warn her in advance."

"Never mind, you! When the time's right I'll make me move."

"Well, the time's never been better, if I may say so myself," Phil replied ear-nestly. "You know I'm not one to tell stories …"

"Yeah, right! Tell me another one."

"Can I please finish?"

"Go ahead! Who's stoppin' ya?"

"Thank you. Like I said, I've never been one to gossip, but from the way it sounded last night, you were havin' just a wee bit too much fun playin' with your wanker. So in my best judgement, Kevin, you really should hurry up. I don't think it can take too much more of that type of punishment."

"It's a lie! It's a horrible lie!" Kevin cried as he jumped on Phil and they began to wrestle. Patrick fell into hysterics as he watched the two men roll back and forth. In less than 15 seconds, Kevin had Phil pinned to the floor. "Take it back!" he panted as he struggled to maintain his hold.

"I can't, it's the truth."

"Recant or die!"

"All right, all right, I take it back! I was only slaggin'."

"Good man," Kevin exclaimed as he loosened his grip.

"You guys are a feckin' riot!" Patrick said, chuckling, as the two men got to their feet.

"Ya think so?" Phil asked, untangling his shirt. "You wanna hear something else?"

"Yeah, sure. Why not?"

"It's all true. He was chokin' the feckin' shite out of it!"

"That's it! You're a dead man!" Kevin growled as he lunged forward. Phil, however, was too quick and evaded his grasp—but the pursuit was on. Around and around the sofa they went. At one point, Kevin even tried jumping over it, but fell in the process. The chase continued, unabated, for close to a minute, until both men, on opposite ends of the sofa, just stopped and glared at each other, beginning yet a new game. This staring contest lasted for another thirty seconds until neither man could take it anymore, and each broke down simultaneously into laughter. After shaking hands and coming to a truce, the two sat down with Patrick and talked for close to an hour more, during which time Phil agreed to accompany Patrick into town the following day to look for work once more.

Sure enough, both men arose early the next morning and set off in search of employment. Unfortunately, however, Lady Luck wasn't on their side that day, nor was she over the course of the next few weeks. And as August approached, both were still without work.

Those were very busy weeks for Patrick, for besides job hunting diligently day after day, each night was spent with Tara, and as the days passed, both found themselves falling in love. And though happy for this, he was more than a little concerned with the way his job search was progressing.

CHAPTER 9

▼

"Rise and shine, lads," Phil shouted, stepping from his room out into the hall-way. "I have a feelin' it's gonna be a great day. The sun's shining. The birds are chirpin'. Who could ask for anything more?"

"How about you shuttin' your feckin' hole!" a voice returned angrily. It was Kevin.

"Good morning," Phil said, opening his friend's door and entering the room.

"Oh, my God! Whadya doing? Six o'clock, Sunday morning, and you're run-nin' off at the mouth? What the hell's your problem?"

"I'm sorry. It's just that it's such a beautiful mornin', I didn't want for you to miss a single moment of it." Phil, too, had begun falling in love with Sandra, and with the way he was feeling, there could have been a tempest raging outside and he would have still thought it a wonderful day.

"Leave me alone! And shut the door behind ya," the tortured man growled from beneath his sheet.

"What's wrong?"

"What's wrong? What the feck do ya think's wrong?" Kevin snapped, whip-ping off the linen and propping himself up.

"I said I was sorry, didn't I?"

"Sorry? Sorry doesn't have anything to do with it, Phil! It's just common decency! You get up, so everyone else has to, too?"

"Yeah, I guess you're right."

"I know I'm right!"

"Well, that's good. At least we agree on that."

"Huh?"

"Never mind. It's not important. So, since you're already up, why don't you come on down and join me for a cup of tea."

"No, Phil! I'm tired! I'm goin' back to sleep!"

"All right, fine. I'm still gonna go have me some, so if you do happen to change your mind, the invitation's still open."

"Bastard!" Kevin grumbled only after Phil had left the room. He tried falling back asleep, but was soon out of bed, wide-awake, and at the table by the time the water was heated. Patrick had also made his way down by this point. "Have ya checked the classifieds yet?" he inquired, taking a seat.

"No, not yet," Phil answered as he stirred in his fourth spoon of sugar.

Patrick left the room but was soon back with the day's edition of the *Globe* in hand. Over the course of the next half-hour, the two men scoured every inch of the want ads, but found absolutely nothing.

"Hey, you know what. Maybe tomorrow we should go in different directions," Patrick said, folding his arms. "The more I've been thinkin' about it, the more I've come to the conclusion that maybe that's the problem. They might not want two friends workin' together. They probably think that we'll be screwin' around the whole time instead of doing our job."

"You think so?"

"Well, it makes sense, doesn't it?"

Phil thought about it for a moment. "Ya know what? You may be right. Then it's set. Tomorrow we go our own separate ways." Well, no sooner had the strategy been decided upon than there was a loud knock at the back door.

"Who the hell—?" Kevin exclaimed, rising from his seat and hurrying over, only to find Tara and Sandra standing there, each wearing a big grin.

"Good morning," both said upon entering.

"Kind of early, aren't we?" Kevin asked, frowning, as he walked back over to the table and once again took his seat. "What if we'd still been sleepin'? You would have woken us up. That wouldn't have been very nice of you, now would it?"

"Well, I guess that's just the risk we had to take," Tara retorted. "Anyway, we had a really great idea and wanted to come over as soon as possible and see what ya thought of it."

"What is it?" Patrick inquired.

"Okay, listen—whadya say about the five of us goin' to the Cape today?"

"Cape Cod? How we gonna get there?"

"By bus," Sandra replied, taking a seat on Phil's lap. "We just called. It's twenty-two dollars for a round-trip ticket, and the ride there only takes about an hour and a half."

"What's there to do there?"

"Oh, it's supposed to be brilliant! Maureen went yesterday with a couple of the girls that she works with, and they absolutely loved it. There's beaches and quaint little shops. Plus, she said the food's really good, too. Come on, let's do it!"

"Yeah, sure. Sounds good to me," Phil returned as he put his arm around Sandra's waist and pulled her close.

"I'm up for it, too," Patrick seconded.

"And you?" Tara asked, looking in Kevin's direction.

"Nah, I don't think so. That's not my idea of fun. Goin' to little shops or lying out on the beach. Besides, I'd just be in the way. No, why don't you four lovebirds jus' go yourselves."

"Don't be silly. You won't be in the way."

"Ah, don't worry about me. Besides, I've got things to do."

"Ah, come on! You'll have a good time," Phil entreated from across the table.

"Oh, yeah? And how do ya know that?"

"Because I just do."

Kevin sighed. "All right, fine, I'll go. But I can promise you this—I'm not goin' to any damn beaches!"

"Excellent!" Tara cheered. She then fell silent for a moment before asking what time it was.

"Five past seven," Patrick answered, looking up at the clock. "Why?"

"Well, there's a bus leavin' at half-past eight. If we hurry, we can catch it. Otherwise, we'll have to wait till ten for the next one. And then, by the time we get there, Christ, the day will already be almost half over."

The five agreed to try and make the eight-thirty departure, and they succeeded with not a moment to spare. The ride there was a scenic and pleasurable one, and they arrived at the Hyannis bus depot at exactly ten.

"So, now what?" Kevin questioned once they had all gotten off.

"Well, I guess the first thing we should do is probably find out when the last bus leaves," Tara replied. "I don't wanna get stranded here overnight."

"Yeah, I would say so! Don't ya think you should've maybe checked on that before we came?"

"Ah, just relax, will ya!" Tara muttered as she turned and headed for the ticket counter. They soon learned that the last bus didn't leave until ten that night.

"Lovely!" Sandra said enthusiastically. "That gives us twelve full hours. That should be enough time, I would think." All the others agreed.

As they exited the terminal, it suddenly occurred to them that they didn't have the slightest idea where they were. They soon returned to the ticket window.

"Excuse me, sir," Phil said politely, "we're strangers to Cape Cod and we really don't know where to go. If it wouldn't be too much trouble, could you please give us some advice."

"Well, what are you lookin' to do?" the old man answered.

"I don't know. What do most people do?"

"Shopping. Antiquing. Goin' to beaches. That's pretty much it, I guess."

"Well, then … that's what we'd like to do, also."

"All right, well, I guess you'd want to head over to twenty-eight, then. That's where everything is."

"Twenty-eight?"

The old man, seeing the puzzled expression on Phil's face, replied, "Yeah, Route 28. It's the main strip of road on the Cape, or at least, on this part, anyway. It's where the majority of all the attractions are."

"Oh, really? Well, then, that sounds perfect. Could you be kind enough to tell us how to get there?" After receiving the directions, they soon arrived at their destination, and for the next six hours they walked and walked and walked, all the while going into shop after shop after shop. By the time four finally rolled around, they found themselves in West Harwich.

"I take it back. Let's go to the beach," Kevin cried as they trudged along the narrow, sometimes unpaved sidewalk. "I can't take much more of this crap. What's the point, anyway? I mean, we've been in every goddamn shop we passed and ya haven't bought a single thing!"

"Ah, the day's not over yet, relax," Tara murmured as she threw her arm around his neck. "Besides, that's the fun part—just browsin'. Don't you know that, Kevin? That's what women like to do. Oh, yeah, that's right, I almost forgot. Ya don't have a woman. How would ya know."

"Get your arm off me now, Tara. Ya just pissed me off with that one," Kevin shot back, while everyone else fell into a fit of uncontrollable laughter.

"I'm … huh, huh! I was only … huh, huh, huh!" was the only response she could muster, for she was laughing so hard.

"Paddy, you'd better come and get your woman right now. Because I swear to God, I'm gonna throw her arse in front of the next large vehicle that comes along!"

"I was only slaggin'," Tara finally managed, struggling, as she bit down on the inside of her cheek. "You know I was. I'm sorry. You're a very good-lookin' man."

"Oh, yeah, a regular Brad Pitt!" Phil guffawed.

"Say whatever you want. It doesn't bother me."

"Look at me!" Tara implored as she grabbed him unexpectedly by the hand and blocked his way. "I'm sorry, Kevin. I truly am. I shouldn't have said it. I was wrong. Will ya please forgive me?"

"Makin' a joke like that at my expense? Tell me, why should I?"

"Because you're my friend. And if you don't … I don't think I'll ever be able to forgive myself. Please?"

Kevin considered it for a moment. "Yeah, all right, fine. I forgive you."

"Thank you."

"It's just that … sayin' stuff like that's mean."

"Yeah, I know," she said, frowning, looking at the ground. "Could I ask ya for another favor?"

"What?"

"Smile. Please. For me."

After doing what she asked of him, and a reciprocation on her part, the five resumed their march, friends once again. They walked on for a short while longer until Kevin abruptly stopped and grumbled, "Can't we at least take a breather, for Christ's sake. Seriously. I'm feckin' beat." In fact, they were all dead tired by this point, and upon hearing his suggestion, all four wholeheartedly agreed.

They immediately began searching for a place to rest, but couldn't find a single spot, not even a bench. After plodding on momentarily, they finally came upon the perfect location: it was called the Mill Store, and there were literally hundreds of picnic tables in a large fenced-in yard about seventy-five feet off the road.

"How about in there?" Tara asked, pointing, being the first one to notice it.

"Yeah, that's as good a place as any, I guess," Kevin acknowledged as he turned and began making his way for the enclosure.

"Yeah, that looks like a pretty good place, all right," Patrick seconded. "Do ya think they'll mind?"

"Mind? They probably won't even notice us. Look at all the people," Phil said as he surveyed their surroundings, and what peculiar surroundings they were. There were doghouses and swing sets scattered about. Sheds, lounge chairs, and miniature wooden windmills dotted the landscape. There was even an item for sale that really amused them, a butterfly house. "Give me a break!" Phil sniggered as he read over the instructions that were stapled to its side. "And they want ten dollars for it, too! Now I've seen it all."

They soon made their way to the extreme back of the yard and collapsed onto a colossal table that was partially hidden behind a huge oak tree. Moments later, a silver-haired man, probably in his early sixties, headed in their direction. "Hello, my name is Norman," he said, smiling. "Is there anything I can help you with?"

"So, no one's gonna notice us, huh?" Kevin muttered under his breath.

"Yes, um … hello. We were just lookin' at a couple of your fine tables, here," Phil answered as he got to his feet and flashed the salesman a big grin. "Could you give us some information on 'em? Especially this monster. What type of wood is it?"

Huge mistake. The man started with a description of the table that lasted nearly two minutes, the entire time not even stopping to get a breath of air. By the time he finished, he had turned what appeared to be a simple pine table into something more closely resembling a work by one of the 'Masters'. However, upon closer scrutiny, the sagacious old man realized that they weren't there to make a purchase, so he ceased the sales pitch. "You're not interested in buying a table, are you?" he asked.

"Honestly, sir? No. We're just really exhausted from all the walking we've done today, and when we saw your store, here, it just looked like the perfect place to take a rest. I hope you don't mind?"

"No, of course not."

Tara smiled. "Thank you, Norman. We promise, we won't stay long. We're just a little winded, that's all. We've been walking for the past six hours."

"Really? Are you kids working here for the summer?"

"No," Sandra returned, "we're from Boston. We just came down for the day."

"Is this your first time here?"

"Yes," they all replied.

"So, how do you like it so far?"

"Oh, it's lovely!" Tara said.

"Lovely, indeed!" the man nodded with an air of satisfaction. "So, have you run into a lot of other Irish so far?"

"No, why?" Phil inquired. "Are there many Irish people here?"

"Are there many? Yes, I would say so! Hundreds, if not thousands. Students mostly. They all come over for the summer to work. We had one last summer, John. Good kid. Not the best worker, mind you, but a good kid," Norman chuckled as he ran his comb through his hair.

"Oh, I didn't know that."

"Yes. My mother was born in England," Norman then said, breaking away from the subject, "right in London. She always used to say, 'I'm not from Europe. I'm from Britain.'"

"Oh, did she?"

"She sure did. I've been to Ireland, though. Six times, to be exact. I used to own a travel agency."

"Oh, really? Which parts?" Tara asked.

Another big mistake! Norman once again began rambling about all his exploits over in the Emerald Isle. By this time, Kevin was just flat-out sorry that they had chosen this, of all places, to stop. "Norman," he said, breaking in, just as they were beginning to be told about how he was almost trampled by a horse during race week back in '71, "sorry to cut you off, but can I ask you something?"

"Yeah, sure. What is it?"

"Well, we're starvin'. Could you recommend a good place to eat?"

"Could I? You're darn right I can! There's this little place, about a quarter-mile up the road, called the Westside Grille. They serve up the best food around. Their crab cakes are to die for!"

"Are they expensive?"

"No, not at all."

"What else do they have there besides crab cakes?" asked Sandra, not a big seafood lover.

"They have everything. Sandwiches. Chicken. Pizza. Everything! Come on," he said, motioning for them to follow. "We have this little booklet inside the store with different things to do in it." The five got to their feet and began to follow him.

"Fast for an ol' bastard, isn't he?" Phil whispered jokingly as they struggled to catch up. Upon entering the small wood shop, they were immediately taken aback by the extreme heat within. "Christ almighty!" he gasped. "Haven't they ever heard of air-conditioning around here?"

By this time, their newfound well-wisher was nowhere to be seen, for he had run off to fetch them one of the guidebooks. "Steve!" he suddenly shouted. "I'd like for you to meet a few people." At once, out walked another man, roughly the same age.

"Steve, I'd like to introduce you to," Norman then said, motioning for Phil to begin the formalities.

"Nice to meet you," the other man replied when all had had their chance. "My name's Stephen Semple. I'm the store's manager"

"They're from Boston," Norman interjected. "Down for the day, and I just thought one of our little guidebooks, here, may be of some use."

"Hey, hey, hey—Boston! I used to go to Boston all the time, about thirty-five years ago, when I was in the Army and stationed at Fort Devins. Had a lot of great times there. Talk about a fun city!"

"Yeah, Boston's lovely, all right," Tara confirmed with a big smile.

"What part of the city do you live in?"

"We live in South Boston."

"South Boston?"

"Yeah, Southie."

"Nah, I don't think I was ever in that section before."

"Well, here's the book I was telling you about," Norman said as he handed the thin publication to Phil. "Look through it. You may just find something in there that catches your eye."

"Okay," Phil answered as he took hold. "Well, thanks for all your help, guys. We really appreciate it. But unfortunately, we really do have to get goin'."

"Well, it was nice meeting you. If you're ever down again make sure you drop by and say 'hello'," Mr. Semple replied as he hurried off to tend to a customer who was currently waiting at the counter.

"We will," Tara shouted, waving goodbye.

"Like I was saying, go to the Westside Grille. You won't be disappointed. And tell them, Norman, Norman Pelletier, sent you, okay? They may even give you a discount."

"Yeah, okay, Norman. Thanks," Phil assured as they turned and headed for the door. When they were about twenty yards from the building, he turned to everyone. "Christ. A little too friendly, weren't they?"

"Stop it, you!" Sandra giggled as she gave him a soft tap on the shoulder. "They were just two nice old men tryin' to help us out, that's all."

"Yeah, I guess."

They walked the short distance to the Westside where they dined that evening, and it did turn out to be every bit as good as Norman had said, but it also turned out to be a little more costly than they had expected. And though they mentioned his name numerous times, they never received a discount.

By the time they finished eating, it was close to seven. With both their funds and their energies pretty well depleted, they all decided to call it a day and catch the eight o'clock bus back instead. Kevin had their waitress call them a taxi, which he paid for with the last of his money, and before they knew it, they were back at the bus terminal.

"What took us six hours took her only fifteen minutes, you know that," Kevin said as he collapsed down onto one of the red padded seats inside the station. "I think I'm gonna save up and buy me a car. I'm sick of walkin' everywhere, anyways."

"Ah, they're more trouble than they're worth," Phil exhorted.

"Maybe, but still … I still think I'm gonna get me one."

"The eight o'clock bus to Boston's South Station is now boarding," a voice announced over the intercom. It was quarter of when they took their seats, and by eight, when the bus pulled away, all five were sound asleep.

Upon arriving in Boston, the driver personally had to wake them. After hailing a taxi, they were soon back in Southie, let off in front of the girls' house. Exhausted, they agreed to call it a night, and within half an hour, all five were in bed, fast asleep.

CHAPTER 10

▼

Everyone was still feeling fatigued the next morning. Kevin, in fact, had over-slept, and was frantically running about the house by the time the other two made their way down. "I'm tellin' ya, Phil. I'm gettin' meself a car, trouble or not!" he shouted as he ran out the door.

"Yeah, okay. You do that," Phil yawned, still half asleep.

Both men plopped down at the table and sat there motionless. Close to a minute passed, during which time not a single word was exchanged, when Phil suddenly got to his feet and began preparing breakfast. Patrick soon got up and lent a hand. After a meal of bacon and eggs, and two cups of tea apiece, both felt somewhat rejuvenated. They lingered in the kitchen for a short time before heading upstairs to shower and dress, and when ready the two men left the house and caught a bus downtown. Upon arriving, they wished each other luck and parted ways.

Patrick headed back over to Newbury Street, on advice from Tara, and applied at each and every place he passed. However, the responses he received were all the same: "You can fill out an application if you'd like, but we're just not hiring at the moment."

Frustrated, he elected to give the financial district another try. *What harm can it do, right?* he thought. So he resolutely began the trek there, but along the way decided to sit for a moment, for his legs were beginning to tire. That moment soon turned into half an hour. As he sat there, he grew more and more disgusted with each passing second. Maybe this whole thing had been a foolish idea in the first place, just as Moses had told him. He was deep in thought when someone began speaking to him. Looking up, he saw the old woman he had met at the airport terminal.

"Good morning," she said, smiling, as she loomed above. "Now, let me see if I remember. Patrick, right?"

"Aye," he nodded. "But I'm sorry to say, I forgot yours."

"Oh, that's quite all right. It's Bridget. Bridget Murphy."

"Right. So … how ya doin'?"

"I'm doing well. And yourself?"

Patrick sighed. "Not too good. I've been here for over a month now already, and I haven't even had a single job offer so far."

"Didn't I tell you on the day you arrived that it might be difficult?"

"Aye," he replied disconsolately.

She sat down beside him. "All I can tell you is to persevere. Sooner or later, something's bound to come along."

"Thanks for the words of encouragement, Miss Murphy, but I don't have much time left. If something doesn't come along soon, and I mean real soon, I won't have any other option than to go back home. I've already gone through half my savings, plus, the rent money's due next week. So, as you can see, I'm really in a bad way."

"Like I said, Patrick. Don't quit looking. Check the classifieds every day, and most of all, take the first job offer you get, whatever it may be."

"Believe me, I will. At this moment, I'd even take a job cleanin' toilets all day."

"Hopefully, it won't come to that!" the old woman chuckled. "Just remember, keep some laughter in your heart and a smile on your face, and in the end, even if it doesn't work out, at least you'll know that you gave it your best. And there's no shame in that."

With this sage advice, Miss Murphy said goodbye and walked off. Patrick thought about what she had said for a moment, and then went job searching some more. However, after about an hour or so, he decided just to give it up for the day. He was disgusted, and would only end up making a bad impression, anyway. He walked all the way back to Southie that afternoon, deciding to forego public transportation, almost as a self-imposed punishment. Upon arriving back at the house, he found Phil and Sandra on the sofa, kissing. Both were drunk.

"Isn't it kind of early for that?"

Phil grinned. "Which one? The foolin' around or the drinkin'?"

"The drinkin' part, Phil."

"Well, come to think of it, I suppose it is. But I was feelin' a wee bit down, so I just said, 'Ah, what the hell!'"

"Yeah, I know the feelin'," Patrick returned, frowning. "So … what time did you get back?"

"About an hour ago, I'd say. I applied at a few places without much luck, and since it was Sandra's day off, I just decided to come home. How about you? Any prospects?"

"What do you think?"

"Ah, don't let it get to you, Paddy. So what if we have to live on the streets and beg for food. Hey, there's worse things in life."

"Oh, yeah? Like what?"

"I don't know. Let me think. How about, um … I've got it! Like, 'not being from Europe, but from Britain,'" Phil replied, trying his best to mimic the voice of the man they had spoken with the day before. All three laughed. "Or what about missin' a limb? That would definitely have to be a whole lot worse, don't ya think?"

"You're wacked! You know that, don't ya?"

"Ah, don't worry about it, lads. It won't come to that," Sandra interposed. "And even if you do happen to get your arse's booted by Kevin, ya know you'll always be able to stay with us."

"Yeah, but that's not fair to Kevin! What? Is he supposed to suffer on account that we can't pull our own?"

"Well, what else can we do?" Phil countered, coming to Sandra's defense. "It's not like we haven't been lookin'. We're just goin' through a bad stretch, that's all."

"I don't know," Patrick said glumly. "And I didn't mean to take it out on you, Sandra. Sorry."

"Don't worry about it."

"Yeah, don't let it faze ya," Phil added. "Why don't you just forget about today, and come on over and join us for a beer."

"No, thanks. I think I'm jus' gonna go up to me room and take a nap." And with that, Patrick turned and began walking up the stairs.

CHAPTER 11

▼

Patrick awoke in darkness. Looking over at his alarm clock, he soon realized that it wasn't ticking. He just lay there for a few moments experiencing that strange sensation of not knowing whether it was late night or early morning. After entertaining this thought for a while, he then began thinking about his encounter with Miss Murphy and her advice. Shortly, he rose and went downstairs to find out exactly what time it was. The clock in the front parlor showed it to be 4:46 a.m.

"Great," he sighed disgustedly, "I've wasted an entire day."

He stood there scratching his head, not fully believing he could have slept for so long a time. Knowing that the lads wouldn't be up for at least another hour or so, and also knowing that it would be fruitless to attempt to go back to sleep, he sat down on the sofa and began planning his upcoming day. Where would he look for work? What would he wear? When he finally decided on the answers, he went into the kitchen and made himself a cup of tea. While sipping at it, he suddenly fell to daydreaming, once again about Miss Murphy. For some reason, he felt intrigued by her, but didn't know why. And this bothered him.

As he finished his cup of tea, the clock in the kitchen showed it to be quarter-past six. Soon, an alarm was heard ringing on the floor above, and knowing quite well that it wasn't coming from Phil's room, Patrick awaited Kevin's arrival. He set out another cup and began heating some more water. Not long after, and much to his surprise, down the stairs flew Phil.

"I thought that was Kevin's clock."

"It was, but it's so goddamn loud, it's like my alarm clock, too. I'm tellin' ya, I'm gonna smash that little fecker some day."

"Ah, he'd kill ya!" Patrick asserted as he went over to the cupboard to fetch yet another cup.

"I'm not talkin' about Kevin. I'm talking about that goddamn Baby Ben of his. Baby my arse! And he always sets it on high. He has absolutely no regard for my welfare or for yours either, for that matter."

"He'd kill ya, nonetheless."

"Yeah, you're probably right. But ya never know. I could land a good one," Phil said, smirking. "Hey, I've done it in the past."

"Yeah, but your little sister doesn't count, though."

"Hey, ya bastard! You were almost the recipient of one, remember?"

"Aye, I do. And it was one of the scariest moments in all me life."

"Yeah, whatever," Phil said derisively, shaking his head. "Enough about me already. What about you? Ya slept your whole entire day away. I guess Sunday really took its toll on you, huh?"

"I know, Jesus—I was shocked meself when I found out. Why didn't you guys try wakin' me or something?"

"We did! But ya just wouldn't come out of it! I even splashed some water on your face, but ya still didn't budge."

"Really?"

"Aye!"

"Yeah, well, I guess I'm out of shape, all right. But still … to sleep all that time?"

No sooner had Patrick finished speaking than in the room walked Kevin. "Hey, lads," he said, taking a seat.

"Good mornin'."

"A little tired, weren't we?"

"Yeah, I know. We were just talkin' about that," Patrick replied as he brought over the two cups and handed one to each of the men. "So, I didn't even budge, huh?"

"No, you were out stone-cold."

"That's pathetic."

The three spoke a short while longer until Kevin got to his feet. "I've gotta get goin'," he said.

"All right. See ya later," Phil returned, sipping at his tea.

"Yeah, have a good one," Patrick added.

Kevin left the room, but was soon back with the morning's paper in hand. "Here ya go, lads. Who knows? Maybe today's your lucky day," he said, smiling, as he tossed it on the table and then hurried off once more.

Patrick picked it up and began looking through the 'Help Wanted' section. The first few pages didn't yield any positive leads, but on page four an ad caught his eye. How couldn't it? It took up almost the entire page. After reading it a couple of times, he called Phil over to take a look.

"Yeah, it sounds good, all right," Phil said upon finishing, "but I wonder what a Customer Service Representative does?"

"Who cares what they do! Look how much they're payin' to start."

The ad the two men were looking at, read, as follows:

> 'AT&T will be opening a new Customer Sales & Service Center in downtown Boston. The positions, 1,000 in all, will be for Customer Service Representatives. Applicants should possess good communication skills and work well with others. Starting salary will be $580.00 per week. Employees will receive full medical and dental coverage after six months. All prospective applicants should call the number below, between the hours of 9:00 a.m.—12:00 p.m., Tuesday through Friday, to make an appointment to test for the available positions.'

"Wanna call?"

"Yeah, sure. Why not?" Phil replied, yawning. "What time is it now?"

"Close to eight. What is AT&T, anyways?"

"It's the phone company."

"That's what it is? A phone company?"

"Aye, a long-distance one."

"Are they any good?"

"Good in what way?"

"You know, like to work for."

"How the feck should I know! They're big enough, all right. I can tell ya that. Probably the biggest in the country. Ya can't turn on the telly without seein' one of their goddamn commercials. And they're so freakin' corny, too!" The two sat there silently for a couple of minutes until Phil finally noticed an angered expression staring back at him. "What?" he asked.

Patrick wasted no time. "You! I ask ya a simple question and you snap at me like that?"

"Oh, God! Not another one!"

"Whadya mean? 'Not another one'?"

"Nevermind."

"But I do! So tell me!"

"Tell ya what?"

"What ya meant by it?"

"I mean ya always have to watch what you say around this place. Ya say something in the wrong tone and you offend someone."

"Who's offended?"

"Well … obviously, you!"

"No, I'm not. I just wanted to know what you meant by it."

"Well, now you do!"

The two men glared at each other for a moment before Patrick finally looked away. "Hey, man. I'm sorry," he said.

Phil smiled and waved him off. With their animosities behind them, the two waited for nine o'clock to arrive, but when it finally did, they didn't have much luck, for the lines were all busy.

"Ah, the whole town's probably callin' right now," Phil exclaimed from his reclined position on the sofa. "You'll never get through."

Patrick persevered, however. He continued calling for close to two hours until the phone was finally answered.

"Kelly Staffing. How may I help you?"

"Yes, I was callin' to make an appointment for the AT&T testing."

"Yeah, you and everybody else," the young woman on the other line giggled. "No, no, I'm only kidding! Um … how about tomorrow at three?"

"Yeah, sure. That sounds good," Patrick replied enthusiastically. After giving her all his vital information, he then asked where the testing was going to be held.

"At the Copley Plaza, on St. James Avenue. Do you know where that is? Or do you need directions?"

Patrick chuckled. "Oh, no. I know it well." And well he did, for he had applied there more than once since first beginning his job quest. "Yes. Yes. All right, well—thank you."

Just as he was getting ready to hang up the phone, Phil suddenly sprung up and yanked it from his hand. "Yes, um, good morning," he said in his most endearing tone to the young woman, while at the same time giving Patrick an evil glare. "My name is Philip Doyle and I too would like to make an appointment for the testing, preferably at the same time as my friend, if that's at all possible?"

"I don't see why not. We just opened that time slot."

After furnishing all of his information and receiving a confirmation of his test time, he asked, "And if it wouldn't be too much of a bother, could I also make an appointment for a friend of ours?"

"Are they there now?"

"No."

"I'm sorry, but they'd have to call in themselves."

"I can appreciate that," Phil acknowledged just before thanking the woman and hanging up. "Didn't mean to rip your arm off, but who knows? It could've been another two hours before I got through."

"Yeah, I don't know what I was thinkin'," Patrick conceded. "Your appointment's for tomorrow at three, too?"

"Aye."

"Good. We can go together."

"You know what? We should tell the girls about this."

"Brilliant idea. Now how come I didn't think of that?"

"Because you're not me, that's why."

"Ah, true, true. Very true."

The two men soon left, with paper in hand, and headed up the street to the girls' house. Upon entering, however, they found that the girls had already seen the ad and were calling themselves that very moment.

"So, I guess you've seen today's paper, huh?" Phil asked as he walked over to Sandra and gave her a kiss.

"Yes, okay, then. Thank you," Joanne said suddenly, as she hung up the phone. She then ran over to her sister. "Guess what?"

"Three o'clock?"

"Yep!" she blurted as they hugged one another and began jumping up and down, hand in hand.

"Tomorrow?" Phil asked, watching their girlish glee disapprovingly.

"Yeah, tomorrow at three," Sandra returned. "Why?"

"Because that's the same time we're scheduled to take it."

"No suh?"

"Seriously. Who else is goin'?"

"Well, the two of us, plus Tara. The others just didn't want to, or thought that they'd get in trouble if they took the day off."

"And you're all tomorrow at three?"

"Aye, we are."

"Give me that damn phone! I'm callin' that place back and settin' up an appointment for Kev. And who knows, maybe it'll be for tomorrow at three, too!"

Wasting no time, Phil gave the staffing agency another ring, and as luck would have it, ended up getting the same girl he had spoken with previously. Amazed, he composed himself and attempted to pull off his best Kevin impersonation—

and it worked! "Very well, then. Tomorrow at three at the Copley," he confirmed, winking. "I'll be there."

"Are you serious?" Sandra asked after he had gotten off the line.

"I am. I guess it's a big place, this Copley."

"Ah, that's wonderful! We can all go together, ya know, and be like some sort of encouragement for one another."

"Hey, where's Tara?" Patrick questioned suddenly.

"Upstairs," Joanne replied. "But she's feelin' a wee bit under the weather, though, if ya know what I mean."

"No, why? What's wrong?"

Everyone started to laugh.

"You'll have to excuse my good friend, here. He's a fine, upstanding young man, but a little naïve about these sorts of things," Phil explained, grinning, as he walked over to Patrick and whispered in his ear, "She's havin' her period. That's what it means."

"Oh" Patrick uttered, looking away in embarrassment. "Can I go see her?" he asked after an uncomfortable moment or two.

"I don't see why not," Sandra answered. "She's probably in the bathroom, though. She didn't look too good the last time I saw her. Plus, you may also wanna be a little careful. She wasn't in the best of moods."

After absorbing all of Sandra's advice, Patrick made his way cautiously up the stairs and, sure enough, found the door to the bathroom closed. He knocked.

"Who is it?" Tara snapped.

"It's me, Patrick. Are you all right?"

There was a brief silence. "I'll be out in a second. Go wait in my room, okay?"

Patrick did as she asked. After waiting what seemed forever, she finally walked in and sank down beside him on the bed. "I'm not feeling too well," she groaned.

"I know, I heard. Is there anything I can do?"

"What?"

"Yeah, Joanne and Phil told me."

"Well, Joanne and Phil have big mouths, then!"

"Don't be mad at 'em. I was the one that asked."

""They still have big mouths, though!"

"So, what's this I hear about you and the others takin' a test for jobs at AT&T?" Patrick questioned, realizing it probably best to change the subject.

"Yeah, Joanne was lookin' through the paper this mornin' and came across the ad. And for that amount of money, I decided to call myself. I was just about to go over and tell you guys. You and Phil should call. The ad said that they were gonna be hirin' 1,000 people."

"We already have. And guess what? Our appointment's for tomorrow at three, too."

"Really?"

"Yeah."

"Cool. We can all go together."

Patrick and Tara soon made their way down and joined the rest of the gang. They all talked for a while, trying to figure out exactly what type of position it was that they were applying for. Before they knew it, they somehow all ended up back at the lads' house with a case of black & tan. The joviality was in full force when the front door suddenly flew open and in walked Kevin. "Hey," he nodded, coming over. "What's the party for?"

"Well, I wouldn't call it a party. Just a little get-together, that's all," Phil replied. "And guess what?"

"What?"

"Sandra, Tara, and Joanne, along with Patrick and I, all have appointments tomorrow to test for jobs with AT&T."

"Hey, that's great! AT&T's a good company. What type of positions are you applying for?"

"Customer Service Representative. Any idea of what that may be?"

"Not in the slightest. Well, come to think, maybe it's some sort of job like an operator. Yeah, that's probably what it is. That would be customer service, right?"

Phil shrugged. "I guess. And ya wanna hear something else?"

"What?"

"We even made an appointment for you, too. Wasn't that nice of us?"

Upon hearing this, Kevin became jarred. "Now ya had no right to do that! I'm perfectly happy where I am now. Besides, I can't get tomorrow off, anyway."

"Come on, Kev, it's a Wednesday. No one gets their checks on a Wednesday."

"Oh, I see. That's all I do is cash checks, right? No, I don't think so! There's a lot more to bein' a teller than cashin' checks, let me tell ya!"

"I know there is," Phil conceded. "It's a very demanding profession. What's that other thing you do? Ah, let me think for a second. You know. Come on, Kev, help me out here. Ooh, ooh, now I remember! You open up that little drawer and hand people money."

"Bastard!" Kevin growled as he got up and began walking away.

"I'm only slaggin'! Get your arse back over here, will ya."

"No!"

"You even said it yourself. AT&T's a great company."

"And what? Sovereign's not?" Kevin retorted, whipping back around.

"Okay, I admit it. Sovereign's good, but it's small compared to AT&T. And the bigger the company, the more job stability, right?" Phil propounded as he looked to his friends for assistance.

"That's correct. Plus, the larger the company, the better the opportunities are goin' to be for its employees, too," Sandra added.

"Ah, you! You're in cahoots with him, anyways. You'd probably agree with anything he said, wouldn't ya? Come on—admit it!"

"Probably."

"That's what I thought. So keep your opinions to yourself, because there's no validity to them," Kevin sneered as he once again turned and began stomping off.

"It pays $580.00 a week, Kev," said Patrick, who had up until that point remained silent.

"How much?" Kevin muttered, stopping dead in his tracks.

"Five-hundred and eighty dollars, plus full medical and dental coverage after six months. That's better than you're making now, isn't it?"

"A little better."

"It's a whole hell of a lot better, and now you admit it!" Phil returned sharply.

"Yeah, okay, it's more. But still … I can't get the day off. So, it doesn't even matter if it was for $1000.00 a week. I'm not gonna jeopardize a sure thing on a long shot. We need money now, and I'm the only one bringin' it in. So, you guys go, and I wish ya the best of luck. But I just can't."

"Why don't ya just call up your boss, what's her name? Nellie, right?"

"Yeah."

"Jus' call her up and see if you can get out a little early, that's all. My God. The test isn't until three."

Kevin sat down for a moment, pondering the idea, before finally getting back to his feet. "Ah, what the heck!"

"Now that's the Kevin I know and love! Just tell her ya have a doctor's appointment for around two or so. She can't fire you for that. I mean, it's not like this is an everyday occurrence or anything. You haven't even missed a single day so far, have ya?"

"No, I haven't," Kevin confirmed proudly as he walked into the kitchen to call. He reappeared a few minutes later. "Well, if we're gonna be takin' a test, we shouldn't be getting' drunk, now should we?"

"She said it would be all right?"

"Aye. She even told me I could leave at one so I wouldn't be late."

"See, I told ya."

"He's right," Patrick interjected. "How can we do well if we're all in bits?"

All agreed. After conversing for a short while longer, the soiree soon broke up and everybody headed to bed early, to ensure his or her success the following day.

CHAPTER 12

▼

The next morning, everyone was dressed and ready by noon. They assembled at the lads' house and awaited Kevin's arrival. All were nervous except Phil. "Relax, guys. It'll probably be a piece of cake," he said, making his way down the stairs from brushing his teeth.

"Probably will," replied Tara, one of the smartest of the bunch, "but I still get nervous whenever I test. Been that way ever since I was a wee girl."

Joanne sighed. "Me, too."

They talked among themselves until Kevin returned; when he did, the six of them caught a bus downtown and got off not far from their destination. Upon arriving at the Copley, the 'Grand Dame of Boston,' each had to show two forms of identification before being allowed to enter a splendid ballroom, 'The Venetian Room,' that had been converted for the occasion with twenty long Formica tables for the test-takers to sit at.

The group got there at around quarter-past two and were among the first to be seated. Slowly, more and more people began to drift in. By the time three finally arrived, there had to have been close to a hundred people.

Phil winked at the outset to all his friends. "Trust me, we'll do fine."

The test, however, was a bizarre concoction of perception and number matching drills that were more like sprints than an actual exam. Upon finishing, each handed in their test booklets and dejectedly retook their seats. Every person in attendance would have bet their life they failed, and most would have been right. Slowly, small groups of people were called out and told their results. Among the first was Tara. In the end, the only ones not to have passed were Sandra and Joanne.

As they exited the luxurious hotel, Phil threw his arms around the necks of both women. "Come on, don't let it bother ya. It was a stupid feckin' test, anyway. Christ, even Einstein could've failed that one! We were just flat-out lucky, that's all. I bet if we all took it over again, the results would be altogether different."

"Stop tryin' to console us, Phil! It's not working! I guess smarts just doesn't run in our family," Sandra cried as she and Joanne broke away and began walking ahead of everyone.

"Come on, stop talkin' like that," Tara implored as she and the rest of the group caught up. "Like Phil said, intelligence didn't have anything to do with it. It was just pure luck we passed. And like they said, you can retake it in six months."

"Screw it! And screw AT&T! I'm not retaking anything! Besides, what makes you think I'd be able to pass it then if I couldn't pass it now?"

"You can't look at it like that! My God … if people looked at things that way, the world would be a bleak place," Phil said philosophically. Finally, he just flat out told her, that as his girl, she didn't need to work—and she shouldn't! Sandra wasted no time, though, stating that she was a modern woman, and as such, didn't believe in that type of thinking. But since she already had a job as a chambermaid at the Ritz-Carlton, this lost opportunity wasn't as devastating to her as it was to Joanne, who had been without work since coming over four months earlier.

As they walked back to Southie that sultry August day, all were quiet. Upon arriving at the house, however, they began talking about the test, and the upcoming steps. For the passing of the exam, they had learned, was only the first of many hurdles along the lengthy road to obtaining employment with the telecommunications super-giant.

Next, there was to be a phone test that would gauge how well they would perform under the pressures that the position would surely entail. This phase was scheduled for the next day. And if they passed this mock role-play, there was still an interview, a drug screening, and a few other determinants that had to be considered before they would be hired.

Each persevered through the grueling days that followed, but in the end, only Patrick, Phil, and Tara remained. Kevin had been eliminated after performing poorly on the phone test. But since he already had a job, he wasn't really too saddened, and said, that with time, he believed he could once again lead a happy and productive life. In fact, everyone who took it agreed that the on-line part was probably the toughest step of the entire process.

Patrick was ecstatic when he learned that he had been hired, and was to begin training the first week of September. It couldn't have come at a better time: he was down to his last three hundred dollars. And even though September was only a few weeks away, it still meant that he wouldn't be receiving a check for over a month. However, Kevin, being the good chap that he was, told them not to worry about the rent. He would cover it as long as they promised to bring him out to dinner at Anthony's Pier 4 when they received their first paychecks. Both men wholeheartedly agreed. Also, upon learning the good news, Patrick called home (only the third time since his arrival) to let his family know that his bad luck had finally turned.

"Ah, congratulations!" Brian cheered after being told. "It's about time, huh?"

"Yeah, I know. I was startin' to get a little worried there, meself."

"Okay, okay," his father said suddenly. "There's someone here that wants to speak to ya."

"Patrick?"

"Yeah, it's me, Ma. Hi."

"Oh, Patrick! It's so good to hear your voice. How are ya?"

"I'm grand. And guess what? I've found a job."

"I know! I heard! Congratulations!"

"Thanks."

"So tell me … what's the name of this company that hired ya?"

"AT&T."

"Right. That's funny. I was just reading an article about them in the paper a couple of days ago."

"You were?"

"Aye."

"What was it about?"

"Oh, something about how they're signing a lot of big contracts with corporations and businesses over here. How they're makin' their presence felt, ya know. Or something like that, anyway, I think."

"How ya feelin'?" Patrick then asked after a brief pause.

"I'm feelin' all right, I guess. You know, doing what I'm supposed to be doing. Takin' my medication. But I'd be doin' a whole lot better if ya called a little more often."

"I've been busy, Ma. You know that."

"I know. I know. I'm sorry."

"Ah, it's all right. Don't worry about it."

"So, tell me about your job. Whadya gonna be doin'?"

"To be honest with ya, Ma … I really don't know. Some type of customer service."

"That's sounds nice. At least you won't have to be breaking your back everyday."

"Yeah, they said it's gonna be a really pleasant environment to work in. Besides, Ma, that's why I went to school. So I wouldn't have to break my back everyday."

"Yeah, I know."

"Oh, and guess what else."

"Go ahead, tell me. I'm listening."

"I've met a girl."

"Have ya now?"

"Aye."

"Is she nice?"

"Oh, Ma—she's wonderful. Her name's Tara O'Malley."

"She's Irish?"

"Born and raised. From Tipperary. Over here with a bunch of her friends. She got hired, too."

"Is it serious?"

"Yeah … I think it is."

"Then she's a very lucky girl!" They talked for a little while longer, and before ending the conversation, Patrick promised that he would call more often.

The next few weeks were carefree ones. With jobs in hand, and no worries on their mind, both Patrick and Phil decided just to kick back and have some fun. They went on a few day trips, including one to Martha's Vineyard, in which Phil got really drunk and nearly fell overboard on the return trip. There was also much drinking and merriment during that period—probably too much to be exact—for when September finally rolled around, both men were nearly broke.

CHAPTER 13

▼

The day Patrick had long dreamnt of finally arrived. He was now employed, and by one of the nation's largest corporations, at that. Yes, it was a glorious day indeed!

It is also safe to say that as the three of them arrived at their new worksite, each was filled with nothing but enthusiasm. However, it didn't take long for their excitement to be replaced by that of yet another emotion—concern. After learning precisely what the job entailed—servicing customers' residential phone accounts—they were then told that over the course of the next six weeks they were to be taught the terminal activities of over twenty different computer screens, emanating from two entirely separate operating platforms, along with all the nuances of exceptional customer service. Sure enough, the following weeks proved to be the most challenging of their young lives, but each persevered and helped one another by quizzing and going over their notes each morning before they started.

As the fourth week of training rolled around, they were set to take their first calls. Simple inquiries were to be routed through the conversant; ones that would allow them to get their feet wet, but at the same time, not dishearten them. The class of eighteen buddied-up for the event. Patrick and Phil plugged into the same phone, while Tara sat with Nicole Gunderson, a girl a few years her senior with whom she had become rather good friends.

As they sat there, all eighteen, including Phil, were apprehensive. Tara received the very first call. It was a basic request, just to tell the customer how much his bill for the month was.

Phil, a few minutes later, also got a rudimentary one: to give an elderly woman a listing for a number on her bill that she didn't recognize. "Piece of cake," he said, smirking, as he pushed the little white button on the phone that temporarily deactivated it.

"Yeah, that was easy enough, all right," Patrick affirmed.

The two men sat there silently for a moment until Phil finally asked him if he was ready.

"No, no. Just give me a second, okay," Patrick replied as he sat up straight in his chair.

Their instructor, Sherry Mohammad, who was close by at the time, noticed the worried look on his face and walked over. "How's it goin'?"

"All right, I guess."

"A little nervous?"

"Yeah," Patrick finally acknowledged as a look of disgust overtook him.

"Don't worry, you'll do fine. Trust me."

"Yeah," he sighed as he took in a deep breath and turned the phone back on. As he sat there awaiting his first call, he said a little prayer for good luck. No sooner had he finished than the phone suddenly beeped and he found himself speaking with a real person. Somehow, though, this call slipped through the system. It wasn't simple, but instead, very involved.

The customer, a man from Lubbock, Texas, who was of Vietnamese descent, was screaming incessantly that he had been charged the wrong per-minute rate for the third month in a row and that he was just plain fed up with it. He wanted the calls re-rated to the correct amount, and when they were, that he was going to leave and go with another carrier.

Patrick tried his best to remain composed, but the whole time the man kept yelling, which in turn, caused Patrick to make an error on the calculation. The man immediately caught the mistake and told him to do it again, which he did, but this time he sent it through for double the correct amount. On hearing the revised total of the adjustment, the man growled, "Make sure Southwestern Bell is notified of this!" and hung up.

"What an arsehole!" Phil exclaimed as he once again disabled the phone and looked at Patrick in disbelief. "Are you all right?" he then asked after observing the flushed look on his friend's face.

"Yep," Patrick answered, taking off his headset and getting to his feet. He was just then heading toward the door when he unexpectedly stopped and began throwing up.

Tara and Phil, along with Sherry, all rushed to his aid and guided him to a seat in the hallway. Tara then ran to the bubbler and got him a cup of water. He took it from her and drank it down in one large gulp, not once lifting his eyes from off the floor. He just sat there, silently, repulsed by the whole incident. Then, suddenly getting to his feet, he went to the men's room, got some paper towels, and headed back to the classroom and cleaned up the mess, despite assurances from both Phil and Tara that they would do it.

Shortly thereafter, Sherry led him to a vacant classroom. "Sure, you'll get an occasional jerk," she admitted once they had both sat down, "but most of our customers aren't like that."

"Yeah, well—still! I just don't think I can do this job, Sherry. In fact, I know I can't. I mean, as soon as that phone beeped, my stomach tightened right up. At one point I actually thought I was gonna pass out. What? Am I supposed to feel that fifty or sixty times everyday? No thanks!"

"Listen to me, Patrick. Okay?"

"What?"

"Please! Don't quit because of one bad call. I personally think that you're one of the brightest and most promising in the class. It just takes some getting used to, that's all. I know how you must be feeling right now. Believe me, I do. I remember when I took my first call. And you thought you were bad?"

"Whadya talkin' about? I've heard ya on the phone. You're brilliant."

"Yeah, but it's taken me eight years to get that way, though! I'm serious, Patrick. AT&T's a really great company to work for. The majority of the people are really nice, plus, I mean … you're not gonna find a better benefits package anywhere. Hey, maybe you're right. Maybe this isn't the job for you. But you'll never know if you quit right now. Just give it a little more time. I promise you, it does get easier."

Patrick, after a short deliberation, told her that he would try and stick it out. And sure enough, the more calls he took, the more comfortable he became. Two weeks later, there was a small graduation ceremony at the completion of the training. Everyone received an official AT&T diploma and a present from Sherry: a small, intricately carved glass jar filled with designer jellybeans.

CHAPTER 14

▼

The next six weeks were spent in internship, a period in which the newly formed teams, each consisting of approximately twenty reps apiece, were assigned a group coach who walked, or more correctly stated, ran around and assisted them with any questions they had.

Those first few days, each and every call posed a new dilemma: a request or inquiry that they had never before encountered. However, as the weeks passed, the coaches were being called upon less and less. Everyone was becoming more knowledgeable with the system they worked on, and friendly with the four hundred or so people they worked with. And although problems were still experienced, they happened less frequently. It was a period of great learning.

Patrick and Tara were doing especially well as their internship came to an end. Phil, on the other hand, was an entirely different story. He was constantly being rebuked, mostly for his excessive talk-time. Whereas the average call was supposed to last anywhere between four to eight minutes, Phil was spending up to half an hour with some customers, just chatting away about everything ranging from the weather to how poorly the Celtics had played the night before.

And his response to the reprimands was always the same: "I can understand your concern. But there's a secret to all this, you see. And that secret is the very root of the word customer—custom. And that's what I'm providing to each and every person I speak with, custom service. And ya can't put a time constraint on that, now can you?"

"Gee, Phil. That's really admirable of you," his supervisor would always reply, "but can you just try and solve the problem as quickly and efficiently as possible. While you're rambling, we're falling behind."

"Okay, if that's how you want it," would always be his final rejoinder, but he could never, for whatever reasons, seem to follow through on his promise.

The following months passed quickly for the entire gang. Kevin had been promoted at the bank to head teller, and Joanne luckily found a decent paying job as a sales clerk at FAO Schwarz. Everyone was working and making money. It was a grand time for them all.

It was also during this period that Patrick and Tara consummated their relationship. They went out to eat one evening at a small, romantic trattoria in the city's North End and shared an Italian platter and a couple carafes of Chianti. By the time they arrived back at Patrick's house, both were feeling a little naughty. They immediately headed up to Patrick's room. "So, you had a good time, right?" he asked, closing the door.

She came up and kissed him. They hugged passionately, then momentarily broke away, staring silently into each other's eyes, before embracing once again. Patrick's hand soon found its way to her breast. Tara moaned with pleasure. Slowly, they began to undress one another, their hands exploring the other's body, until they found themselves in bed, united in the rapture of their amorous desires. Their bond was at last complete and it only continued to strengthen as the months passed.

Everyone continued working as hard as they could, and as Patrick and the others' six-month anniversary on the job rolled around, they decided to throw a lavish party to celebrate the occasion. Not only were they now permanent employees with benefits and all, but they were each also going to be receiving a forty-dollar-a-week raise. They planned the gala for over three weeks and spent close to five-hundred dollars on kegs of various beers, bottles of fine liqueurs, and enough food to feed a Roman legion.

It was a cold Friday in March when they completed their sixth month, but the extravaganza was planned for the following evening. All their friends from AT&T were invited, along with all the neighbors whom they were still on good terms with—which weren't many by this point, due mainly to all the loud, raucous parties they had thrown over the last year.

The event began promptly at seven, and it almost seemed as though everyone who was invited actually showed up. By eight, the house was jam-packed and the partygoers had even begun to stream out onto the porch. Patrick, Phil, Tara, and Maureen also ventured out, despite the frigid chill, to momentarily escape the congestion within. They found sanctuary at the very far corner of the porch.

"My God! There has to be at least a hundred people in there," Tara whispered in disbelief.

"And half of 'em I don't even know," Patrick murmured in response.

"Ah, don't worry about it," Phil exclaimed, lifting himself up onto the railing. "Everyone's havin' a good time, right?"

"I know, but … it's only been goin' on for an hour and the food's already almost gone."

"But there's still drink, and much of it, so let's stop worrying about triflin' little things and start havin' a good time. After all, isn't that the reason why we're having this party?"

"It is. And we will. But I just can't believe the food's almost gone, that's all."

Phil groaned. "Unreal! Hey, Tara—why don't ya just get him loaded and take him upstairs and make long, passionate love to him. At least then he won't be worrying about the goddamn food so much!"

Tara shook her head. "Ya pig!"

"No, ya know what. That doesn't sound like too bad of an idea, after all," Patrick said as a slight grin slowly began to play over his lips.

"My God, you're just as bad! Can't live with 'em, and ya can't live without 'em."

"Isn't that the truth," Maureen confirmed, sipping at her vodka and Coke. The four returned shortly to the party and began mingling with the mob within that appeared to be growing with each passing second.

True to his word, Patrick soon joined in the festivities. He started with a can of beer, followed immediately by a few shots of E&J Brandy. After meeting up with Tara once again out on the front porch, they decided to head on over to the keg of Guinness and pull themselves a glass. As they were making their way towards the kitchen—the keg's resting place—Patrick tripped over someone's foot.

"You're drunk already, aren't ya?" Tara asked, helping him up.

He grabbed her by the waist and stole a quick kiss. "Just a wee bit."

"Come on, Paddy, stop it," she said, pushing him away. "You're embarrassing me."

"Tara O'Malley, embarrassed? Now I've heard it all!"

"You'd better watch it, lad. If ya don't slow down, you're gonna end up feelin' like shite in the morning."

"Ah, who cares about the mornin'! I'm havin' a good time, now."

"Hey, it's your head. Do what ya want. I'm just tryin' to help ya."

"Yeah, I know you are, Tara. I'm sorry. It's just that … I'm just feelin' really good right now, ya know. I'll be all right. Trust me," Patrick said assuringly as they entered the kitchen and joined ranks with the dozen or so people who were currently waiting in line at the tap. When their turn finally arrived, Tara was in the process of filling her glass when she suddenly looked up and saw Nicole Gunderson walk through the front door.

"Finish this for me, will ya?" she asked as she extended the foam-filled glass in Patrick's direction.

"Why? Where ya goin'?"

"Nikki's here." She then walked over to where her friend was standing and the two women hugged. "Thanks for coming."

"Thanks for having us."

"Ah, that's right. So this is the one, huh?"

"Yep. Tara, I'd like for you to meet my husband, Eric."

"Eric. Well it's nice to finally meet you!"

"No, the pleasure's all mine," he replied, as the two shook hands. "I've heard nothing but 'Tara this' and 'Tara that' for the past six months."

"They better have been all good things ya heard!"

Nikki looked to her husband and gave a big, visible wink. "Oh, of course."

"Ah you!"

They all began to laugh.

"So, where's your better half?" Nikki asked momentarily.

"In the kitchen, getting our drinks. Come on." Tara motioned for them to follow. Upon entering, however, she was appalled—for there on the floor, lying directly below the keg, was Patrick himself. He had the hose leading from the barrel stuffed in his mouth, and was drinking directly from it as a mob of onlookers cheered him on.

Tara scowled. "Would you please excuse me for a moment?" Not waiting for a response, she broke through the mostly inebriated crowd, grabbed Patrick by the hand, and dragged him to the far corner of the room amid a host of boos.

"Stop it, will you! You're makin' a fool out of yourself! And in front of all the people we have to work with!"

"Ah, relax, will ya! I'm just havin' a good time, that's all."

"Good time or not, will ya just take a breather, for Christ's sake! I want ya to meet Nicole's husband over there. Oh, and please, Patrick … try not to make too much of an arse out of yourself."

"Ah, don't worry about it," he grumbled, breaking free from her grasp and marching over. After being introduced, and after making a surprisingly good impression, he soon excused himself and rejoined Kevin, Phil, and a bunch of the other lads for a round of Quarters in which Jack Daniels was the poison of choice. The reveling was in full swing by midnight, when Patrick, after momentarily blacking out, finally realized that he had better stop before he ended up killing himself.

He walked over to where Tara was sitting and told her that he was going to call it a night. She said that that was a good idea, but that it would have been even wiser had he come to that conclusion an hour or two before. He just nodded.

As he was making his way up the stairs, Patrick suddenly stopped and shouted loud enough for all to hear: "Okay, I'm goin' to bed now. But I just wanna thank each and every one of you for comin' and making this night such a memorable one. Who knows? Maybe we'll do it again in six months when we get our next raise. All right, well … good night everybody."

A chorus of "Good night" and "See you on Monday" greeted him.

After standing there for a moment, holding on tightly to the handrail—his body swaying and his head spinning—he finally turned and stumbled up to his room.

CHAPTER 15

▼

No sooner had Patrick closed his eyes than he was abruptly awakened by cries from below. "Ah, Christ, what the hell's goin' on now?" he grumbled agitatedly as he dragged himself out of bed and headed down the stairs to see what all the commotion was about. To his surprise, though, not a single person was in the house. He found this especially odd, since only minutes before, or so it seemed, there had been people lining the walls. Concluding that there was something taking place outside, most likely an argument between Sandra and Heather, he went to look. The whole night they had been going at it, bickering back and forth about a crass statement Heather had made at Sandra's expense: "It's too bad you're not celebrating with them."

"I knew it," Patrick said aloud as he opened the front door, and, sure enough, there everybody was. He immediately realized, however, that it was more than a fight: people were screaming and through the crowd he could see a body lying on the pavement.

Running over, he pushed his way through the horde of onlookers only to be stupefied by the sight his eyes fell upon—for there in the middle of the mass, was Patrick himself. His body lay lifeless, and there was blood flowing from a large gash on the top of his head.

"Someone, call for an ambulance!" Tara cried, taking hold of his hand. "Oh, please God, don't let him die."

Without delay, Phil bolted into the house as fast as he could.

Patrick, still confused by the entire scene that was now taking place, turned back towards the house and saw shattered glass lying all over the sidewalk. Looking up, he noticed that his bedroom window was broken. Slowly, the truth began to sink in. Instead of making it to his bed and passing out, he must have some-how crashed through the window and fallen to his death. He sank to the ground and began crying, only two things on his mind, his family and Tara.

"Tara!" he screamed, but there was no response. Finally, picking himself up, he tottered over to the front porch and was just about to take a seat when the door unexpectedly flew open and Phil ran out. Patrick lunged to his side, trying to get out of his way, but he wasn't quick enough. Amazingly, though, Phil ran right through him. "They're on their way!" he shouted, making his way back over.

The ambulance soon arrived, but after a brief examination, the young man was pronounced dead. Tara, upon hearing this, passed out. The paramedics revived her with some smelling salts, and not long after, Kevin and Phil guided her back into the house and sat her down on the sofa. Everyone was silent until Kevin got to his feet. "I'll call his family," he said numbly.

Patrick, who had been there the entire time watching everyone's reaction, had always wondered what it would be like if he died. Would anybody care? Now see-ing all the sadness, he changed his mind. No! He didn't want to see or know. As hard as he tried, however, to escape this heart-wrenching scene, he couldn't. It was almost as though he was being held in place for some unknown purpose. He soon fell to thinking about his family once again and his mother in particular. She wouldn't be able to take this. She just wouldn't. With nostrils flaring and upper lip quivering, he raised his clenched fists toward the heavens. "Why?" he screamed. Suddenly, his body began to shake violently and he was whisked away.

Arriving at his apparent destination, Patrick looked around, perplexed, as a strange feeling slowly began to engulf him. "Am I in Hell?" he muttered, for the scene he now saw before him perfectly portrayed that image. He stood on a dark and muddy shore, which looked out upon a murky body of water, with yet another shore lying beyond it. Instantly, the Greek myth of Hades and the river Styx popped into his head. "What is this? Have I not lived a good life? Where am I?" he cried. At this, he was lifted and transported by some unseen entity across the river to the shore beyond.

After standing there quietly, for a moment, examining his new surroundings, Patrick then set off to find out exactly where it was he now stood. He had been walking but a short time when he suddenly noticed a small door-like opening in a craggy, mountainous rock that lay to his left. *Where did that come from?* He looked back. However, everything was dark, so he concluded that even though he had just spotted it, it must have been there all along.

He lingered a short time before venturing in; then, to his amazement, he saw a wide, rocky path that went on indefinitely. And all along both of its sides were hundreds of peculiarly shaped openings. Glancing up, he noticed that this mammoth edifice had no real roof, but instead, only more of the strange caverns, some reaching as high as thousands of feet up into the air. He began going into every grotto he passed, looking for some form of life. Then, ever so softly, there came a noise. At first, it almost sounded like an infant's crying, but as he walked on, and it got louder, he could tell it was that of a man.

It was around this same time that Patrick passed through a huge fissure in the rock, and after a few more moments of searching, he finally thought he saw something. Yes, it was a man. He was sitting on the ground in the fetal position, and had his face hidden between his knees. And although this man was also weeping, it was not *his* lament Patrick had come in search of. No, the cries that had guided his exploration were that of a much deeper and sadder element. He walked up slowly to the man and after a brief hesitation said, "Excuse me, sir."

Not realizing that there was anyone with him, the man jumped up in alarm. "Who are you? What do you want?" he demanded.

"Hello. My name is Patrick Quinn. I think I just died and came here, but ... I don't know where here is. Could you please tell me?"

The man studied him for a moment and then said, almost contemptuously, "You are in Heaven. And my name is Jesus, Jesus of Nazareth."

Upon hearing this, Patrick lost consciousness. When he eventually came to, he looked around but found himself all alone. As he returned to the walkway, the gut-wrenching cries suddenly started up once again. Determined, he set out to locate this man claiming to be the Christ, and to find out, once and for all, exactly what in the hell was going on.

After about twenty minutes more of continued pursuit, he finally spotted him. Walking up cautiously, so as not to alarm him, Patrick questioned softly, "Why is it that you're afraid of me? I won't harm you. I wish only to find out the truth about this place you call Heaven. For in my dreams, Heaven was nothing like this. But instead, it was a wonderful place. A place filled only with happiness. It was where all those who were good went when their lives on Earth had ended. This to me is more of how I envisioned Hell. The sadness, the gloom, the despair. Was I wrong? Were we all wrong?"

Jesus glared at Patrick, this man who was now standing before him, asking all these questions. "You wish to know everything about this place where you now stand?" he finally answered, sarcastically. "Very well. You'll soon receive your wish. But first let me ask of you a question, if that's all right?"

"Yes, of course. Ask me anything you want."

"The thing that I wish to know is how you died. What was the cause of your death?"

"I fell out of a window."

"Were you pushed?"

"No, I wasn't. Some friends and I were having a party on account of a raise we had just received. We were having a great time, but … I guess I went a little overboard. I got really drunk, and when I went upstairs to go to bed, I guess I just fell out the window. Or, at least, that's what I think happened."

Upon hearing this, Jesus exploded into laughter.

"You find that funny?" Patrick cringed, stunned by his Lord's reaction.

For a moment, both men just stared at each other, neither of them giving, until Jesus finally stood and motioned for Patrick to follow him. While they were walking, Jesus resumed the conversation. "Very well, you told me what I asked of you. Now I shall tell you what you desire to know. But first, let us go to my sanctuary, the only place here where I can find even a glimmer of peace."

The two men headed down the walkway and came to a small shaft in the rock. They entered and immediately began following another narrower path, which eventually led to a small grotto that was completely lit up by a glowing, candle-like object in its center. "Welcome to Valhalla," Jesus exclaimed.

Valhalla? Patrick thought. *Where have I heard that word before?* Somewhere in school, he concluded, but he just couldn't remember anymore.

"Before we talk, though, let us eat. For I am hungrier than a camel after a long journey," Jesus said, pulling a small wooden box from behind a rock. The two men sat down on the ground and Jesus opened the container and took from it a round, greenish object. He broke it into two equal pieces. "Here, this is Trubeem. I think you will enjoy it."

Patrick took the nourishment from his Lord's hand and examined it briefly before taking a bite. It instantly reminded him of a sort of bread but was much hardier than any bread he had ever before eaten. He also thought he tasted a slight hint of wine in it. Jesus was right—he did enjoy it. They both ate their Trubeem without speaking. When they had finished, Jesus came over and sat directly in front of Patrick, so that their faces couldn't have been more than two feet apart. He looked straight into the young man's eyes and smiled. "Now … let us talk."

Patrick sat forward and readied himself.

Jesus moved closer still. "What I am about to tell you, you will not believe at first. But it is true. All of it. So be prepared to hear horrible things, for through the millennia, the stories that have been told, and the things that people believe to be as fact … are not."

"What are you talking about?"

"This is what I'm talking about," Jesus replied and then proceeded to tell the young man seated before him how history had really transpired. "Through mistaken oracles and storytellers all of what you know about the past or, what I knew, for that matter, is wrong. In the beginning of time, many billions of years ago, through some truly wonderful miracle, life began. And from that one seed of human existence, two people came to be—God, my Father, and Lucifer … his brother."

"Lucifer's your Father's brother?"

"Yes," Jesus nodded shamefully. "They traveled the newly-forming planet for many years, searching to find other signs of life, but they didn't succeed in their search. Both were saddened by this, so my Father and uncle decided to try and create their own world, with people of their own likeness. And it worked! They created a beautiful Kingdom and many people with whom they could talk and play. It was a wonderful time for them both. But after many years of happiness and peace, my Father and his brother had a falling-out. Lucifer wanted all the people to be their slaves. He figured that since they gave them life, it was only logical for them to do as they said. My Father disagreed. And although he was good and cared for the people, and Lucifer was evil. *This*, my friend, is where the story was mistold. For it was Lucifer, and not my Father, who was the stronger of the two."

"What are you saying?" Patrick murmured.

"What I am trying to tell you," he went on, "is that this is when factions arose. Most of the people allied themselves with my Father, obviously, but a lot also backed my uncle. Then there was one incident where one of Lucifer's followers called my Father a terrible name. And even though he tried to convince the people that the insult didn't bother him, and pleaded with them just to dismiss it, it was too late. There was a great battle that raged on for many years between the two sides. There was much bloodshed and many lives were lost. In the end, it was my Father and his followers who were defeated and cast out of the beautiful Kingdom."

Patrick just sat there, mouth agape.

"What you believe Heaven to be, is not what it really is. And, yes, though Lucifer resides in Hell, Hell is the place of immense beauty. This, where we now sit, is Heaven—and it always has been. Heaven has always been the Kingdom of

God, wherever he may be," Jesus said, all the while paying close scrutiny to the expressions that flickered across the young man's face.

Sickened, and not knowing what to now say or do, Patrick finally asked, "What about Adam and Eve? Was that all just made up, too?"

"Yes. They never existed. It was just a fable some wise man created many, many years ago to try and explain the beginnings of life, how Man came to be. And though Man was created in the image of his Maker, that image was basically that of Lucifer, and this is why Man by nature is mostly bad."

"That's not true. Most people are good."

"No, they aren't, Patrick. Believe me. I know people a lot better than you do."

"And what? All the other stories from the Bible are false, too?"

"I'm sorry to say, but—yes. The majority of them never occurred. And the ones that did, well …"

"Then tell me! Tell me the truth about what did happen."

"Very well, I'll tell you. But why do you torture yourself so? It's obvious you aren't up to hearing."

"Just tell me."

Jesus sighed. "Very well, then. If we must, let us start near the beginning. You're familiar with the story of Noah, I assume, and the great flood?"

"Yes."

"Well, that was an actual event. Noah and his family were forewarned about the forty days and forty nights of rain that were to come. And, yes, they did indeed build a great ark. And upon that ark they did indeed place seven pairs of every clean, and one pair of every unclean animal and bird species known to man as they were commanded to do. And, yes, they were spared from that horrific cataclysm. But you see, Patrick, Noah and his family were extremely evil people. And it was only because of their wickedness that they were chosen, and it was none other than Lucifer, himself, who did the choosing.

Not waiting, Jesus continued. "The story of Abraham, the Chaldean, was also a true one, but it occurred a lot differently than you believe. Abraham did bring his son, Isaac, to the top of Mount Moriah as was asked of him, but there was no intervention. The sacrifice took place! He slaughtered his own son, and he did it to honor my uncle. So, do you see now, my friend, what I am trying to tell you?" he questioned, but there was no response.

"Most of the stories from antiquity are wrong. Done so intentionally, I would assume, to leave mankind with at least a little bit of hope. But whatever the reason, they were told and people believed. Another account incorrectly handed down through the ages is that of the two towns of Sodom and Gomorrah.

Though both were indeed leveled by fire and brimstone, it was Lucifer who did it, and he only did it because most of the town's inhabitants were good and kind people. They had many temples, and they prayed to my Father all the time, and for that … Lucifer hated them!"

Patrick was just about to speak when they suddenly heard a violent crash. The two jumped to their feet. They were silent for a moment, listening keenly, until Patrick finally whispered, "What was that?"

Jesus put his finger to his lips. "Come quietly. It's probably one of his henchmen."

"Whose henchmen?"

"Lucifer's. He's constantly sending one or another of them to terrorize me, but they're not very smart. They never find me. But there's always a first time for everything. Now come!"

They frantically began searching for a place to hide. Jesus soon called Patrick over to a long, flat rock about ten feet in length and four feet high that lay in a nearby cave. Both men quickly knelt behind it and prepared themselves for whomever or whatever it was that was now pursuing them. A few minutes passed, and thinking that they were now out of harm's way, Patrick was beginning to get to his feet to try to ease a cramp that had developed in the back of his thigh, when Jesus suddenly grabbed him by the arm—and just in the nick of time.

For at that moment, standing in the cave's passageway, was the most hideous sight Patrick's eyes had ever beheld, and almost altogether impossible to look at. It was surely a beast, and one standing close to nine feet tall, at that! He, it, or whatever it was, had reddish-brown skin and white, streaming hair falling half-way down its back. It had a long, pointed nose, was muscular in frame, and was now heading directly towards the rock. Both men prepared themselves for the encounter. Patrick could hear his heart pounding, but somewhere in the back of his head, he thought, *What can he do to us? We're already dead.*

The massive beast came within a few feet of them, when, for whatever reason, it looked towards the entrance and ran out. The two men stayed in their crouched positions for a couple of minutes more. Standing, both looked at each other and groaned, relieved that the creature hadn't found them.

"What in the world was that?" Patrick asked.

"That was the giant, Goliath. You know, the Philistine spoken of in lore. Now that is a true story, and one I enjoy very much, for it is one of the few instances in history where good overcomes evil. Yes, Goliath is sent here probably more than any of the others, but he definitely has to be one of Lucifer's dumber henchmen. He looks and looks, and just about when he is always ready to find me he runs off and goes searching somewhere else. Sometimes I think he knows where I am but just gets a laugh out of terrifying me in my Father's Kingdom," Jesus said glumly and then fell into thought. He was quiet for a few moments before turning to Patrick. "The years haven't been kind to him. He really is of the strange sort, don't you agree?"

"Yeah, I would say so!"

At this, both men began to laugh.

"Though I don't like the things you've told me," Patrick soon said, "I believe you speak the truth. For what benefit would you get out of deceiving me? Please, tell me everything about this place. I need to know."

"Ask me anything you wish."

"Okay, there is one thing that I don't understand."

"And what is that?"

"Does everyone that goes to Heaven come here? I mean, since I've arrived, I haven't seen anyone else besides you. Shouldn't there be billions, if not trillions, of other people here?"

"There are. But as soon as they arrive, they immediately go up to one of the top caves and seek refuge. What else can they do? Only a few have been down here with me, and they've only stayed for a fraction of the time that you have. I don't know why it is you still remain, but I'm sure we'll learn the reason for it soon enough. But for now, come, let us enjoy this time together." The two returned to Valhalla and had just taken seats on the ground when Patrick said, "There are so many more questions that I still have."

"As I said before, ask me anything you wish and I will try to answer it, for I feel quite comfortable around you, my friend. I can tell you are a truly good man."

Patrick thought for a moment. "What is Hell like?" he then questioned.

"Well, obviously, I've never been, but I have heard stories about it from my Father. It's beautiful! Close your eyes and try to picture this scene: As far as the eyes can see there is a rolling, grassy plane, and all around its perimeter, and scattered within, are beautiful trees. They are the tallest, most perfect trees one will ever see. Giant oaks. Hemlocks. Flowering ashes. There are also many wonderful olive gardens that produce only the finest, purest oils. In the middle of the plane, there is a huge palace, magnificent in its grandeur. It's made of pure white marble and is trimmed with the finest gold. It's called Atlantis, and it's where Lucifer lives. It has hundreds of bedrooms, with the most extravagant belonging to Lucifer himself.

"On the main floor there is a huge banquet hall, and within that hall sit five thrones. One massive, golden one, and four smaller ones cast from silver. Well, I guess I don't have to tell you to whom the one made of gold belongs, but the three farthest from Lucifer's belong to the three people who in their human lives caused the most sorrow, men named Shalmanon, Nero, and Hitler. Because they were so wicked, Lucifer made them his most trusted confidants," Jesus said and then began staring blankly ahead. He was silent for a moment, then unexpectedly covered his face with his hands and began to weep.

"What's wrong?" Patrick asked, confused by the sudden show of emotion.

Jesus soon took down his hands, and with tears streaming from his eyes, replied, "I cry now because I am thinking about whom the throne closest him belongs. That throne is reserved for his queen, and that queen is ... my mother, Mary!"

"No, don't say that! Why is she there? She wasn't evil."

"No, you're right, she wasn't. She was very kind and gentle, and it was because of that reason that he brought her there. To inflict this terrible grief upon my Father and me. It would have been too easy for him to have chosen someone deserving, but he thought it a wiser and much crueler thing to do to the two of us. He was right! Not a day goes by I don't think about her, or wish that she was here with us. He had no right in taking her. Those are the rules! If you're good, you come here," Jesus cried and then once again fell silent, engrossed in reflection as Patrick sat quietly, allowing his Lord to contemplate this injustice. No words were exchanged between the two men for what seemed an eternity.

Unbelievable! Patrick kept thinking. *The Virgin Mary lives with the Devil!* While marveling at this most unfathomable of thoughts, this vicious, but apparently true realization, his mind began to wander. Answers. He needed all the answers. There were so many more questions that he still had, but where would he begin? He suddenly broke the silence. "Do any other people live in Atlantis?"

"Yes ... of course," Jesus answered momentarily. "Thousands live inside with him, but only the cruelest people ever to walk the face of the earth. The rest of the demons live and sleep outside, including his twelve henchmen. Those like Goliath and Telamahri, the Cyclops. Lucifer uses them as he sees fit, uses them to carry out his will both in Heaven and on earth. Some are men, and some are monsters, but they all serve the same purpose—violence and destruction. Whenever there is a disaster on earth, whether it be an earthquake or the introduction of a horrible pestilence, you can be sure it's because of one of them."

No sooner had Jesus finished speaking than Patrick asked, "Is there a purgatory?"

"Yes, there is, and it's the saddest place of all. It's where all the people who have lived mostly good and righteous lives go before coming here. They arrive with such wonderment, ecstatic at the mere notion that they are finally going to meet their God. However, instead of happiness, they are thrust into torment. For them, it is almost like being suspended over a crocodile pit, just waiting to be lowered. They can see all the sadness that is awaiting them, but can do nothing to escape it. They sometimes remain for many years. It is so very heart wrenching. Many tears are shed for them."

"Why did I avoid it?"

"You must have lived a very good and pious life."

"I tried, believe me, I did. But I sinned. I wasn't the best brother or friend, and God knows, I definitely wasn't the best son I could have been. Yes, I sinned in my life!"

"Don't do this to yourself, Patrick. People make mistakes, act in ways they sometimes regret, but that doesn't make them bad. What matters is …"

"But still. I could have been a better person."

"As could've I," Jesus avowed, rising to his feet. "May I pose to you a question?"

"Yes."

"What makes man good?"

"What makes man good? I don't know."

"Think," Jesus retorted, almost tauntingly, "the answer's quite simple."

Patrick pondered this challenge for a moment and then said, "I guess what makes a person good is his actions. How he treats others, both friend and stranger alike. Going out of his way to lend a helping hand. Showing love, even when it sometimes shouldn't be shown. I guess just by trying to be the very best person he can be."

"And is that how you lived your life?"

"I think it is."

"Then that's why you avoided it," Jesus said, placing his hand on the young man's shoulder. "See, I told you the answer was a simple one. Now, are there any other questions you have?"

Patrick thought for a second. Yes, there were still many questions. More than he could possibly ever ask. However, one in particular, suddenly came to mind. "Yes, I have another."

Jesus flashed an amused grin. "I kind of figured you would. What is it?"

"Well, before I met you, I was searching. Searching to find the source of this deep, mournful crying that I heard when I first arrived. But it wasn't you. Whom did it belong to?"

"The crying that you heard, my friend, was that of our Father."

Patrick now leaned back against the cold stone wall, absorbing everything he had just been told. His body ached, and his limbs were sore. No more words were exchanged between the two, and they were soon asleep. Patrick had spent his first day in Heaven.

CHAPTER 16

▼

When Patrick awoke the next morning, he found himself all alone. He immediately exited Valhalla and stood silent, listening for footsteps or any other noise that might give indication as to where Jesus now was. However, all was quiet.

A few seconds passed, when, without any warning, the crying started up again, this time even louder and sadder than before. At that same moment, Patrick felt a hand on his shoulder. Whipping around, his eyes fell upon the Christ, who was standing there with a sickened look on his face.

"What's happening?"

"Come with me, Patrick. We need to talk."

The two men walked over to a nearby slab of granite and sat down. At first, neither said a word as they just stared at one another. Jesus finally broke the silence. "There is something you need to know," he said. "I have just been talking with my Father and he has told me something terrible. It appears as though … it's about to happen once again!"

"What's about to happen?"

"In the not so distant future, there is going to be a major catastrophe. And it shall be one which will eventually lead to the annihilation of nearly all mankind."

"What?"

"Yes, it's true. I don't know what it'll be, or when it will happen, only that it will occur and that nothing can be done to stop it. So, my Father has decided, to let the people know. And he wants for you to be his messenger and deliver the word."

"Me?"

"Yes, Patrick—you. He knows how good you were and he believes that the people will listen to you. So, I guess *this* is the reason you remain."

"What—what am I supposed to tell them?"

"The truth."

"I don't think I could do that. I'd be betraying Him. Wouldn't it be wrong to tell the people? All those who have lived good and honorable lives? Sure, I mean, they wouldn't be going to the place they dreamt about, but still … they'd still be with the same God they loved and prayed to.

"Will you not honor His wish?"

"I don't know if I could live with myself if I did."

"Why, you're not living now, you're only existing. You'd still come back here afterwards. Why not just tell the people the truth and let them decide for themselves?"

"I'll have to think about it," Patrick answered distractedly, as he turned and began walking away.

"That's fine."

"Right now I have to be alone."

"I understand," Jesus replied, watching him stumble off into the darkness. "Take your time. Oh, and yes … be careful."

Patrick wandered aimlessly for hours through the rocky labyrinth, deep in thought, images racing through his head faster than his mind could process. Why did he have to be the chosen one?

As he wrestled to find the answer, a strange feeling slowly began to overtake him. He steadied himself against the rocky wall. It was only after this near delirium had finally passed that he found the strength to look for a place to sit. His head was still spinning, and he was sweating profusely when the sensation returned. This time he wasn't so fortunate: he passed out. While unconscious, more visions darted through his head. And then, unexpectedly, he heard a voice beckon, "Come to me, my son."

Patrick began walking towards it, almost as though he was being pulled by some magnetic force. Then, right before his eyes, the gloom and despair were transformed into a scene of radiant splendor. Beauty more wonderful than he had ever before imagined. His first impression was that everything that had previously occurred was all just a delusion, most likely brought on by the traumatic injury to his head. And that now, finally, he was about to enter the Kingdom of Heaven.

So it was with great eagerness that he walked through a high, arching gate that stood before him, and ran up a grassy incline that it led to. Upon reaching its plateau, he looked down and saw it—the Kingdom of God! It was just as he had always imagined it would be. He cried in relief as he marched down the hill, taking in all the sights.

Magnificent flower gardens dotted the landscape. Awe-inspiring waterfalls, some falling hundreds of feet, could be seen in the distance. Beautiful birds, some of species he didn't recognize but wondrous nonetheless, flew overhead.

There were children running around playing, and adults sitting in groups, talking. And all that he passed smiled and waved to him. He rejoiced. Not knowing really what to do or where to go, he walked over to an attractive, young woman who was sitting by a stream. "Hello, my name is …"

But before he had the chance to finish, the girl smiled and said, "I know who you are. They've been expecting you."

"They have?"

She nodded. "Yes. There, see that trail over there? Follow it. It'll lead you to where you need to go."

After thanking the woman for her help, Patrick began following a narrow, worn-out path. He hadn't gone too far when suddenly, through a brush-cleared opening, he saw a beautiful castle rising in the distance. He hurried the rest of the way, and upon reaching the marvelous structure, found himself standing before a door of immense proportions. It was probably close to fifty feet high and at least twelve feet wide. He stood there for a moment and waited. Nothing happened. Deciding that the only logical thing to now do was knock, he gave it a few short raps. Slowly, it began to creak open.

Patrick entered but couldn't see anything, for it was pitch dark inside. Using the wall as a guide, he inched forward gingerly, arm outstretched; then, all at once, the darkness gave way to brilliant sunlight that filtered through a huge stained-glass window immediately to his left. The sudden change of light made it necessary for Patrick to refocus his vision, and what he soon saw captivated him: mosaics, frescoes, and tapestries lined the walls. There were many exquisite sculptures and vases all along the floor. Mesmerized by their beauty, he proceeded up a long hallway and came to yet another massive door. Once again he knocked.

"Come in," a voice answered.

With great haste, Patrick obeyed, and quite naturally, once inside, the first thing he did was try to see whom it was that had just spoken. However, there didn't appear to be anyone there. He soon fell to surveying the room. Here, too, were many wonderful pieces of art. Patrick was so happy, but a little nervous, for he believed that at any moment his eyes were going to behold the Divine Architect, his maker, the Creator of All! But in an instant, his exhilaration was shattered. For there, in the very far corner of the room, sat five thrones. One huge one and four smaller silver ones. The hairs on the back of his neck began to stand on end as he shivered involuntarily. At that moment, he felt as though he was about to faint once again.

Dear God, please—don't let it be! he cried to himself.

All of a sudden, from somewhere behind, a voice said, "I'm sorry, my son, but I'm afraid it's true."

Patrick spun around to see who it was, but deep down, he already knew.

"Welcome. Let me introduce myself. My name's Lucifer."

"No!" he shrieked. Then darkness came.

Awakening, Patrick found himself drenched in perspiration. He looked around and noted that he was still back in his bed on W. Fourth St. Could it have been all just a dream? He pinched himself—and felt it!

Getting out of bed, he went over and examined the windowpane he thought he had fallen through, but it was still intact. At about this same time he also realized that he had a raging hang over. He walked back over to his bed, sat down, and began reviewing the nightmare he had just had. It was too realistic for a dream, he thought. Wasn't it? Maybe this was a dream now. No. In dreams your head doesn't pound like this.

Patrick finally accepted that it must have been a dream, and a truly bizarre one at that. Arriving at this conclusion, and in an agony of throbbing pain, he lay back on his pillow and soon slept like the dead.

BOOK 2

CHAPTER 17

▼

Awakened by a sudden, shaking sensation, Patrick opened his eyes only to find both Tara and Phil standing over him, each wearing a big grin. He immediately remembered his dream and after a few moments asked, "Am I alive?"

His friends began to laugh.

"Poor thing. I told ya not to drink so much, didn't I?" Tara replied as she sat down beside him on the bed. "Oh, I can handle it. Don't worry about me. I'm just havin' a good time, that's all," she mimicked.

"Yeah, now that ya mention it, you do look a little more dead than alive," Phil joked. "Christ, you're a madman. You know that? Ya should've seen yourself."

"Yeah?" Patrick murmured as he began to prop himself up, but he immediately realized that it wasn't in his best interest. The throbbing in his head once again returned, now coupled with a feeling of intense nausea. He soon fell back. "Oh, God, I feel like shite! Could one of ya get me some aspirins, please?"

"I'll get 'em," Tara answered as she motioned for Phil to stay seated. She left the room and was soon back playing the role of mother. "Why'd ya have to drink so much, huh, Paddy?" she questioned after he had taken both the pills and handed her the glass. "Ya made a fool out of yourself. Everyone was talking. You should've heard 'em."

"Ah, be easy on him, Tara. Christ, the lad's in bits. He doesn't feel like hearing ya preach. Besides, I don't think he made too much of a fool out of himself. Well, on second thought, maybe he did, but we all did."

"You mind your own! I'm allowed to speak me mind!"

"Come on, not now," Patrick pleaded. He lay silent for a few moments before asking, "Why, what were they saying?"

"What were they saying? What weren't they sayin'!" and she went on. "Well, I heard Christy Lynch say something to the effect that you were acting like an arse."

"Ah, she's a prude!" Phil scoffed. "I wouldn't worry too much about what Christy Lynch thinks. No one else does."

"It wasn't just her, Phil! Even Darryl commented about it," Tara added, referring to Patrick and Phil's supervisor, Darryl Pompey.

"What did he say?"

"That he never saw Paddy act that way before. How he thought he was so quiet. Didn't think he had it in him."

"Oh, please! Darryl's cool. He knows it was just a party, and that's what we were doin', partying. Whadya think he's gonna do, counsel him or something? Besides, I've seen Darryl drink a wee bit too much, and it wasn't a pretty sight, either, let me tell ya. It was right after we got out of internship and went over to his team. He invited us all out to that Mercury Bar place to get acquainted. Remember? Well, the whole night he was pounding down his Korbel, and then he went out on the dance floor with his wife, Lori, and I'm tellin' ya … your man made a complete arse out of himself! The whole team was roaring. But I mean, we knew he was drunk, and people act that way when they're drunk. It's not like we don't respect him now or anything."

"Well, ya never know. A promotion could come up, and he might not support him after thinking back about last night."

"Never happen! I'm tellin' ya, Darryl's not like that."

"Oh, I know. You know him so well."

"Good enough, I'd say."

"Help me up, will ya?" Patrick muttered suddenly, deciding that it would be better to face the headache that was surely awaiting him than to continue listening to the two of them squabble back and forth.

After going downstairs and lying on the sofa, he found out that it was half past two that afternoon. Kevin, who had gotten up only a couple of hours earlier, had spent the entire time cleaning up. He came into the room and sat down beside Patrick on the sofa.

"Let me tell ya something. I'm happy I didn't get that job. You work with a bunch of savages. Each and every one of 'em."

"Then you're a savage, too," Phil said, smirking, "because you were acting the same exact way."

"I was not."

"Ya were."

"That's a lie!"

"Whatever!" Phil shot back, deciding just to give up on it for—God knows—the lad was a stubborn one, and when his mind was set on something, as it was now, there was just no changing it. After a few moments of uneasiness, Patrick brought up the dream he had had, and then proceeded to recount it as vividly as he could.

"I'm tellin' ya, it just seemed too real to be a dream."

Phil chuckled. "Damn. That sure was a good one, huh? And what did ya say? Mary's chillin' with Lucifer?"

"That's what I said, all right! And that's the way it happened!"

"Christ, I'd love to have a dream like that. Ya know what. I don't even think I dream anymore. Haven't had one in a long time, anyway. I miss 'em. You guys still dream?"

"I was wishin' I was feckin' dreamin' when I came down this mornin' and saw the condition the feckin' house was in, let me tell ya!" Kevin complained as he got to his feet. "Utter savages. And with absolutely no regard for our house. Christ, there was even freakin' tomato sauce all over the kitchen ceiling! How do you suppose that got there, huh? I had one hell of a time getting it off, too. Nearly broke my neck doin' it!"

"Was there? Now that you mention it, I do kind of recall one of your buddies from the bank juggling some lasagna. I wonder if it could've possibly been from that?"

"I don't think so! We're a little more civilized than that."

"Oh, that's right. I'm sorry. I almost forgot. You're a professional, aren't ya?" Phil gibed, trying to rile him up. Unfortunately, Kevin wouldn't play along.

The rest of the day, Patrick, with the aid of Tara, nursed his hangover. He took two aspirins every four hours and tried to get in a good meal or two, but it really didn't help too much, for when he awoke the next morning, he still felt lousy.

After taking his first call of the day, a call in which he got into an argument with a Middle-Easterner who was demanding that he remove over two-hundred dollars worth of calls from his bill, Patrick could tell it was going to be one of those days. And, sure enough, his intuition was correct. Call after call turned out to be complicated and lengthy. No one had gotten what they were promised. Everyone was yelling. And as noon approached, he was thinking about just asking Darryl if he could take the rest of the day off.

I'll give it till after lunch he told himself. Which, in fact, turned out to be a sound decision. For after taking some more aspirins and eating a large bowl of chowder from the cafeteria, he finally began to feel better. And by the time four rolled around, the effects of the liquor were completely gone. He even had a customer on the line that was born in Ireland, but now lived in Oklahoma City, and they were in the middle of a delightful little chat when Darryl came over and told him to put the conversation on hold.

"What's up?"

"You've got a call."

"A call? I wonder who'd be callin' me here?"

"I think they said it's your father."

"My father?"

"Yeah," Darryl nodded. "I'll take over the call. What were you doing?"

"Oh, nothing. She's all set. We were just talkin'."

"Okay, well, tell her you've gotta get going, all right."

"Yeah, okay."

As Patrick logged-off and headed down to the Operations desk, a terrible sense of foreboding overtook him. Why would his father be calling him here? Something must have happened. He tried not to let his imagination get the best of him, but by the time he reached the phone, he was an absolute mess.

"Hello?"

"Patrick? Is that you?"

"Yeah, Dad, it's me. What's up?" But there was no response. "Hello?" he repeated.

Through a cracked voice, Brian began to speak, "Patrick, there's been an accident."

"An accident? What kind of accident?"

Trying to compose himself, his father continued, "It's your mother. She had a seizure this afternoon. A severe one."

Patrick gasped. "Is she all right?"

Silence.

"Da, is she …

"No, she's not all right! She's gone!"

"What? Oh, God! Don't say that, Dad!"

"I'm sorry, Son, but it's true. She was all alone when it happened. I found her. I called for an ambulance but she was already dead by the time they arrived." After what seemed an eternity, both men composed themselves the best they could. "Come home as soon as possible, all right, Paddy? We need you. I need you."

"Yeah, sure. I'll be there as soon as I can."

From the moment Patrick returned to his zone, it was apparent to anyone he passed that something was wrong. He immediately sat down at his cubicle and began putting his things away.

Phil, too, had noticed the tortured expression on his face. Realizing that something really bad must have happened, he told the customer that he was currently speaking with that he would have to call him back.

"Call me back? No, you're going to help me now!" the man growled, but Phil hung up on him anyway.

By the time Patrick finished straightening up his workspace, Phil and Darryl were standing there beside him. Both men waited. Finally, Patrick looked up and said despondently, "My mother—she's dead. I've gotta go home now. And I don't know when I'll be returning."

"Sure, Patrick, that's fine. Don't worry about it," Darryl replied.

"Jesus, Paddy. I'm sorry," Phil gasped as he put his hand on his friend's shoulder. Patrick didn't respond; he just sat there, staring blankly ahead. After a few moments, he abruptly got to his feet and began to stumble off.

"Hey, man, he's in no shape to be goin' alone," Phil winced as he began to follow him. "I'm gonna go with him, all right?"

"Yeah, sure. No problem. Go."

"Thanks." He then turned and hurried off.

After stopping at the bank to withdraw some money, the two men headed back to the house so Patrick could pack for his trip home. In the meantime, Kevin returned from work, only to be horrified by the terrible news. Wasting no time, he bounded up the stairs and was soon standing outside his friend's door.

"Patrick?"

"Yeah."

"Can I come in?"

"Yeah."

Upon entering, Kevin walked over to where Patrick now stood. He struggled to find the right words, but there were none, so he just said, "I'm sorry."

"Thanks."

"What ... what happened?"

"I don't know. Something about a seizure."

"Jesus."

Around this same time, Phil entered the room. The three men conversed briefly before calling for a taxi and heading off to Logan. They got off at the Aer Lingus terminal, where Patrick purchased the last remaining ticket for a flight that was departing at 8:40 that evening. All three sat silently until boarding time. After saying their good-byes, Patrick took his place in line and was soon in the air.

The whole flight back he reflected on all the good times he had had with his mother throughout the years. He began damning himself for ever leaving.

When the plane finally touched down in Dublin, it was daybreak. Patrick hailed a taxi outside the terminal and was back shortly in Loughshinny. As he walked through the ancient, cobblestone streets, he thought how good it felt to be back home. But why did it have to be for an occasion such as this?

He soon found himself standing in front of his house. There really wasn't much to it, but he still looked upon it with pride. His father did the best that he could for the family. Maybe that's one of the reasons he went to the States—so he could give his parents a better life. A little bit more. Maybe even one day a nicer house. But that dream was now shattered.

Looking up, Patrick tried to see if he could spot any movement within, but it was dark. And not wanting to wake anyone, he decided just to sit on the stairs and wait. What he didn't know, however, was that his father had never gone to bed that night, and when Brian heard stirring on the porch, he looked out only to see his eldest son just sitting there, gazing at the ground. Patrick was so deep in thought that he never even heard the door open. Suddenly, he felt a hand on his shoulder. He looked up only to see his father standing there, smiling down at him.

Patrick rose and the two men embraced. After a long, emotional hug, they went inside and sat down at the dining room table. At first, neither man spoke, happy enough just to be in each other's presence once again.

"It's good to have you back, son," Brian finally said. "We missed ya. We all missed ya."

Patrick smiled and shook his head in agreement. After another brief silence, he asked, "What the hell happened?"

"I don't know, Paddy. I guess she wasn't as diligent with her medication as I thought she was. The doctor's said it progressed, into a more serious condition. Hyperglycemic coma? Or something like that anyway."

Patrick sighed. "So, when's everything gonna take place?"

"Well, the wake's set for tomorrow. We're gonna have it here, at the house. And the funeral's Thursday."

"How are the little ones doin'?"

"Oh, I don't even wanna think about them. It breaks my heart too much. It's been horrible. They took it really bad, especially Paul. He couldn't stop crying when he found out. Sinead cried, too, but I mean … I think she's really too young to fully comprehend the magnitude of it all."

Patrick was just about to ask how the rest of the family was doing when he suddenly heard footsteps on the floor above. And not long after, down walked Paul and Sinead, hand in hand. On seeing their brother, both ran over and hugged him.

"I can't believe it! It's not fair!" Paul whimpered, which in turn, caused his little sister to start crying. Patrick held both in his arms as tightly as he could. The whole time Brian fought back the tears at the unbearably sad scene that was now taking place.

"Come on, guys. Ya have to be strong," Patrick said but immediately thought what a ridiculous thing it was to say. Here were two children who had just lost their mother. They could damn well cry if they pleased!

Soon, family members began arriving. The first, quite naturally, was Catherine.

"Oh, Patrick," she sobbed as they embraced, "it's good to see ya. It's been so long."

"It has, hasn't it?"

"Yes, it has! So … ya look good. How's Boston and AT&T?"

"All right, I guess," he replied and then paused before saying, "I'm sorry."

"Sorry? Sorry for what?"

"I don't know. First ya lost your mother and now your sister. I just feel bad for ya, that's all."

Catherine cleared her throat. "The last couple of years have been rough for us all," she acknowledged, "but I'll be all right. Trust me. I've lived long enough to know how life can be. I'm more worried about the wee ones. The poor things!"

At that moment, Moses walked through the door. He briefly surveyed the room and upon spotting Patrick exclaimed, "Come here, lad, and give your uncle a hug."

"Hey, Moses. It's good to see ya," Patrick said as they heartily grabbed hold of one another.

"Aye, it's good to see you, too! How ya holdin' up?"

"Ah, I'm doin' the best that can be expected, I guess. I really don't think it's sunk in yet, though."

"It's a hard thing to lose a parent, especially one like Moira. I remember when our mother died. I didn't think I was gonna be able to take the pain, but in time, it does get easier. You just remember that, okay? Besides …" he whispered out of the corner of his mouth, "she was a spark plug. Wouldn't go for any of this cryin' shite, ya know."

"Yeah, I know."

"Not too many people can get the best of me, but she always could. Put me in me place every time. She was a classic, all right."

Patrick smiled. "Yeah, she sure was."

CHAPTER 18

▼

The day turned out to be a busy one for all involved. While Catherine and the others stayed at the house and watched the children, Patrick, his father, and Moses went to make all the arrangements.

The first place they headed was the funeral parlor in Skerries to purchase a casket. There, they were greeted by the parlor's owner, a regal-looking man in his early fifties, who led them down a long, winding staircase to the building's basement.

Upon reaching the lower level, they were then guided into a large room immediately to their right, which housed all the coffins for sale. There had to have been close to two dozen different models. Each man went his own way and began looking. Brian soon called the others over.

"How about this one?" he asked, pointing to an attractively carved and finished pine casket bearing the price of 425 pounds. Patrick was reluctant to reply, but Moses had no problem stating his mind.

"What's wrong with ya, man?"

"Whadya mean?"

"What do I mean? Look at it. It's a piece of shite! I wouldn't bury my dog in that!"

Turning towards the owner, who was by this point staring uncomfortably at the floor, Brian asked, "Could you please give us a few moments alone?"

"Of course," the man replied graciously as he turned and left the room, closing the door behind him.

When they were finally alone, Brian said, "Listen, Moses. I'm not you. I don't always have to buy the very best of everything. Now there's absolutely nothing wrong with that one over there."

"I can't believe you," Moses grumbled, shaking his head.

"Can't believe what?"

"I told ya, it's a piece of shite! Just take a look at it, for Christ's sake."

"I have, and I don't think it is."

"Well, it is! And that's the end of the conversation, little brother. Now listen to me. I know she wouldn't want for you guys to go into debt over this, but she deserves better. A whole hell of a lot better. I'll tell you what. I'll put up the rest of the money and we'll get something a little more fitting, all right?"

"No! She was my wife and I'll be the one to decide! Now that's the one we're getting, and that's that!"

Moses clenched his brother by the shoulder and looked him straight in the eyes. "Yes, she was your wife," he said, "that's true. But I loved her, also. Isn't my opinion worth anything? Listen, if it has anything to do with the money, you can pay me back."

Pulling free, Brian walked to the far corner of the room. After a few moments, he called Patrick over. "What do you think?" he asked his son.

"I don't know. The choice really isn't mine to make, Da. That's your call. But if I did have to give my opinion, then I'd have to agree with Moses. It's all right, I guess. And the price is reasonable enough, but … price shouldn't have any bearing at a time like this." He paused briefly. "And I know what you're thinkin'."

"Oh, yeah? What's that?"

"That Moses is right. It does have something to do with the money. And ya wanna know something else?"

"What?"

"He's right. It is a piece of crap. And it'll be rotted-out come five years," Patrick blurted but immediately wished he hadn't, for when he looked into his father's eyes, all he could see was shame and disgust, not toward his son for speaking the truth, but toward himself for allowing it to be the truth. "I'm sorry, Da."

Brian smiled. "Don't be sorry, Paddy. I asked for your opinion and you gave it." He then walked over to where his brother was standing. Patrick followed.

"I'll tell you what. Okay, fine. We'll get something a little better, but I will have to borrow some money. I promise you, though, I will pay ya back every penny. I mean it. I don't want any hand-outs."

"No one's offering charity, Brian."

"Okay, well … what did ya have in mind?"

"I knew you'd see it my way!" Moses exclaimed joyously as he threw his arms around the necks of both men. "Now come on, let me show you my choice." He then led them over to a mahogany casket bearing the price of 5,500 quid.

"Have ya gone mad?" Brian murmured.

"Ah, it's grand, don't ya think? And quite fitting, too."

"Fitting? No, I'd have to agree with Da, Moses," Patrick said. "It's too expensive, plus, it's ugly as hell. Looks like something out of a Dracula movie." After much debate, the three finally agreed upon a handsome cherry coffin that cost 3,000 pounds.

After everything was at last finalized, they then headed over to St. Brendan's to make arrangements with Father Munroe to speak at the wake, and offer the mass on the day of the funeral.

Finally, they drove to the florist, where Patrick and his father ordered a beautiful arrangement of white roses in the shape of a cross. Moses also made a purchase, but in keeping true to his nature, he ordered not one but five exquisite flower arrangements.

By the time they were finished with everything, it was close to half-past seven that evening. After arriving back at the house and eating a lovely ham dinner that was prepared by Catherine and Leona, Brian's eldest sister, everyone soon went to bed.

CHAPTER 19

▼

Patrick awoke the next morning to the familiar sound of rain pelting against the window. He immediately remembered that it was Wednesday, the day of the wake, and the day that he would at last see his mother after close to a year. As he lay in bed thinking about her, family members slowly began arriving. And by one, almost everyone was there. The reason for the gathering, however, combined with the bad weather, made for a rather somber time with very little conversation.

Moira and the casket were supposed to be delivered by two, but by two-thirty, they still hadn't arrived. Brian was starting to get a little concerned when he finally heard the sound of a car outside. Looking out the window, he saw a hearse pull up in front of the house and two men get out. One was the gentleman who had sold them the coffin, and the other was a much younger one, in his mid-twenties, who bore a strong resemblance.

Most of the men, and quite a few of the women, went out to lend a hand. Within minutes, the casket was out of the car and inside the house resting on supports lent to them by the funeral home. After thanking the two men, who left shortly thereafter, everyone sat down on one of the many wooden seats that had been rented for the occasion and just stared at it. Finally, Brian walked over and opened the lid. Everyone could hear him fighting back the tears.

Catherine was the next to rise. She broke down and nearly collapsed the instant she saw her sister. Luckily, though, Brian noticed her beginning to sway out of the corner of his eye and held her shoulders.

"Oh, God," she sobbed after steadying herself, "she looks so beautiful."

One by one, family and friends went up and viewed the body. Everyone was either crying or on the verge. Even Moses, who wasn't a particularly sentimental man, nearly broke down.

Interestingly, Patrick was the last to leave his seat. He was scared. He didn't know what his reaction would be. When he finally decided that the time had come, he apprehensively stood and walked over.

Catherine was right. She did look beautiful, and so at peace. To his amazement, though, he didn't cry. This lack of emotion sort of confused him. But he brushed it off.

At precisely three-thirty, Father Munroe arrived. After viewing the body, he too became teary-eyed, for he had known Moira her entire life. He had baptized and confirmed her, and had also married her and Brian. When four finally struck, he stood and began speaking.

"Today we gather here in the memory of Moira Quinn, a woman whose love for others was only overshadowed by the love we all felt for her. She lived her life according to the teachings of our Lord, helping all the people she could, while at the same time forsaking her own needs.

"I personally saw her grow from an infant into a warm and caring mother, wife, and friend, and I enjoyed the pleasure of her company. I would just like to take a few moments now to speak about an incident that occurred many years ago that will attest to the type of person she was. It was probably back sometime around 1959 or '60. Moira was just a wee thing, maybe nine or ten, I would have to say, and we were celebrating mass for the first day of Lent. Well, about halfway through, suddenly the church doors flew open and this drunken man, who I'd never seen before or since, stormed in and began screaming that there couldn't be a God, and if there was, then he was a son-of-a-you-know-what. Well, everyone, including myself, just sat there horrified. But do you know what? Moira stood up and walked over to that man who was drunk out of his mind and hugged him. No one else in the entire church that day, myself included, had either the love or the understanding—but she did. That was just her nature. I recall that day very vividly, as I'm sure some of you here today do also," he said while looking in Catherine's direction, who immediately smiled and shook her head. "I remember that day not so much for the act itself, but instead, for the feeling I had toward her afterwards. And that feeling was," at that moment he abruptly stopped and took in a deep breath. "I remember thinking that if I could ever have a child, I would hope that she would be just like Moira Meehan."

And after looking up to the heavens, he finished by proclaiming, "May God grant you everlasting love and peace, Moira. We will all greatly miss you, but will never, ever forget you!"

It was a very touching speech—even more than he had rehearsed—but instead of bringing tears, it brought smiles. Looking around, he saw the response and thanked God that he could help alleviate some of their pain, and in a way, some of his own, too. After giving his condolences to the family, Father Munroe left. Not long after, Patrick and Paul questioned Catherine about the validity of the story told of their mother, and sure enough, she confirmed it.

Spirits were much brighter after the speech, and laughter resulting from fond reminiscences could be heard resonating from the walls within. To anyone passing by on the street, it would have sounded more like a celebration than a wake, but as is the case with many of the Irish, they try to make joyous affairs such as these.

Friends and relatives stayed till close to nine that evening. And by eleven, everyone in the house was fast asleep.

At some point during the middle of the night Patrick awoke. He lay there motionless but found himself unable to fall back asleep. Finally, getting to his feet, he headed downstairs. After pouring himself a large glass of milk, he sat down at the kitchen table and began to reflect. Different visions began racing through his head, and before he knew it, he was standing in front of his mother's coffin.

He looked down at it and marveled at its construction: the joints meshed in such a way that it almost appeared to be fabricated from a single piece of lumber. Patrick ran his hand along the glistening wood. And then, as though almost in a trance, he slowly began to lift the lid. He hesitated momentarily, before opening it completely. Staring down at his mother's lifeless body, he began to tremble, and unlike before, the tears now came.

"I'm so sorry I wasn't here for ya, Ma. I should've been. I knew how sick you were, and that ya didn't want me to go. But no … I was off chasin' some feckin' rainbow! Thinking only of myself," he wept as he rubbed her cheek with the back of his hand. "Paul was right. It's not fair! God had no right takin' you at so young an age. Plus, ya suffered so much this past year with Gram's death and everything. You poor thing. It's just not fair, Ma. It's just not! And I know you're up there looking down at me, probably embarrassed as hell in front of all your new friends that I'm talkin' this way, but I just can't help it. Oh, God—why'd ya have to take her? Why!" After a moment, Patrick wiped the tears from his eyes and closed the lid.

He walked over to the couch and sat down and soon began weeping once more. And he cried until there were no tears left. He felt weaker at that moment than at any other time in his life. After dragging himself back up the stairs, he quickly fell asleep.

CHAPTER 20

▼

The day of the funeral finally arrived. Spirits were at an all-time low that morning, and if the saddening reality of the burial wasn't bad enough, everyone's dejection was intensified by the fact that it was still raining.

After getting dressed in their finest outfits, the four drove to St. Brendan's where during the service they heard a eulogy by Father Munroe that was so powerful and touching, there wasn't a single dry eye in the entire church by the time he finished (his own included).

When the mass ended, the procession headed to St. Catherine's cemetery in Rush, the family's ancestral burial ground. After closing prayers, everyone went over to the Quinn house for the reception.

Moses had brought over a couple of bottles of whiskey, and everyone was soon easing their anguish—Catherine included, which was a rare thing since she hardly ever touched the stuff. Before long, laughter filled the room as they talked for hours about everything ranging from lovely old times to how poorly this year's football team was doing.

By five o'clock, most of the people had left, and by six, the only ones still remaining were Patrick, his father, and Moses. Paul and Sinead were spending the night at their Aunt Patricia's house. It was apparent to both men that Moses was intoxicated when he brought up the notion of Patrick possibly not returning to the States.

"Well, I just can't get up and quit, Moses. They need me."

"What about your mother? Don't ya think she needed ya?"

"That's enough, Moses! This isn't the time to be speaking like that!" Brian growled.

"What's wrong? Can't I speak me mind?"

"Not now you can't!"

Moses chuckled. "Why? You know it's true."

"Listen, I'm serious. Stop it now. You're in my house and you'll do as I say."

Moses continued, however. "Ya know something, Paddy. Every time I'd see your mother, I'd ask her if she heard from ya, and it was on a rare occasion to hear her say yes. It's almost like you forgot about us. The last days of that poor woman's life were spent worrying about you, you selfish son-of-a-bitch!"

Upon hearing this, Patrick left the room.

In the meantime, Brian grabbed Moses with both hands and looking crazily into his eyes, seethed, "If you weren't such an old man and you weren't piss drunk, I swear to God, I would hit you right now. Now get the hell out of my house!" Moses left without saying another word.

Patrick remained in Loughshinny for another week, lending a hand around the house and just trying to help his siblings, and himself, deal with their devastating loss. Yes, it was a very trying time for the entire clan, but everyone contributed something, whether a cherished memory or an act of kindness to hasten along each other's healing process.

One disturbing fact, though, and one that was noted by each and every family member, was the conspicuous absence of Moses Quinn. In fact, not once did he show his face that entire week, and when questioned about his brother's whereabouts, Brian would lie and say that he was battling a really bad head cold, most likely brought on by the terrible weather the day of the funeral. Deep down, however, Brian was both disgusted and enraged with Moses, but for the good of the children he kept his emotions in check.

It was a dreary Sunday afternoon when Brian drove his son to the airport to see him off. After parking the car, they proceeded to the Aer Lingus terminal where Patrick was to board a 4 p.m. flight. Both men were relatively quiet as they sat there and awaited the boarding call. At twenty of, when it was finally heard, both simultaneously rose to their feet.

"Try to keep in touch, okay?" Brian said as he placed his hand on his son's shoulder.

"I will."

Both men looked at each other, and after a brief lapse, they embraced. Upon breaking away, Patrick picked up his luggage and walked off. However, he suddenly stopped and returned to where his father was still standing. "Do me a favor, will ya?"

"Yeah, sure, Paddy. What is it?"

"Forgive Moses? I have. He was drunk and didn't know what he was saying. And besides … I guess most of what he did say was true."

"Ah, Paddy. Don't do this to yourself. You didn't have anything to do with your mother's death. And like you said, he was drunk and talkin' out of his arse."

"Yeah, but still …"

"Let me tell you something, all right?"

"Yeah, what?"

"Even though your mother was sick, I never saw that woman as proud as she was with you. Yeah, she missed ya. Christ, she missed ya something fierce," he chuckled. "But in the end, she knew you were doin' what ya had to, and she respected you for that. She loved you. She loved you, Paddy, with all her heart— and so do I. So don't worry about Moses. Things'll work themselves out. They always do, right?"

"Yeah, I guess."

"Yeah, well, um … now see what you've gone and done," Brian said, referring to his sudden show of emotion. "You'd better get goin'."

"Yeah, I know." They hugged once more and Patrick said goodbye.

After touching down at Logan and retrieving his luggage, Patrick walked outside only to have his dormant senses suddenly revived by the stinging, frigid chill. He hopped into the first taxi he saw, and before he knew it, he was back at the house. Upon entering, however, he found it completely empty. Or so it seemed. This struck him as particularly odd, seeing how Sunday was the day Kevin cherished so dearly, his relaxation day. He headed upstairs to see if one, or possibly both, were napping. But soon found this wasn't the case, either. After going to his room, Patrick had just begun unpacking when he suddenly heard the front door slam and the voices and laughter of what sounded like many people.

It was the lads and the girls. They had just come back from a Bruins' Sunday matinee at the TD Banknorth Garden where they watched in horror as the home-town-team got pummeled, 8–2, by the Philadelphia Flyers. Patrick caught them all by surprise as he descended the stairs.

"Paddy!" Tara shouted enthusiastically, being the first to notice him. She was overjoyed, and had long since overcome any animosity she felt towards him for not calling her the entire time he was back home in Ireland. In fact, she hadn't seen or heard from him since the day after their party, but she knew, that although he loved her, he was totally distracted by his problems.

"Hey, guys," he said, smiling, as he reached the foot of the stairs.

Tara walked over and hugged him. He buried his face in the sweetness of her hair and returned the gesture. Looking into her eyes, he said, "It's good to see ya." He then acknowledged that it was good to see them all.

"It's good to have ya back, Paddy," Kevin said as he now also came over. "And I know it's not much, but ... my prayers have been with you and your family every day."

"Thanks, Kev. I appreciate it," Patrick answered while staring off into space. It was true: he was happy to see them, and to be back, but his mind was just someplace else.

"Everyone at work's been askin' about ya," Phil said suddenly, drawing back his attention. "How you're doin'."

"Have they?"

"Yeah, everyone feels really bad for ya. The company even made arrangements to have a mass said in your mother's name."

"Oh, that was nice of 'em, but it was probably Darryl, and not AT&T that set it up, though."

"So ... I guess it's gonna be awhile before you go back to work, huh?"

"Well, actually—no. I was plannin' on going back tomorrow."

"Tomorrow? No, Paddy. You don't have to go back right away. They said you could take as much time as you needed to mourn. For God's sake, it's a law! You can take up to a month, I think. Or, at least, something like that."

"A month? What the hell am I gonna do for a month?" Patrick scoffed as he made his way toward the stairs. "Just sit around and feel sorry for myself and probably end up goin' stark-ravin' mad, that's what. No, thanks. I'm goin' back tomorrow and getting back into the swing of things. If I don't, I'll probably never end up goin' back. Besides, I think it'll be good for me, ya know. Something to take my mind off her."

And with that said, he went upstairs to his room and finished unpacking. Tara spent the night and they made love. However, there was an emptiness inside of him, a void so palpable it worried her.

CHAPTER 21

▼

Sure enough, Patrick returned to work the following morning. Throughout the course of the day, people were continually coming up to him to offer their condolences. To each one he just smiled and said thanks.

He worked hard that day to keep his mind from straying and to help his customers as well as he could. And it worked. Only twice while he was working did he think about his mother, but the images were soon replaced by a new customer with a new request or a new problem.

He decided to follow this same mindset the next day, and sure enough, it worked once more. And before he knew it, the week was over. He had made it through in one piece and in relatively good shape. Concluding that idleness would only encourage sadness, he decided to fill every moment of every day with activity; so when the weekend arrived, he and Tara headed over to South Station and boarded a bus for Vermont.

It had been midweek when Patrick overheard two managers talking in the lunchroom about an elegant turn-of-the-century bed and breakfast one of them had taken his wife to a few weeks before. The idea caught Patrick's fancy, so he had asked for all the particulars and that's where they were now headed.

The ride up was to take a little over four hours, and the entire time Patrick rambled on about everything under the sun. At one point, Tara actually became concerned and asked him if he was feeling all right.

"Yeah, I feel grand," he said, seeming to mean it, and assured her that he was only excited about the trip.

It was close to three-thirty by the time they finally pulled into the station. Upon retrieving their suitcase from the bus's storage compartment, they headed inside the terminal and called for a taxi, which arrived promptly. After a short ride, they turned onto an unpaved trail and slowly began ascending a long, tree-lined drive, when a beautiful Victorian mansion suddenly came into view.

"See, I told you it was gonna be nice," Patrick said, squinting, as he tried to get a better look.

After paying the driver, the two of them got out and just stood there examining the house and all its surroundings: situated in the heart of a small glen and flanked on all sides by the majestic Green Mountains, it looked like something out of a storybook. This, coupled with the fact that it had been flurrying the entire ride up, and that the landscape was now completely covered with a thin dusting of newly fallen snow, made for a truly enchanting experience.

"Oh, Paddy, it's beautiful," Tara murmured. "Like some winter wonderland."

"I know," he acknowledged, also spellbound. They soon went inside and checked in.

"Here you go. Room #10," an attractive woman in her late-thirties said, smiling, as she handed Patrick the key. "Just go up those stairs, hang a right, and it's the last room on the left."

"Thank you," they replied in unison and then turned and headed upstairs. They found their room easily enough, and what a charming room it turned out to be! Jutting out from the west wall was a large canopy bed, with an exquisite, hand-stitched comforter and what appeared to be at least a half-dozen pillows. An intricately carved crystal chandelier hung overhead. And there was even a massive, stone fireplace in the room's far corner.

"Pretty romantic, huh?" Tara leered as she sauntered over to the window and threw open the drapes. "Oh, my God, Paddy. Come take a look at this view. It's brilliant."

Patrick walked over. The sun was just beginning to set at that moment, and the radiant hues of pink, blue, and crimson bathed the distant, snow-capped peaks. After marveling at the glorious panorama for a short time, they began unpacking. When finished, they headed downstairs.

Upon reaching the lobby, they learned from the receptionist that dinner wasn't served until six each evening. Both were dismayed, for neither had eaten anything since that morning. But if it wasn't served until six, it wasn't served until six. After thanking the woman for the information, they went outside for a walk. They explored the surroundings for close to an hour, the entire time captivated by the beautiful, tranquil setting.

By the time they arrived back, all the other guests, sixteen in number, were getting situated in the grand dining room. Patrick and Tara had just taken their seats, when the doors to the kitchen suddenly flew open and out walked three tuxedo-clad men to take their orders.

The menu that evening was a choice of two entrees: Beef Wellington with truffle sauce, or grilled, herb-marinated swordfish with peach chutney. Most in attendance, including Patrick and Tara, selected the Wellington. And it turned out to be a sound decision. The meat was so flavorful and tender it nearly melted in their mouths.

When everyone was finished with their main course, the waiters wheeled out three large, silver-domed carts, each bearing a vast array of sumptuous-looking desserts. After a very difficult deliberation, Tara finally decided on key lime pie with a dollop of whipped cream, while Patrick feasted on a slice of pecan pie, with a double scoop of vanilla ice cream.

After finishing their desserts, and letting it be known to the proprietors, a pleasant, elderly couple named Robert and Sara Reynolds, that the meal had been absolutely delicious, the two excused themselves and went back up to their room. They both plopped down on the bed upon entering and sighed. Stuffed, they just lay there. After a short while, Patrick called down and ordered a bottle of white zinfandel (Tara's favorite). It seemed that no sooner had he hung up, when there was a knock on the door.

"Yes?"

"Room service."

"Feck off! Now that's what I call excellent customer service!" Patrick exclaimed as he walked over to the door, only to find the amicable receptionist standing there, smiling, with their bottle of wine in hand.

"Here you go. One bottle of white zinfandel."

"Christ, they've got ya doin' everything around here, don't they?" he muttered as he took it from her and began fishing in his pocket for some sort of tip. She abruptly stopped him, though, by softly grabbing his forearm and shaking her head.

"Why not?"

"Because …"

"Because? No, come on, please. Just take it."

"No! I'm not taking it," she giggled as she pushed away the ten-dollar bill that was now being held in front of her.

"Please," Tara implored, taking her place beside Patrick. "You've been so nice to us since we've arrived. We really want for you to have it."

"Listen. I appreciate it, and it's a really nice gesture, but I don't do this for the money."

On hearing this, a perplexed look came over both their faces, which caused the woman to begin giggling once more. "Listen, maybe this will make things a little clearer. It's Mr. and Mrs. Quinn, right?"

"Yes," Patrick answered, trying to keep a straight face.

"Okay. I just wanted to make sure. Well, Mr. and Mrs. Quinn, my name is Alexandria Reynolds."

"Reynolds?"

"Yes," she nodded. "My parents own this place."

"Oh, I didn't know you were their daughter."

"Yeah, well … it's not like I go around broadcasting it or anything. I'm content just staying in the background. Let them get all the limelight. God knows, they deserve it. They've worked so hard, both of them, over the years keeping this place up and running. And let me tell you, it hasn't been easy. I only wish I could help them out more than I do."

"More? Why, it seems to me like you do enough."

"I guess I do as much as I can, but … sometimes it just doesn't seem like enough, though. At least not to me, anyway. I'm a sixth-grade teacher a few towns up. I'm just here on the weekends."

"Still, though. It's nice of you to come and help 'em out like you do," Tara asserted.

"Yeah, well … as I said. They deserve it."

"And you deserve this. Please, won't ya just take it?" Patrick asked once again, trying to hand her the money.

"Thanks but no thanks."

"You're a stubborn one, aren't ya?"

"More than you know. Now goodnight." With that, she turned and left the room, shutting the door behind her.

"Good night," they both replied, but she was already gone.

"Yeah, she was a stubborn one, all right," Patrick said, shaking his head. "Kind of reminds me of someone I know."

"Oh, really? And who might this someone be?"

"Ah, just some girl."

"A special girl, I hope."

"Nah, there's nothin' really special about her. She's just average."

"Ya bastard!"

"I'm only slaggin'."

"You'd better be!" Tara warned as she sat on the bed.

"Ah, relax, woman. There's nothin' average about you. You know that," he conceded as he opened the bottle of wine and poured them each a glass. They finished it in no time and soon poured themselves another. Meanwhile, Patrick walked over to the hearth, and after a few futile attempts, finally managed to get a fire blazing. Shortly, they undressed one another and began making love. When they finished—their passions quenched—both just lay there, exhausted.

"That was great, Paddy," Tara whispered momentarily, but there was no answer. "Paddy?" she repeated. Still no response. Turning to see if he had since fallen asleep, but finding that not to be the case, she became alarmed. "Paddy, what's the matter?"

"I don't know," he finally murmured. "I just feel numb all over."

She giggled. "Well, isn't that the way you're supposed to feel afterwards."

"I'm not talkin' about my body, Tara. I'm talkin' about my heart. My head. Everything."

"Listen, Patrick. Your mother just died in a horrible, horrible way. Of course you're gonna feel like that. And it's probably gonna last awhile, too. You wouldn't be human if you didn't. That's what they mean by a broken heart. You're in pain, and it's a deep pain, but time will lessen it. I can tell ya that."

"How do you know? Have you ever lost anyone close to ya?"

"No, I haven't, but … that's what they say."

"That's what who says?"

"I don't know?" she retorted, somewhat caught off guard. "It's what everyone says, I guess. Don't tell me you've never heard it before."

"Oh, I've heard it said, all right. But who are the people saying it? It's not the ones in pain, but those trying to do the consoling. So there's really no validity to it."

"I think there is, if ya think about it. You'll always have your memories. Just keep thinkin' about all the good times ya spent with her. They'll help you cope. And cry! That's supposed to help, too."

"Oh, I did cry. The night of the wake. And I cried long and hard, too. I'm not sure, but … I think something inside me broke that night. I don't know. I'm scared, Tara. I'm afraid I'll never feel again."

"What brought this on all of a sudden?"

"I don't know. Maybe it was the wine."

"Well, don't worry, okay? You've got me and the lads. We won't let ya go down. We'll take care of you. I promise."

"Yeah?"

"Yes!"

They made love once again and both slept peacefully. When they awoke the next morning and looked outside, both were amazed to see what had to be at least two feet of snow. After packing everything up, they then hurried down to the lobby where they called the terminal and were relieved to learn that, yes, at least for the moment, everything was still up and running. But the man who answered also told them that if the snow didn't stop soon, then they would have to put a halt on all outgoing traffic.

So it was with great urgency that Patrick called for a taxi. After paying their bill and saying goodbye, they hastily jumped into the cab and were soon back at the bus station. They were fortunate to arrive when they did, for they caught the last bus leaving that morning; all the others were to be detained until conditions improved. And by the way it looked as they pulled out, their bus very well may have been the last one leaving for a good many days.

The four-hour ride ultimately turned into a seven-hour ordeal as the bus crept slowly along. So by the time they finally arrived back, it was dark out. Boston, too, was in the midst of a major nor'easter, and they soon learnt that the city's buses were at a standstill.

"Ah, feck off!" Patrick grumbled as they headed outside and began searching for a taxi, but the streets were deserted. Realizing that the only mode of transportation left remaining was the T, that's where they were heading when they suddenly saw a yellow cab hydroplaning around the corner. They hailed it, but were informed by the driver, a pleasant Nigerian, that unfortunately he wasn't taking any more fares. Patrick, however, succeeded in changing his mind by offering him twenty dollars for the short ride home. They soon arrived back in Southie, and as they pulled up in front of the house, they found both Kevin and Phil outside, shoveling.

"Need a hand?" Tara asked, getting out.

"Not now we don't. Where were you guys a couple of hours ago before I got this goddamn hernia! Christ, this stuff weighs a ton!" Phil exclaimed as he reached down and grabbed a handful of snow. After packing it tightly together, he then threw it gently at Patrick, hitting him in the arm. And before they knew it, all four were in the middle of a heated battle. But the funny thing was, everyone was attacking Phil. He was continuously heard shouting that it wasn't fair that he didn't have a partner, but sadly, no one felt any pity for him and continued the onslaught until he finally got mad and went inside.

The next morning, Patrick arrived at work an hour before he was scheduled, and began looking through his handbook.

"Kind of early, aren't we?" his supervisor questioned, walking up.

"Yeah, a little, I guess. Jus' thought I'd go through the handbook, ya know, and see if anything's changed."

"Nah, it's just the same ol', same ol'," Darryl answered and then went on to ask him how he was feeling.

"Like shite."

"Yeah, I know what you're goin' through. When I was twelve I lost my father. It's tough. All you can do, brother, is just take it one day at a time," his boss advised as he turned and began walking away. "One day at a time."

I hate those damn sayings, Patrick thought as he went back to what he was doing.

As the days and weeks passed, Patrick began arriving earlier and earlier, and was delving more and more deeply into his work. In his mind, it was the only way he was going to be able to get through his ordeal.

And when he wasn't working, his weekends were all spent either going somewhere or doing something with Tara or the lads. But even his days of rest could be something of a torture, for he had time to think, to let his mind run free, and that was a bad thing. There were even times where he would just sit in his room, staring blankly at the wall, sometimes for hours on end, until either Tara or one of the lads would knock on the door, and break him free from his spell.

As the months dragged along, instead of getting better, Patrick was falling deeper into a depression that was becoming more and more evident to everyone with whom he came into contact. While at work one day, Darryl had to send him home two hours after his shift ended, saying that he was going to hurt his eyes staring at the computer monitor for so long a time.

Ultimately, there came a point where Tara called Brian up. She, of course, didn't tell Patrick this, so it came as somewhat of a surprise when the phone rang the following evening and his father asked him how he was doing.

"All right," he replied, and all right he basically was, for it wasn't as though he was sick or deranged. He wasn't. He was just having a pretty rough time coping with the reality that he'd never see his mother again. To compound the whole matter, he still felt partly responsible, and kept continually replaying in his mind what Moses had said to him the last time they had spoken.

Patrick persevered, though, taking each new day as it came, praying that he'd feel something—good or bad, it didn't really matter. He just wanted to be normal again. Unfortunately, as the days passed, the hollowness remained.

He tried a host of different remedies during that time, also. There was a stretch when he went to mass everyday imploring that the Lord or some saint would miraculously lessen his suffering, but when that failed, he decided to call home and request that some pictures of Moira be sent. They arrived by express mail two days later and were soon propped up on his dresser. They didn't help, either.

Patrick even tried starving himself over the course of a four-day period, hoping that his privation might somehow ease his despair. The only thing that resulted from it, however, was a large lump on his head that he got while passing out at work one day.

And to make matters even worse, his emptiness was now even beginning to poison his relationship with Tara. He loved her so much at one point, but now felt absolutely nothing towards her—and this worried him. He attempted to rekindle his feelings for her, thinking about all the good times they had shared, but no matter how hard he tried, it just didn't work. And as the six-month anniversary of Moira's death approached, Patrick just couldn't take anymore of the pretense.

CHAPTER 22

▼

It was a muggy Saturday afternoon, in early September, when Patrick called Tara on the phone and asked her to come over. She was soon at the house, being led up the stairs to his room. By this time, she could tell something was amiss, but she remained quiet and waited for Patrick to speak.

After staring at her intently for a moment, he finally said, "We need to talk."

"About what?" she asked, taking a seat on the bed.

"About us—our relationship."

"What about it?"

He sighed. "I've been thinkin' about it quite a bit, ya know, and um … I don't think we should see each other anymore."

"You're jokin', right?"

"No, I'm not."

"Why? Is it something I did?" she questioned, her upper lip beginning to quiver.

"No, of course not. You didn't do anything. It's me. The way I am now. The way I've been ever since it happened. It's not fair to you, Tara. You shouldn't have to go through this crap, too. I'm draggin' ya down with me and I just don't want that to happen."

"I don't mind, Paddy," she answered as the tears now began to fall. "I wanna be here for you. I love ya! Please, don't do this."

Patrick walked over to the window and looked outside. He had expected this and had made up his mind beforehand to stand firm on his decision. "I'm sorry, Tara," he soon said. "I really am. I don't wanna hurt you. You know that. But it's gonna be a whole lot better for both of us this way."

"Better for you, maybe! Not for me! Goddammit, Paddy ... I thought you loved me?"

"Come on, Tara, please—don't make this any harder than it has to be."

"Harder than it has to be? How'd ya expect me to react, huh? I can't believe you. All these months I've been here for ya, doin' everything you've asked of me and not saying one goddamn word!" Tara shouted as she sprung to her feet and just stared at him, unable to believe what was now happening. She soon composed herself, though, and wiped the tears from her eyes. "Okay, fine. If that's the way you want it, then so be it. But I just wanna hear you say it."

"Hear me say what?"

"That you don't love me anymore. Say it and I'll be on me way without another word," she demanded as she stood up straight and awaited his response.

Gazing up at the ceiling, Patrick asked himself why life had to be so freaking complicated. He was silent for a moment, then looked her straight in the eyes and said, "You wanna hear me say it? Then I'll say it. I don't love ya anymore, Tara. I'm sorry, but it's true. I don't love anything. That's how horrible life is. And to be honest with ya, I wish I was feckin' dead!"

On hearing this, Tara ran from the room, crying. Within seconds, both Phil and Kevin were standing outside his door.

"What the hell was that all about?" Phil questioned.

"I just broke up with her."

"Ya did what?"

"Please, Phil, not now, all right. I'm not in the mood."

At that moment, Kevin gave Phil a slight nudge to let him know that it was best just to leave him alone. Now wasn't the time. Phil nodded in compliance, and the two men went downstairs, where they discussed the matter.

After closing the door, Patrick walked over and collapsed onto his bed. He began replaying the scene that had just transpired over and over in his head. The look in her eyes. The expression on her face when he told her that he didn't love her anymore. *Shouldn't I feel like shit?* he thought. And he was right. Of course he should—but he didn't. And that's because he couldn't feel at all. Patrick spent the rest of that day, and all of the next, holed up in his room, leaving only to go to the bathroom or to eat.

The next day at work, while heading to the lunchroom to get a bite to eat, Patrick unexpectedly ran into Tara and Nicole Gunderson, who had just finished eating themselves. Not knowing what to say, but feeling that he should say something, Patrick smiled and said hello. Both walked past without even acknowledging him.

He just frowned and continued on.

Autumn soon arrived, and with it, Patrick, for the first time since the terrible tragedy, finally felt as though he was beginning to break free from the frailty and torment that had ravaged him for so long a time. Maybe it was the crisp, invigorating fall air that had descended upon the city over the past couple of weeks, but he no longer felt as powerless. Sadly, though, as the days passed, and his anticipation grew, it was all to no avail. Shortly, it was winter, and Patrick settled into a deep depression. He really began to believe that he would never be the same again. Maybe something in his head did burst the night of the wake, possibly a blood vessel, for he surely wasn't the same man now that he was prior to that night. But whatever it was, it most definitely wasn't anything controlling intelligence; for despite being void of emotion, he noticed his faculties were sharper than ever. So much so, in fact, that he was promoted to a Customer Service Specialist after only one year on the job—quite a remarkable feat.

The promotion was due chiefly to two reasons: the first being the doggedness and hard work he had shown since his mother's death. And the second, and probably more important factor, was the recommendation submitted by his supervisor. Darryl had always liked Patrick, and that combined with the grief that he now felt for him probably swayed his decision. Whatever the determinant, though, he had the job, and with it came a raise. It also brought a little more prestige. No longer was he in the trenches, in the heat of battle. He was now going to be upstairs, sitting in a larger cubicle and answering questions from other C.C.A.'s on how to perform functions not done on a regular basis. All the long hours spent scouring the handbook, reading up on topics everyone else thought foolish, now came in handy. Most people would have been ecstatic at being given this opportunity so soon in their careers, but Patrick's response on hearing the good news was just, "Oh really?"

After arriving early the Monday following his promotion and gathering all his equipment, Patrick proceeded to the floor above and took his place at his new desk. As he sat there awaiting his first call, he marveled at his calmness and began reflecting on his very first call, the year before. While he was reminiscing, the phone suddenly beeped. "Yes, hello. This is Tara O'Malley. I was wondering if you could pull up an account with me? I'm havin' a wee bit of a problem with it."

"Hey, Tara," he answered reluctantly, when the phone suddenly went dead.

CHAPTER 23

▼

As the months passed, Patrick excelled at his new position, so much so, in fact, that he soon began attracting the attention of certain managers, and even some higher-ups. As they watched his progress, they were amazed at his knowledge and efficiency. He seemed to know as much, if not more, than most of the regular managers who had been with the company for years, and who had transferred out East when the Boston-area center first opened.

Eventually, he even caught the eye of Phyllis Jorgenson, the site-leader and basically everyone's boss. She was heard one day questioning Michael Tucker, the head manager, as to how the quiet, young man had become so proficient. Mr. Tucker didn't have an answer, but he began paying close attention to him, and within a week, he too became astonished with Patrick's aptitude.

Deciding it prudent, and much to the benefit of the company to retain the young man, Mr. Tucker offered Patrick the position of full-time C.S.M. He would be a manager, doing a job that consisted of mainly taking over calls from customers who were upset and demanded on speaking with someone higher up the totem pole than just an ordinary representative.

At first, he declined the offer, but after a long and heated discussion with Darryl, during which time he was told that he'd basically be a "goddamn fool" not to take it, he reluctantly accepted the position. On the 15th of December, Patrick became a Customer Service Manager.

During those same few months since his break-up with Tara, Kevin and Phil had taken on the monumental task of trying to bring back the old Patrick, the Patrick they both knew and loved. But after realizing that that man was gone, probably never to return, they set out to help the new Patrick. And they went about it in a variety of ways.

One of the first things they did was bring Patrick to Foxboro to see a Patriots game. They had a good time even though the Patriots got trounced, 37–14, by the Dallas Cowboys. Another outing they took one Sunday was up to Loon Mountain in New Hampshire to go skiing. However, the majority of their free time was spent just exploring their adopted home. They did a lot of sightseeing those chilly, late autumn days, visiting the city's many parks, museums, and historical sites, such as Bunker Hill and Faneuil Hall. After each excursion, Patrick would smile and say that he had wholeheartedly enjoyed himself, but Kevin and Phil saw through the façade. They knew they were still far from their desired objective, but they persevered nonetheless.

The Christmas season quickly approached, and with it, the three of them took to the streets of Downtown Crossing and hit all the major department stores in search of gifts to send back home. Patrick purchased an exceptionally nice, chrome-plated Citizen Eco-drive watch for his father. Paul received a Sony Discman, and Sinead ended up with basically the entire Barbie collection. With overnight express shipping costs, just to ensure that everything arrived on time, Patrick spent close to $600.00, and that didn't even include the money he was to spend on presents for Kevin, Phil, and Darryl. All told, he paid out over $800.00, but with his new position there had come yet another small raise, so this large amount of money really didn't faze him as much as it did his friends, who felt he had gone a little overboard.

At last, it was Christmas Eve, and at precisely one that afternoon, Patrick called home to wish the family well. The phone rang and rang, and just when he was about to hang up, it was finally answered.

"Hello?" It was Sinead.

"Ho! Ho! Ho!"

"Who is this?"

"It's Santie! Could I please speak with Sinead Quinn?"

"This is she," the girl replied nervously, truly believing that St. Nick was on the line. Patrick could tell he had her right where he wanted her, and after having a laugh or two, finally told her the truth.

"I'm sorry. I was just messin' with ya," he said after she told him that she didn't think it was funny. She soon forgave him, though, and began thanking him for all the wonderful gifts."

"So you like 'em, eh?"

"Oh, they're grand! I love 'em!"

"Well, that's good. I'm happy." They spoke for a little while longer until Patrick finally asked to speak with their father.

"He's not here now."

"Where is he?"

"He went to collect Paul in Skerries."

"Let me guess—he's just finishing up his Christmas shopping, right?"

"Yep!"

Patrick groaned. "Unbelievable! So … how long's he been gone for?"

"I don't know. Maybe half an hour."

"Great. That means he's not gonna be back for awhile then."

"Guess what, Paddy?" Sinead said abruptly.

"What?"

"We went by Mommy's grave today."

"Did ya?"

"Yeah, I cried. I still miss her so much, but I'm happy she's up in Heaven with God."

"Who ya talkin' with?" a voice was suddenly heard asking in the background. It was Brian.

"Daddy, Daddy, it's Paddy!"

"Is it?" he whooped and was soon on the line. "Patrick?"

"Yeah, it's me, Da. Merry Christmas."

"Ah, it's good to hear your voice, son! Merry Christmas! How are ya?"

"Grand. And yourself?"

"I'm doin' well, thanks."

"That's good."

"Oh, yeah, and by the way, thanks for the watch. But ya know, you really shouldn't have. I mean, it's brilliant and all, and I'll cherish it for the rest of me days, but you need that money to live on."

"Ah, don't worry about it, Da. I got another promotion a couple of weeks ago. I'm a manager now. Got a raise, too."

"Really? Hey, congratulations. That's great."

"Yeah, things are goin' pretty well, all right," Patrick replied and then went on to thank his father for his present, which was a boxed set of *Father Ted* tapes, a popular Irish sitcom, which Patrick missed greatly. After being briefed once more about the family's visit to the graveyard, Patrick then asked to speak with his brother.

"He's not here right now."

"He's not? I thought Sinead said you went to collect him."

"I did, and then I dropped him off in Lusk."

"Lusk? What the hell's he doin' in Lusk?"

"Would you believe it if I told ya the lad's got a girlfriend?"

"Are you serious?"

"Aye, it's the truth! The fair Grania Plunkett. She's adorable. Long red hair. Freckles. It's innocent enough, though. Plus, she comes from a really good family."

"Wow, I can't believe it. Paul has a girlfriend."

"Hey, the lad's growin' up. He is sixteen, ya know."

"He is, isn't he?"

"Yep. Two months ago."

"Ah, Christ, that's right. Bollox! And I never even called to wish him a happy one."

"Ah, don't worry about it. He knows how busy things are for ya right now."

"But still … I should've at least remembered, don't ya think? I guess I really haven't been too good of a brother or son lately, have I?"

"What did I say, Pat? Don't worry about it. And enough about Paul already. How are Tara and the lads doin'?"

"The lads are great."

"And Tara? How's she?"

"I don't know. We're not seein' each other anymore."

"Ah, that's too bad. What happened?" Brian asked but immediately apologized, saying that it wasn't his business and that he had no right in asking.

"Of course ya have the right to ask, Da," Patrick answered and then paused briefly before saying, "I broke up with her a few months ago."

"You broke up with her? Why? You seemed so much in love."

"I was, but … things change, I guess. People change. Back in September, that's when it happened, well, back then I was still havin' a pretty tough time dealing with Mom's death. I was in a really bad way, ya know, and um … I was draggin' the poor girl down with me and obviously I didn't want for that to happen, so I just broke up with her."

"But you're doin' better now, right?"

"Oh, yeah. Back to me old self."

"Well, why don't ya ask her back out then?"

"Yeah, maybe I will." Another lie! No, he knew he wouldn't ask her back out because he was still the same man, still feeling the same way. "Well, I guess I'd better get goin'," he said after a moment. "This call's gonna cost a fortune."

"Yeah, you're right about that. Okay, well—we all wish you were here."

"Yeah, me, too. Well, okay, um … I'll try to call back again tomorrow, but if I don't, you have yourself a good Christmas, Da. And tell Paul and the rest of the family that I said hello, all right?"

"I promise, I will. And you have yourself a merry one, also. Ya hear?"

"Yeah, I will. Don't worry." And right when they were about to end the call, Sinead was heard shouting in the background, "Daddy, gimme the phone!"

"He' gotta get goin', Sinead! This type of call costs a lot of money, ya know."

"Ah, it's all right, Da. Put her on."

"Patrick?"

"Yeah, I'm still here, little one. What is it?"

"I love you," she whispered softly.

"I love you, too. Now you'd better get goin' to bed soon so Santie can come, all right?"

"All right. Bye-bye."

"Bye."

After hanging up the phone, Patrick sat down at the kitchen table and began thinking about home. He missed it more that moment than he ever had. What in the hell was he doing with his life anyways? While pondering this question, he began to drift into one of his spells that were now beginning to occur more and more frequently. Suddenly, it occurred to him that he was feeling really sad. That was a good sign, right? At least he felt something. Concluding that things might not be as hopeless as he thought, he smiled and shortly thereafter joined the lads in the living room. They were watching the Father Ted tapes that his father had sent him. The three men shared a case of Samuel Adams' Cranberry Lambic and a whole lot of laughs that evening, and everyone went to bed happy.

CHAPTER 24

▼

The next afternoon the phone rang in the Quinn house, and much to Brian's delight, it was his son Patrick on the line.

"Hey, Merry Christmas, Pat!"

"Merry Christmas to you, too, Da."

"So, how's your day been thus far?"

"Well, I just woke up, but … it's been grand so far, I guess. And yours?"

"Busy!"

Patrick chuckled. "Yeah, I can imagine." He then paused momentarily before asking if Paul was there.

"The whole gang's here!"

"Are they?"

"Aye. Hold on for a second, all right?"

"Okay," Patrick replied, and before he knew it, he had talked with every sibling, aunt, uncle, and cousin, including Moses, who apologized continually the entire time they spoke. The call lasted a good twenty minutes, and after wishing everyone well, Patrick said goodbye and hung up. He then went upstairs and woke the lads. Not long after, all three were in the kitchen preparing their Christmas dinner: roast pork with all the trimmings. It was finished by two that afternoon, and the three of them, along with Sandra, sat down and ate. During the course of their meal they spoke about different things, but the core of the discussion centered around something that had become sort of a neighborhood ritual over the past couple of years: their New Year's Eve party.

"You're gonna have it, right?" Sandra asked, initiating the topic.

"I don't see why not," Phil surmised, raising an eyebrow. "Why? Ya dig my parties, don't ya, babe?"

"Our parties!" Kevin corrected.

"Whatever."

"Yeah, they're good craic."

"Yeah, I guess we're gonna have it, right?" Phil shrugged, looking over at Kevin.

"I don't see why not."

"Cool!" Sandra exclaimed.

Over the course of the next week, news of the party—the third annual one to be exact—could be heard resonating from the halls of AT&T, to inside the safe at Sovereign, and everywhere in between. Everyone was looking forward to it, everyone that is except Tara O'Malley. She had seen Patrick only twice since their break-up, and was unsure about whether or not to make an appearance, let alone if she'd even be welcome. Ultimately, though—after a lot of coaxing from the girls and even a phone call from Patrick himself—she decided to attend.

On December 31, people began arriving at around eight, but the girls didn't head over until close to nine. As the five of them walked along, reveling could be heard mixed with the gritty, melodic pounding of Rancid's "As Wicked." Tara was extremely nervous as she ascended the front steps, which were already jam-packed with people.

Upon entering, the girls were greeted by Kevin and Phil, who were making the rounds, trying to ensure that everyone felt at home. Sandra soon joined them while the rest began to mingle with friend and stranger alike. A short time had passed when Joanne suddenly noticed Tara standing by herself, looking apprehensively about. Walking over and taking her by the hand, she led her over to the sofa and sat her down. They were immediately joined by Heather and Maureen.

"Just relax, will ya," Joanne said as she gently rubbed her friend's back.

"Believe me, I'm trying, but it's just not workin'. Oh, God, I'm so nervous."

"Listen—I'll go make you a drink, all right? That should help loosen ya up," Maureen said as she began getting to her feet.

"No, no," Tara cried, grabbing her by the arm. "I'm not drinkin' tonight."

"Why not?"

"Because …"

"I know why," Heather interjected, causing everyone to turn in her direction. "You're afraid you'll get all mushy and sentimental when ya see him, huh? Tell me I'm not right."

"Yeah, well … kind of. Maybe. I do kinda get that way when I drink. I don't know. I guess I'd just rather be safe than sorry."

"Well, Christ, we're not tellin' ya to get locked, just tryin' to help you relax, that's all," Joanne exclaimed. "And right now the only way it appears you're gonna be able to do that is by havin' a drink or two. Am I right or am I right?"

"I guess."

"I know I'm right! And besides, Tara, it's a party, and for God's sake … ya have as much right to be here and to be enjoyin' yourself as anyone. So sit back, relax, and let's have some fun."

"Yeah, all right."

"Now that's a girl," Maureen said, grinning, as she began to rise once more. "So, what'll your poison be?"

Tara sighed. "A vodka and Coke, I guess."

"Okay. You've got it. One vodka and Coke comin' right up." After taking Joanne's order, the two girls walked off. A few moments passed, when over scurried Sandra.

"How ya doin' so far?" she asked Tara.

"So far, so good."

"Have ya seen him yet?"

"No, not yet. Have you?"

"No, I haven't seen him all night. I wonder where the hell he is?"

No sooner had Sandra finished, than the girls returned with their drinks. Tara took her vodka and Coke and began sipping at it, and before she knew it, it was gone. The girls were right. She did feel more at ease. As she sat there, looking around at all the people, her mind suddenly started to wander. She began remembering all the good times spent in this house. In this very room. Her reminiscing was interrupted by Maureen asking her if she wanted another drink.

"Yeah, sure. Why not?"

"Same thing?"

"Yes, please."

By eleven, Tara found herself as relaxed as could be. This was due, in part, to the four drinks she had already consumed, coupled with the fact that she had yet to see Patrick. The girls had just settled back with round number five, when a curvaceous blond suddenly walked down the stairs, all the while adjusting her bra. It was obvious by that, and from the tousled condition of her hair, as to what she had been doing.

"What the hell's that bitch doin' here?" Tara snarled.

"You know her?"

"Yeah, I know her. That's Courtney Bennett. She works with us. She's a snob and a real slapper. Probably done half the guys at work! She lives in the Beacon Hill district. A real little rich girl. Supposedly her family came over on the Mayflower or something."

"Ooh, I'm impressed!" Heather snickered.

"Yeah, I had words with your woman when I first started. Listen to this. I'm standing in the lunch line one day, waiting to get served, and right when I'm about to give me order, she cuts in front of me. So I said to her, 'Excuse me, but it's my turn.' And guess what she says?"

"What?" all three replied simultaneously.

"She smiles and says, 'So?' real cocky-like and continues placing her order."

"Are you serious?" Joanne asked.

"Yes, I'm serious!"

"And what did you say?"

"I think I might have just laughed and shook my head or something, but mind you, it was only the second or third day of training. What was I gonna do? Get into a fight?"

"Yeah, I guess there really isn't much ya can do in a situation like that," Maureen conceded. "Except … possibly catching her away from work and beatin' the livin' shite out of her. Now that's an option."

Tara began to chuckle. "Yes, a very viable one!"

"I wonder who the lucky lad is?" Joanne asked suddenly. "She really is rather attractive, though."

"Yeah, I guess, but … bein' attractive's one thing. Walking around with your tits pushed out, acting as though you're God's gift to men is something altogether different. It's uncalled for, I mean—it's not as though she's flat chested or anything. Look at 'em! They're huge! And what's more, sometimes she doesn't even wear a bra and you can see everything. It's just disgusting if ya ask me."

Everyone agreed.

"Well, no one came down before her," Maureen said. "I would've seen 'em if they did. So that means the culprit's still up there."

"And while we're waiting to see, why don't we all have another drink?" Tara replied, turning towards her.

"Sounds grand, but why ya lookin' at me?"

"Because you're a saint, that's why!"

Heather cleared her throat. "Aren't we forgetting something?"

"Where's me manners? You're both saints. Now come on, please. Joanne and I will get the next round."

"And this comes from the one who wasn't even gonna drink at all!"

"I promise. Won't we?"

"Of course we will. And are we not women of our word?"

"There'll be no comment on that!" Maureen shot back jokingly as the two of them walked off.

Soon, all four, with drinks in hand, squeezed onto the sofa and waited. It had been about ten minutes since Courtney first made her appearance, and they were now starting to get a little perturbed.

"For cryin' out loud, lad! Show your face!" Joanne grumbled.

Another minute or so passed when the hallway light came on and footsteps were heard. All four girls sat up straight and waited with great enthusiasm.

"Ooh, this is so exciting!" Maureen squealed. "Like a goddamn soap opera!"

Suddenly, down the stairs walked Patrick. Upon seeing him, Tara sank back heavily, absolutely floored. The truth is, the thought never even crossed her mind that it might have been Patrick. He despised Courtney Bennett. Didn't he? She tried to think; however, the alcohol combined with the sudden flood of emotion, made it difficult. *Yes. Of course he does* she finally remembered. It was her ridiculing one of his ideas during a team meeting that caused him to feel that way. Tara tried making sense of it all. Maybe their paths had just crossed. Yes, of course. That had to be it.

Patrick had yet to see Tara by this point, but Courtney noticed her and the stunned look on her face, and she laughed to herself in satisfaction. She considered herself a seductress and enjoyed turning men on or trying to steal them away from their girlfriends or wives, just for kicks. It was all a big game, and one she always seemed to win. And realizing that she was close to victory yet once again, she went in for the kill! Walking slowly over to where Patrick now stood, she came up, grabbed him aggressively by the back of the neck, and gave him a long, passionate kiss. When the embrace was over, she headed towards the kitchen to make herself a drink but made a point of catching a glimpse of Tara's expression. And what she saw was exactly what she had hoped to see: a woman destroyed.

As he stood there, using the back of his hand to wipe away any lipstick, Patrick finally spotted Tara. All at once, he felt both embarrassed and dirty. And even though they had only made out, Tara didn't know that. Ashamed, and not knowing what to do, he quickly turned and walked out onto the front porch.

Dammit! Haven't I caused her enough pain? Why'd she have to see that? he scolded himself. He pondered what to do next. Should he go say hi, or try to avoid her altogether. The latter would probably be easier, but ultimately, he decided on the former. After a few minutes—during which time he mustered the necessary courage and decided what he would say—Patrick headed back inside. Wasting no time, he walked over and asked how everyone was doing.

"We're havin' a grand time, thanks," Tara replied.

"And it looks like you're especially enjoying yourself, huh?" Heather added. It was obvious what she was referring to, and it caused both Patrick and Tara to throw an irritated glare in her direction. A moment or two of uneasiness ensued before Tara finally said, "I heard about your promotion, Patrick. Congratulations."

"Thank you."

After another uncomfortable silence, Joanne got to her feet suddenly. "Come on, girls. Help me get the next round, okay?" They both nodded and followed her out into the kitchen.

Once alone, the two felt extremely uncomfortable—Patrick especially so. He had only consumed a couple of beers by the time he and Courtney went upstairs, and both had long since worn off, so he was pretty much sober and much more cognizant of the awkwardness of the moment. In fact, by the time the girls returned with the drinks, neither had uttered a single word to one another. Now determined, Patrick got to his feet and said, "Can I talk with you for a moment?"

"About what?"

"In private."

"No. I don't think that's a good idea."

"Please."

Tara was about to decline once more when she suddenly felt elbows being pressed into her from both sides. "Okay, but only for a second. It's almost midnight. I wanna watch the ball drop in Times Square." As she got to her feet and began following him up the stairs, she wondered what all this was about, just as she had done that fateful day when her entire world had been shattered. Patrick led her to his room, and securely closed the door when they were both inside.

"So, what's so important?" Tara asked, surveying the room. She immediately noticed the disheveled bed, which both angered and upset her, but outwardly she remained composed.

"I don't know. Us. What happened. Why it happened."

"Well, there isn't an 'us' anymore. And it doesn't really matter why, I guess, only that it did happen. The reason's obvious, anyway. You said it yourself. You didn't love me anymore."

This caught him off-guard. But it was true. That's what he had said all right. He searched for the right words. "There isn't a single day that goes by that I don't think about you, Tara."

"Oh, I'm sure you were really thinkin' about me when you were screwin' Courtney, huh?" she blurted out. It was the liquor, though, and not reason, that caused her to say what she had secretly been thinking. And even though drunk, she still felt ashamed, so she apologized.

"I know that's probably how it looks, but I swear, nothing really happened. We just kissed."

"Listen, Patrick. You don't have to explain yourself to me. Really. You're a free man now. You can do whatever you want."

"I know I don't have to explain myself, but still … there's a few things that I want you to know."

"Listen, you don't …"

"Will ya just let me say what's on me mind, woman, for God's sake!"

"Go ahead! Who's stoppin' ya?"

"Well, you're not makin' it easy."

"Nothing in life ever is. You taught me that."

"Yeah, I know I did. And I'm sorry."

"Are you? Are ya really?"

"Look at me. I didn't wanna hurt you. You know that. Ya have to know that! You meant everything to me. Maybe ya still do, but I just can't feel it. That's why I broke up with you, Tara. Not because I didn't love ya anymore, but because I couldn't feel anymore. For you or for anything. I tried so hard all that time to love you like I once did, but I couldn't. And I felt guilty for it even though it wasn't my fault. I still do." He fell silent for a moment, staring intently at the floor, before looking back up. "I don't think I'll ever love another woman as much as I once loved you."

Suddenly, the one thing she had hoped wouldn't happen, did: no longer able to contain her true feelings, she burst into tears and began sobbing uncontrollably. "Oh, God! I miss you so much!"

"I know ya do," Patrick said softly as he came up and hugged her. He, too, was becoming emotional and it felt really good, he thought.

"Do you miss me?" she wept.

"Yeah, sometimes."

"I miss you all the time—still! Why'd we have to end up like this, huh?"

"I don't know. Things just happen, I guess."

"Do you think you'll ever love me the same way again?"

"I don't know, maybe. I would like to think that I could, but I can't say for sure. At least not right now, anyway. I'm still not well. Let's just try bein' friends for a while and see what happens, all right? But if things don't work out, ya have to promise me something."

"What?"

"That you won't hate me."

"I could never hate you, Patrick. And I know you can't help the way you feel, and how hard of a time you've had since your mother's death, but … it's just gonna hurt being your friend when for a time we were so much more."

"I know," he answered consolingly as he ran his fingers through her hair. The two talked a little while longer, and when they finally descended the stairs five minutes before midnight, they were hand in hand. Everyone who saw them was stunned, especially Courtney, who immediately came up to Patrick and tried planting another kiss. However, he pushed her away.

"I thought you kicked this one to the curb a long time ago," she said, sneering, while looking Tara straight in the eyes.

"Yeah, well … I guess ya thought wrong!" Tara retorted.

"Please! Just save it, all right. Because you are not all that." The two women glared at each other. And then, without another word, Courtney retrieved her jacket from the other room and left.

"Okay, everyone, here we go!" Phil no sooner shouted. "Ten!"

Everyone in the entire house festively joined in. "Nine! Eight! Seven! Six! Five! Four! Three! Two! One! Happy New Year!"

"I hope so," Tara said, turning to Patrick.

"Yeah, me too."

CHAPTER 25

▼

As the new year began, Patrick felt as though it might actually be possible to escape the wretched hell he had spent most of the previous year trapped in.

Tara, who once again became a regular over the lads' house, on a platonic basis only, helped Patrick's healing process through simple acts of kindness and frequent talks. Slowly, his emotions appeared to be reviving. In addition, he felt that his weekly calls back home to his family were also helping.

Another factor, he believed, was his new position as C.S.M. Although the responsibilities could be taxing at times, he embraced the challenge of his new job and excelled at it. He also seemed to enjoy the prestige the new appointment brought him. He was a manager now and was treated with a certain respect that he hadn't gotten before. And even though he told Tara that it made him feel uncomfortable at times that people he had started with, some who were even twice his age, began deferring to him, deep down, he really did enjoy it.

The first couple of months of the new year were truly a magical time. Patrick and Tara appeared to be falling back in love, and although they hadn't made love, or even kissed—through pure friendship—their feelings for one another were quite obvious. There were also many parties and much laughter. The gang was back together and it seemed as though nothing had ever changed.

Despite all of this, though, somewhere in the back of his mind, Patrick knew that March 10th, the one-year anniversary of his mother's death, was fast approaching, and this worried him. Nevertheless, he believed that if he could just make it through that day in one piece, he'd be recovered, and if recovered, he would ask Tara out again. She, of course, didn't know this, nor did anyone else.

CHAPTER 26

▼

It was the first weekend in March when the girls invited the lads over for a couple of drinks, which quickly turned into a few more, until all eight were completely inebriated.

"Hey, why don't we all do something next weekend?" Tara suggested as she made her way from the kitchen, carrying two bottles of Corona beer. She handed one to Heather and the other to Phil.

"Like what?" Maureen hiccupped.

"I don't know. Something," Tara replied, plopping down on the couch. She knew full well what the following Monday would bring, and although she never mentioned anything about it to Patrick, she feared that it was going to be a considerably rough time for him and wished to get him out of the house. It didn't really matter to her what they did, just as long as he was kept busy.

"Something to do? Something to do?" Phil pondered out loud. "Hey, I've got it. Why don't we all go skiing?"

"Nah, screw that!" Kevin exclaimed.

"Why? What's so horrible about skiing?" Joanne asked her man. Yes, it was she, in fact, that Kevin had alluded to many months earlier when he said he'd had his eye on someone. And although she hadn't been particularly excited about the idea at first, through some coaxing from her sister and Phil, she agreed to date him. She was now happy that she had listened to their advice, for the two had recently begun falling in love.

"I just don't like it!"

"Not even for me?"

"Uh-uh, not even for you. I mean … it's just not natural to strap two thin pieces of wood to your feet and fly down a large mountain. It's feckin' dangerous!"

Patrick chuckled. "Yeah, I second that. It was nice, I guess, to have tried it. But I can't see doing it again. Once was enough. Like some people at work—I think that's all they do on their weekends is ski. And I can't understand why. I didn't see anything particularly impressive about it, except maybe the price. It's expensive as hell!"

"Yeah, plus, not to mention, ya freeze your arse off," Kevin added. "Nah, anything but skiing."

"Hey, it was just an idea."

"But not a very sound one."

"Well, what do you propose, huh? I haven't heard any good ideas from you."

"There isn't very much to do."

"Well, not with a mindset like that there isn't! Ooh, I'm so cold, and not to mention, afraid of the big hill!" Phil mimicked.

"Ah, feck off!"

The two sisters, seeing that the current antagonism was on the brink of escalation, went over and sat on each of their significant others' laps—a telltale sign for them to stop their arguing right away.

"How about a game?" Maureen asked, trying to break the tension.

"Hey, now that's an idea. We can go see the Celtics play," Phil replied. "Good thinkin', Maureen."

"Basketball? I don't wanna go to a basketball game. Talk about expensive," Sandra grumbled. "One of the girls I work with, Erika, she went to one a couple of weekends ago with her boyfriend and said it was something like eighty dollars per seat."

Phil made a face. "I think you're wrong. Why would it be so expensive?"

"I'm not wrong! That's what she said! And why would she lie?"

"They must've been some pretty good seats then."

"Nope. She said they weren't anything special. At least not what you'd expect for the price, anyway."

"Well, I guess that chalks that up," Kevin said, yawning, as he placed his can of beer down on the coffee table.

"Why does it chalk it up? It's not that much. Christ, we paid close to that to see the Patriots."

"Phil, I'm not gonna go and spend eighty dollars to see something that I don't even care about! Football was different. Ever since I was a small boy I wanted to see an American football game in person. My grandfather loved the Chicago Bears, for whatever reason, so that's all I grew up hearing about. Basketball, on the other hand, is something I have absolutely no desire to see, whatsoever."

"See what I'm talkin' about."

Kevin glared at him.

"Well, let's do something," Tara entreated suddenly. "Christ, the weekends have been so boring lately. I mean, you can only party so much. I'm startin' to get worn out."

"Yeah, me, too," Maureen seconded. "I mean, don't get me wrong, the parties have all been great. But they do tend to take their toll on ya after awhile."

Phil jumped to his feet. "Speak for yourselves. I feel fine."

"But that's because you're the world's best party animal," Kevin shot back in his best 'stoner' voice, which caused everyone, including Phil himself, to begin laughing.

"Well, I'm sure we'll come up with something," Joanne said as the group began to disperse.

"Yeah, but let's decide soon though, okay? So we have enough time to plan everything," Tara urged as she walked the lads to the door. Everyone, including Patrick, promised her that they'd spend the next couple of days thinking something up.

On their way home, Phil inquired as to why Tara was so hung up on doing something the following weekend.

"I have no idea," Patrick answered. However, he knew quite well what her intentions were, but never let on.

As the days passed, and the weekend approached, Patrick became anxious. He tried not to think about it too much, but the harder he tried, the more he found himself lost in thought. Tara could sense his apprehension and sought to help lessen it during the course of the week by baking him chocolate chip cookies and by drawing funny, little pictures and leaving them at his desk, but it soon became apparent that her efforts weren't having the desired effect.

When the weekend finally did arrive, no definitive plans had been set. Tara had feared this would happen. Disgusted that no one, including herself, had followed through on their promise, she decided just to brace herself for the days ahead and whatever outcome they yielded.

Patrick had also taken on this approach by midweek. *How bad can it be? It's just another day, right?* he kept telling himself. *Just be strong and you'll be all right.* But unbeknownst to him, strength wouldn't be a factor; nothing would—except fate.

CHAPTER 27

▼

It was half-past one, Saturday afternoon, by the time Tara finally left her house and began walking down the street. She felt troubled the entire way as to what type of mood Patrick might be in but made a point to be cheerful regardless of his state of mind.

After ringing the doorbell and knocking countless times without an answer, she had just turned and was about to try her luck around back when the door suddenly opened. It was Patrick.

"For a moment there I didn't think anyone was home."

"Why? Have ya been waiting long?"

"Nah, only about a minute," she replied as they entered the house and sat down on the sofa, while Patrick finished watching an episode of his favorite American TV show, *All in the Family*. "I'm tellin' ya, that Archie's a feckin' riot!" he roared, finally turning off the television. "Ya hungry?"

"No. I already ate."

"Well, I'm starvin'. Come on." They walked into the kitchen and Patrick began making scrambled eggs. As the butter sizzled in the pan, he asked her how her day had been.

"Broke up Sandra and Heather again. Watched the news. I guess you can say it's been a typical Saturday."

"They're still goin' at it, huh?"

"Oh God, worse than ever! The problem is—the girl just doesn't know when to keep her mouth shut!"

"Why? What did she say now?"

Tara groaned. "The question should be what didn't she say. Well, Sandra was nice enough to make us all breakfast this mornin', and keep in mind, her cookin' sucks. But it's the gesture, ya know. So we just eat it and keep quiet. Ask Phil. He probably knows better than anyone. Well, anyways, to make a long story short, halfway through breakfast, Heather decides, for whatever reason, to tell Sandra how the toast tastes like brick and that the pancakes somewhat resemble cardboard. Or something to that effect, anyway. And God knows what followed. Joanne called her a bitch and said she had no manners. Heather called her a bitch back. And then Sandra just flipped! I mean, you should've seen the look on your woman's face. I thought she was gonna kill her. I really did. So me and the girls jumped in between them, and then the next thing ya know, we're all rollin' around on the floor!"

"Why? What happened?"

"Well, by the time we stepped in, we had pretty much defused Sandra, but Heather—she took a swing at her! If you can believe that! And that's when all hell broke loose. Yeah, it wasn't a pretty picture, let me tell ya. Someone even stuck a finger in me eye!"

"Are you okay?"

"I am now, but it stung like hell at the time! I swear to God, though, the next time Heather offers one of her little insults, I'm just gonna let her get what's comin' to her. I'm sick of it! She has absolutely no gratitude. Never even thanks me for helpin' her, either."

After turning off the burner and ladling the eggs onto a large ceramic plate, Patrick took a seat at the table. He took a few bites, then, looking up, said, "I don't think I'm much better than Sandra," which caused both to smile.

"Do you wanna do something?" Tara questioned.

"Like what?"

"I don't know. How about Rummy?"

Rummy had been their game of choice the entire time they had been dating, and they had even once played up to 25,000 points over the course of a two-week period. Tara had won that game, along with most of the others. As a result, Patrick wasn't particularly excited about the idea, but he agreed to play nonetheless. It wasn't long before he was losing once again. The cards had just been dealt for the third hand, when they suddenly heard a series of loud thuds coming from what appeared to be the front porch. They quickly got to their feet and were heading to the door, when it unexpectedly flew open and in darted Phil, drenched in beer. "Christ almighty!" he cried. "Will ya look at me!"

"What the hell happened?" Tara asked, trying not to laugh.

"I feckin' tripped comin' up the stairs and one of the cans of beer exploded! I tried salvaging it, but … it doesn't look like I did too good of a job, now does it!" Phil guffawed as he lowered two cases of beer onto the floor and then sprinted up the stairs. He was soon back down with a thick pink towel. "Come lend a hand, all right?" he said to Patrick, while wiping himself off.

"With what?"

"With the rest of the beer. There's another four cases out in the car."

"In the car? Who ya with?"

"Tommy Catalano."

"Tommy Catalano? What the hell are ya doin' with him?"

"Whadya mean? What am I doin' with him?"

"I don't know, I mean … I don't really trust the lad. Isn't he in the Mafia or something?"

"Ah, that's bollox!"

"Well, that's what I heard!"

"Yeah, and I heard it too," Tara added. "That's the rumor goin' around, anyway."

"And that's all it is—a rumor. There's no validity to it. It's his father who's in the Mafia. Not him."

"Well, that puts my mind at ease."

"Ah, don't worry about it. I met his father. He's a nice enough guy. And enough about Tommy, already! Will ya just come on and lend a hand, for Christ's sake!"

"What's wrong with him?" Patrick grumbled, motioning outside.

"He can't. His hand's broken."

"How'd he do that?"

Phil grinned. "He went to some club over on Lansdowne Street last weekend and forgot his I.D. They wouldn't let him in so he got pissed off and punched the wall. Jacked up his hand and wrist pretty bad."

"So I guess he's got a temper, too, huh? Sounds like a really pleasant bloke!" Tara quipped.

"Will ya just give the lad a chance, for God's sake!" Phil exclaimed while the two put on their jackets. "I'm tellin' ya, he's sound enough."

The moment the front door opened, Tommy got out of his black Mustang GT. "Hey, what's up guys?" he shouted.

"Hey, Tommy. How's it goin'?" Patrick asked as he walked around to the back of the car and lifted one of the cases.

"Can't complain. And yourself?"

"Oh, I'm grand. Thanks."

Tommy suddenly noticed Tara also reaching for one of the boxes. "My hand may be broken, Tara, but not my manners. Now you go bring yourself inside. I'll help them."

"Thanks, Tommy, but I'm grand. Really. Besides, it's only a case of beer. I've lifted things a whole lot heavier," she said, glancing over in Patrick's direction. After carrying all the cases into the house, the four of them then sat down in the living room.

"Nice place ya got here," Tommy said, looking around.

"Has anyone eva told you that you're a terrible liar?" Phil shot back jokingly, which caused everyone, including Tommy himself, to begin laughing. They chit-chatted for a short while about work until Patrick finally asked about Kevin's whereabouts.

"We dropped him off at the video store about twenty minutes ago," Phil replied.

"And ya didn't wait for him? It's freezin' out!"

"No, he told us not to. Said he was just gonna browse around for awhile and then head over to Joanne's."

Patrick then fell silent for a moment before finally asking, "By the way, what's goin' on tonight, anyways?"

"Ah, not too much. Just some drink and a few flicks."

"Who's comin'?"

"Just the girls and us. Oh, and yeah, I also invited Chris and Devon from up the street. They said they'd try to make it, but hey, you know those guys. So it's only gonna be about eleven of us at the most."

"Make that ten," Tara corrected. "I don't think Heather's gonna be comin', either. Your woman almost killed her this mornin'."

"She did? Why, what happened?"

"Well, Sandra cooked us all breakfast …"

"Ya poor things! You need not tell me anymore. Let me guess. And Heather, being the charming creature that she is, told her how delicious it was, right?"

"Yep! Ya hit it right on the head."

"Sounds like my mother," Tommy said, frowning. "It's a rare thing for an Italian woman not to be a good cook, but my mother's the exception to the rule. I'm serious, the woman's horrible. But me and Dad, we just eat it and keep quiet."

"I know the feeling."

"Oh, come on!" Tara giggled. "It's not that bad."

"Yes it is! You try eatin' it on a regular basis, and I guarantee ya, you won't feel the same way." Everyone had just begun laughing when the front door suddenly opened and in walked Kevin and Joanne, shivering.

"Jesus, it's cold!" Kevin bellowed, rubbing his hands together.

"Hey, Joanne," Phil called over.

"Yeah?" she replied as she took off her jacket and placed it on the radiator.

"I'd like for you to meet a friend of ours. This is Tommy Catalano. He works with us."

She walked over and extended her hand. "Nice to meet you."

"No, the pleasure's all mine."

"See, I told ya he's all right," Phil whispered to Patrick out of the corner of his mouth. "Just a little misunderstood, that's all."

"So, what movies did ya get?" Tara questioned.

"You don't wanna know," Joanne replied, grimacing.

Kevin shook his head. "Oh, come on! Don't be a baby!"

"What the hell did you get?" Tara asked once more.

"Well, let's see," Kevin responded as he removed three tapes from a yellow, plastic bag, "we have *Halloween. The Texas Chainsaw Massacre.* And *The Evil Dead.*"

"Fuckin' A! Those are great movies, Kevin! Nice goin'. Especially *Evil Dead.* There's this really cool scene where this chick gets raped by a tree," Tommy said enthusiastically, but as he looked around the room, he immediately noticed that the women in attendance didn't appreciate his fervor. "Sorry, ladies. Didn't mean to offend anyone, but it really is kind of hilarious. I guess you have to see it, though, to appreciate it."

By four, everyone who was going to be there had arrived, which was everyone except Heather, Chris, and Devon. With drinks in hand, and everybody situated comfortably in front of the television, Kevin popped in *The Evil Dead* to begin the night's festivities. In the end, the lads loved it, but the girls found it too ridiculous and crude, and not the least bit scary.

"Which one do you guys wanna watch next? *Texas Chainsaw* or *Halloween*?" Kevin asked as he grabbed the controller and began rewinding the tape. The group was divided, but from a spirited endorsement by Tommy, who was basically the evening's guest, *Halloween* won out.

"Now I can partially understand you not liking *Evil Dead.* True, it was a little more vulgar than I remember. But I know you'll love *Halloween.* I'd bet my life on it. The acting is superb! I think Jamie Lee Curtis even won an Oscar for it,"

Tommy said while opening another bottle of Guinness. "Hey, you know something. This stuff isn't bad."

"It's the first time you've eva had it?" Sandra muttered in disbelief.

"Yeah, I'm more of a Bud man, but I think I've found a new love. Excuse my French, but ... this stuff is freakin' awesome!"

Before they knew it, the streets of Haddonfield, Illinois came into view and all seemed mesmerized by the haunting, sinister music emanating from the TV—all that is except Patrick, who was battling a stomach ache that had come upon him a short time earlier. As was his nature, though, he kept quiet about it. An hour or so passed before he finally beckoned Tara to the kitchen.

"What is it?" she asked, taking a seat at the table.

"I don't feel too good. My stomach's botherin' me." He then paused. "Would you mind it if I just got goin' to bed now?"

"No, no, I don't mind. Are you gonna be all right?"

"Yeah. I don't think it's anything serious. Just an upset stomach, that's all."

"Do ya want anything for it? Like Pepto-Bismol or something"

"Nah. The best thing's probably just to sleep it off, don't ya think?"

"I guess," she answered dejectedly. She wondered if now would be a good opportunity to tell him that she knew the anniversary of his mother's death was fast approaching but decided against it. No, she wouldn't bring it up unless it was absolutely necessary. And if that time ever did come, then, and only then, would she say something.

"Ya sure you don't mind?"

"Of course not."

"You gonna be all right?"

"Yeah, I'll be fine. It's you that I'm worried about. Are ya sure you don't want anything?"

"No. I just feel like goin' to bed, that's all."

"Right. All right, then."

They walked back out into the living room.

"Watch out! Watch out! He's in the bushes! Don't ya see him?" Sandra screamed at the top of her voice as she clenched Phil tightly with both hands. "I'm tellin' ya right now, this one's gonna end up dead."

"Nope!" Tommy said proudly for all to hear.

"For God's sake, man, will ya shut the feck up!" Phil barked disgustedly. "You told us the entire plot to the last story! Will ya at least let us enjoy this one! We haven't seen it yet!"

"No problem!" Tommy snapped. He was pissed. It was evident by the look on his face, but he kept his anger in check. And it was a good thing for Phil that he did! Tommy stood close to 6'3" and was covered from head to toe in rippling muscle. He was a very good-looking man with jet-black hair, olive skin, and classic Roman features. And although he was 100% Sicilian on his father's side, and half Bolognese on his mother's, his maternal grandmother had been a Wexford woman, so he had a deep love for the Irish, especially since she had lived with him up until her death three years earlier.

"Hey, good night everyone. I'm goin' to bed," Patrick said as he began walking up the stairs.

"No, no, no, get down here! You're not goin' to bed yet. The night's still young," Phil shouted over the blaring television.

Patrick stopped. "It's not because I'm tired. I just don't feel well."

"I don't care! Now get your arse down here!"

"Say what you want, Phil. But I'm goin' to bed. Now good night."

"All right, fine. Good night," Phil shot back as he took a handful of the popcorn that Sandra had just made.

"Yeah, good night, Pat," Kevin and the others hollered up the stairs.

Patrick had just reached the landing, and turned the corner, when another voice suddenly called to him. It was Tommy.

He looked down. "Yeah?"

"I just wanna thank you for having me over tonight. I really appreciate it."

"Ah, don't worry about it. It was fun."

"Well, just the same—thanks," Tommy said once more and then turned and rejoined everyone in front of the television set.

Patrick stood motionless for a moment, reflecting on how maybe Phil had been right all along, before retiring to his room.

CHAPTER 28

▼

It was close to noon the following day by the time Patrick awoke. As he lay there, an overwhelming sense of sadness began to take hold. And by the time he finally got out of bed, an hour later, he could tell the day was going to be a difficult one.

"Hey, how ya feelin'?" Kevin asked cheerfully as Patrick made his way into the living room and sat down beside him on the sofa.

"Better, thanks."

"Good," Kevin rejoined as he continued reading the morning's edition of the *Globe*. A few minutes passed in silence before Patrick finally inquired on Phil's whereabouts.

"He's workin'."

"Working?"

"Yeah, he changed his schedule. He's gonna work Sundays now and have Wednesdays off instead."

"Oh, I didn't know that."

"Yeah, I guess he needs the extra cash."

"So, what time did the party end last night?" Patrick asked, changing the subject.

"I don't know. Maybe midnight."

"How about Tara? What time did she leave?"

"Oh, I'd probably say about twenty minutes or so after you went to bed."

"Did she? She told me she was gonna stay and enjoy herself."

"Well, don't blame yourself, Paddy. I don't think your goin' to bed was the only reason she left. I just don't think she likes horror movies."

"Yeah, maybe," Patrick murmured, while staring off into space. He soon snapped out of it and went to the kitchen. After making himself a cup of tea, he sat down at the table and had just begun sipping at it, when, out of the corner of his eye, he suddenly noticed two full cases of beer lying near the back door. He stared at them intently for a short while before walking over and opening a can. It was warm but he drank it down anyway. He soon had another. Then another. And by the time Tara came over, at around three, he had consumed an entire six-pack.

"Kind of early for that, don't ya think?" she asked, frowning, as she took a seat directly across from him and pointed to the can.

"Just tryin' to make up for last night."

"Well, ya didn't miss much, let me tell ya."

"Oh, yeah? And how would you know? I heard you went home pretty early yourself."

"Yeah, well … I was tired."

"Want one?" Patrick asked suddenly.

Deciding that now was as good a time as any, she looked him straight in the eyes and said, "Ya know something, Paddy. Your getting' drunk isn't gonna make this day any easier. I know what tomorrow is."

"Yeah, I know you do."

"Don't do this to yourself! Your mother wouldn't want this! You think she's happy lookin' down, knowing that she's the cause of so much grief?"

Patrick chuckled. "Listen, Tara, my mother's not lookin' down from any-where. She's dead. And probably the feast of some maggots as we speak. And that's the reality of it." However, he quickly apologized after observing her horri-fied expression.

"I'm just worried about you, Paddy. I'm afraid you're gonna break."

"Don't. I'll be all right," he assured her as he leaned over and softly kissed her lips for the first time in over six months. She closed her eyes and savored the moment. "I just have to deal with this me own way, that's all."

"And what way is that, huh? Drinkin' yourself to death?"

"I'm not gonna drink myself to death, Tara, believe me. It's just that … I just have to be alone today and overcome these demons once and for all."

"So you want me to leave?"

"If you wouldn't mind."

"No, of course not," she replied as her upper lip began to quiver. All week long she had planned on being by his side during this trying time, and now, here she was, being asked to leave. Of course she minded!

"Now come on, don't look at me like that. Like I said, I have to do this me own way."

"Very well, I'll leave. But only if ya promise me something."

"And what's that?"

"That you'll cool it with the drinking. Please. You're gonna feel like shite at work tomorrow."

"Oh, yeah, that's right—work. I almost forgot about that. I don't think I'm gonna go. I'll just call in sick."

"And that's how you're gonna feel if you don't slow it down. I'm serious, Paddy! Please, just give me your word, okay?"

"All right, all right, I give you me word! I'm just gonna have one or two more and that's it."

"Listen, Patrick. I'm not tryin' to be a pain. It's just that … I'm worried about ya, ya know."

"Yeah, I know ya are. But don't. Like I said, I'll be fine."

"I hope so," she said pointedly. "All right, well … I guess I'll get goin'. If ya need anything, give me a call."

"I will. Don't worry."

They kissed once more and then she left without saying another word.

At last, he could drop the façade. After calling into work and letting them know that he wouldn't be coming in the following day, Patrick then checked under the sink and found an untouched pint of Smirnoff's vodka. He took it out and placed it, along with six cans of beer, in a brown paper bag and headed upstairs.

Over the course of the next three hours, he drank in the silence and privacy of his room. And by the time he finally passed out, at around seven, all the liquor was gone.

CHAPTER 29

▼

Roused from his sleep by a soft yet steady pounding that sounded as though it was emanating from the floor below, Patrick opened his eyes and looked around. A few moments passed before it finally dawned on him what day it was.

He was quickly out of bed and hurrying toward the stairway when his over-zealousness caused him to stumble. Luckily, though, the fall was only a short one—three steps. The landing below, and its plush carpeting, softened the impact. Picking himself up, he continued hurriedly the rest of the way down. And no sooner did he enter the front parlor than his intuitions were confirmed: for there, under the tree, was Paul gently shaking a gift-wrapped box.

Patrick was only dreaming, of course. For this relapse in time that he was now experiencing was that of a Christmas Day long since passed, the Christmas following Sinead's birth. He was thirteen, and Paul was only five, and for reasons too numerous to name, it had been his most enjoyable and memorable one. But why did it come upon him now? On this of all nights?

"Put it down!" Patrick whispered as he came up quietly from behind. The surprise caught Paul off-guard: he jumped, and the present flew from his hands and found its way into the tree and was saved only by a quick-acting older brother who lunged forward and caught it before it hit the floor.

"Now ya promised you weren't gonna do this, didn't ya?" Patrick chastised as he laid the box back under the tree and looked sternly at the innocent, who now appeared to be visibly shaken. However, he couldn't maintain it for long and a smile soon crept across his face.

"He came! He came! And he ate all the sweets, too!" Paul enthused as he jumped to his feet and pointed to a plate that had been covered with cookies and candy only the night before.

"I can see that," Patrick said, chuckling.

"Let's go wake up Mommy and Daddy!"

"No, now come on. Just be patient, will ya. I'm sure they'll be down soon enough. You most likely woke 'em up with all your noise."

On hearing this, Paul quickly turned and was running for the stairs, when Patrick grabbed him by the shoulder. "What did I say? You're not wakin' 'em up! They've been up all night with Sinead. They're exhausted. No, we're gonna sit right here and wait for them. Now come on!" Patrick commanded. And it was the truth. Sinead had been born only a few weeks earlier on the 7th, and was currently suffering from a severe case of colic. As a result, neither Moira nor Brian had gotten very much sleep over the past two nights.

Paul just looked up, devastated, as Patrick took him by the hand and sat him down on the sofa. This authoritative stance was due chiefly to concern for their parents, but there was another motive, a much more sinister one, and that was to see Paul squirm. And did he ever! The poor little thing agonized as he sat there, and rightly so. Can one imagine a boy of five-years being made to sit patiently within the midst of a mound of toys on the most magical day of the year?

Thankfully, however, footsteps were soon heard on the floor above, and moments later, their parents walked down the stairs. On seeing them, Paul lunged from the sofa and ran in their direction. "Santie came!" he screamed at the top of his voice.

"Paul, no!" Brian yelped, but it was too late. Sinead, who was now lying peacefully in her mother's arms, woke up and began crying. They had finally just gotten her to sleep not more than an hour ago, and had questioned whether or not to leave her upstairs. But in her current condition, decided to bring her down. They now regretted their decision.

Brian's stern reprimand—uttered mostly out of fear, though, and not anger— caught the young boy by surprise, and he too appeared to be on the verge of tears. On seeing that he had caused his son unnecessary alarm, Brian scooped him up and gave him a big hug. "It's all right. I'm not mad at ya," he assured the boy with a big smile. "She was bound to wake up sooner or later."

"Oh, she was?"

"Yeah, she's been fussin' all night," Moira acknowledged as she went over and gave him a kiss on the cheek. "Merry Christmas! Now come on, it's supposed to be a happy time. Give your mommy a big smile."

Paul did so exaggeratedly, as children often do, and then gave her a big kiss also.

"And Merry Christmas to you, too, over there," she said, smiling, while looking in Patrick's direction.

"Merry Christmas."

"Why the long face?" Brian questioned.

"Ah, just tired, I guess."

"Hi, Sinead!" Paul blurted out as he suddenly leaned over and gave his little sister a kiss, which only caused the infant's crying to intensify. Moira soon had to leave the room; she headed to the kitchen where she succeeded in calming the baby by singing a soothing lullaby, but it took a good ten minutes.

The entire time they were gone, Paul pleaded with his father to open just one of his presents, but Brian said for him to wait until his mother and sister returned. Paul did as he was told, but it was excruciating. Shortly, though, the entire family was together and the time had finally arrived for them to see what wonderful surprises old St. Nick had brought. As the two brothers were at last given the ok, and each hopped from off the couch and were heading towards the tree, Brian unexpectedly shot to his feet. "Wait a minute! Not yet!" he shouted.

"What is it?" Moira asked.

"Aren't we forgetting something?"

"Are we?"

"The camera."

"For Heaven's sake," she muttered as Brian began mounting the stairs.

It was a ritual to take pictures of the children opening their presents on Christmas morning, and with this being Sinead's first, it would have been an absolute shame had they forgotten. But luckily, thanks to Brian, that wouldn't be the case this day. He was soon back down, and as each present was unwrapped, a picture was taken to remember the moment.

"Here's one for you, Sinead," Patrick said softly as he brought over a small, flat box and handed it to their mother. Moira opened it and inside was a crushed red velvet suit with white lace trim and a little white bow—her Christmas outfit.

"Oh, now isn't that adorable," Brian said as he snapped a photo.

Meanwhile, Patrick had returned to the presents and immediately spotted a large box bearing his name. He slowly unwrapped it and then to his astonishment saw that it was the Atari 5200 video game system. He had always wanted it, but never in his wildest dreams did he ever expect to get it.

"Now that's a great picture!" Brian exclaimed with a big grin. "The best one so far, I think."

"What is it?" Paul asked.

"It's Atari."

"Really? Can I play?"

"Don't be silly. Of course you can."

"Thanks!"

Looking over at his parents, Patrick saw that they were both smiling. He wanted so much to thank them at that moment, but he couldn't, not with Paul in the room.

"Paddy, give me another one!" Paul said suddenly, jumping up and down.

After finding one with his name on it, Patrick was just beginning to hand it to him when the little boy spluttered, "Wait—not yet—I—I have to go to the bathroom." As Paul raced upstairs and vanished from sight, Patrick walked over to where his parents were sitting. "You didn't have to get it for me," he said. "It costs too much money."

"Believe me, I know how much it costs," Brian chuckled. "But we also knew how much ya wanted it, and to us that was more important."

"Of course I wanted it. Everyone wants Atari! But still … ya just shouldn't have."

"Listen, Patrick," Moira began, "the last couple of years have been pretty rough for us. You know that. We haven't been able to give you and Paul the things we would've liked. But with your father's new job, now we can. Or at least a little more, anyway."

Brian had just gotten a job with Wilde Seafood delivering fish throughout the Republic, and on certain occasions, even up North. And although the pay wasn't spectacular, it did provide them with a little more disposable income than that of his previous employment as a farm laborer.

This fact, coupled with an idiosyncrasy common to many Irish—a total disregard for money—swayed their decision to make the purchase. Neither Brian nor Moira received a single present this day; this was something that they had both agreed upon. No, they would spend all their available funds on gifts for the children and other family members, for this type of giving filled them with more joy than they could ever get from the receiving of a present.

Finally, after everything had been opened, and all the wrapping paper picked up, everyone got ready for church.

St. Brendan's was only a short distance from their house, and even though it was winter, the day was a pleasant one so they decided to walk instead of taking the car. They made it to the church in about seven minutes and were greeted inside by Veronica and Peter, Patrick's maternal grandfather who would die the following year. Also with them were Aunt Catherine and Aunt Patricia. The mass that day was a beautiful one, and when it ended, everyone headed over to Brian and Moira's for Christmas dinner.

As the women set about helping Moira prepare the goose and all the trimmings, Brian and Peter began working on the Atari, but since neither was very mechanical, they were having quite a bit of trouble. An hour later, they were still struggling with it, when there was a loud knock at the back door; however, since the women were right there, they didn't pay it much heed and continued with what they were doing.

"Ho! Ho! Ho!" a voice suddenly guffawed from the kitchen.

Paul, on hearing it, looked to his father in bewilderment. "What was that?" he whispered.

"Why, it sounded like Santa to me. Didn't it, Peter?"

"It sure did."

"Is there a Paul Quinn here?" the booming voice then questioned.

"Why yes," Moira replied, "he's in there."

Soon, in the door walked the plump, jolly old elf. Paul, and it was quite comical to see, looked as though he was about to burst, amazed by the idea that Santa Claus was now in his very house. He studied him from head to toe, this King of Christmas joy, and then walked over and inquisitively began a closer examination. "It's only Moses!" he soon giggled. Everyone, including the women, who were now peeking in from the kitchen, began laughing.

"Come here, lad! I'll give you it's only Moses," his uncle roared as he began chasing the little boy around the room. He finally grabbed hold, and was just about to start tickling him when he suddenly looked down and asked, "What are you guys at?"

Brian moaned. "We're tryin' to set up this god-awful video game system. But we're not havin' much luck."

"Sweet Bridget!" Moses exclaimed, shaking his head. "Grant the lad the serenity to accept the things he just cannot change!"

"And what's that supposed to mean?"

"Brian, you've never been known to fix a single thing in your entire life. And I know you can't help it, and God knows ya try, but … it's just not in ya. You end up breakin' more things than you fix."

"Oh, is that true now?"

"Aye! It is! You name me one thing you've ever fixed or put together properly."

A few moments passed, and Brian still hadn't responded, when Moses asked again.

"Don't rush me! I'm thinkin'!"

"You're gonna be there all day then."

"Here, be my guest if ya think you can do any better. Come on, Peter. Let's go help the women."

"I can't believe I'm sayin' it, but … it sounds good to me!" Peter replied as he got to his feet and animatedly wiped the sweat from his brow. "Technology, me God—it's the work of the devil!"

"If that's true then I'm right in me essence," Moses smirked as he began taking off his costume.

"You can have it," Peter shot back, walking away.

Not more than five minutes passed when Patrick entered the kitchen and said, "He got it up and runnin'."

"Did he now?" Brian answered. "Well, he probably just connected something we missed."

"No, I don't think so. He took everything apart and started fresh."

"Well, then, good for him!"

"Ah, don't be sore, Da. You're still my hero," Patrick said as he came up to his old man and smiled. He then went over and sat down next to his grandmother, who was peeling potatoes, and just watched her. She just looked at him and smiled. That was the type of relationship they had. It was almost as if they could communicate with one another without actually speaking, and he cherished this special bond.

No, he loved his mother more than anyone, and believed Catherine to be the kindest, saintliest person in all the world, but he had an almost telepathic relationship with his grandmother—a relationship that caused him many a night just to lie in bed and ponder it. Yes, she was his grandmother and he loved her, and, for whatever reason, he felt a closeness and a kinship with her that he didn't feel with anyone else.

Well, as the day progressed and dinner hour was approaching, Patrick suddenly began feeling nauseous. He lay down on the couch and watched as his little brother tried his hand at the video game, Pac-Man.

"So, do ya like it?" he asked.

"Aye, it's grand! Ah!" Paul squealed as his Pac-Man was just then swallowed.

Patrick soon felt his condition beginning to worsen. After taking a few deep breaths, he rushed upstairs and had just begun vomiting, when Moira called him down to dinner. He didn't respond, but instead, just knelt there, his head reeling.

"Patrick!" she hollered once again.
"All right, I'm comin'!"
"Patrick?"
"Ma?"

CHAPTER 30

▼

"Ugh!" Patrick gasped as he looked around and tried to comprehend what was now taking place. He was in his room, lying on the floor (that much he knew), but his body was limp and his head felt as though it was about to explode. Never in his entire life had he ever felt so disoriented.

He just lay there, moaning, until he finally gathered enough courage to try and sit up. And when he did, what he found was an egg-shaped lump on the left side of his forehead, with remnants of dried blood all around it. Moreover, he noticed that the lamp that had previously sat on his night table was now lying on the floor, in hundreds of little pieces.

He soon came to the conclusion that at some point during the night he must have fallen from his bed and cracked his head on the nightstand. That would explain both the swelling and the shattered light. And this, coupled with the excessive drinking the previous night, was the cause of his current condition. He had brought it on himself and was now reaping what he had sowed.

After struggling to his feet and collapsing onto his bed, it suddenly occurred to him what day it was. Before he knew it, he began crying. "Oh God, Ma, I miss you so much! Why'd ya have to die?" he wept. Patrick knew this day was going to be a test, but he never expected to react like this. He just couldn't help it, though. He cried himself back to sleep that morning. A few hours passed, when there was a knock on the door that once again woke him.

"Patrick, are you awake?" a voice asked. It was Tara.

He remained silent.

"Are you in there?"

Once again no response. Slowly, the door began to creak open and Tara peeped her head in only to find that the answer to both her questions was 'yes.'

"Did I wake you?"

"No," he answered despondently.

"Oh my God, Paddy! What happened?" she cried, noticing his injury.

"I don't know. I must've fallen and hit my head on the nightstand."

"Does it hurt?"

"Of course it feckin' hurts! I split my head open, didn't I?" he snapped but immediately apologized.

"Maybe you should have a doctor look at it. Ya know, you may need stitches."

"Nah, I don't think so. It's not that bad. Just a little sore, that's all."

"Do you want me to get ya anything for it?"

"No …" he began, but then thought better. "On second thought, could ya get me some aspirins?"

Tara quickly left the room and was soon back with the aspirins and a small glass of water, plus a plastic sandwich bag filled with ice and a wet face cloth. As he was taking the pills, she knelt down beside him and began wiping away some of the caked-on blood.

"It's a good one, all right," she exclaimed as she inspected the wound. With most of the blood now gone, she could see that it was almost an inch long, and rather deep. "Paddy, you need to go to the hospital. This is gonna scar."

"I told ya! I'm not goin'!"

"Hey, it's *your* head. Do what you want," she retorted while handing him the bag of ice. As he was applying it, something suddenly occurred to him. "Why aren't you at work?" he asked.

"They were given E-Time (excused; unpaid), so I took it."

"On a Monday?"

"Yeah, can you imagine."

He looked up at her, that moment, searchingly, as though he wanted to say something, but didn't. Instead, he just winced and began moving his jaw slowly back and forth.

"What are you doin'?" she asked after watching him for a short time.

"I don't know. It just feels better when I do this."

"Did ya hit your jaw?"

"No, Tara, my jaw doesn't hurt, it's my head. And for whatever reason, doin' this just makes it feel better, all right?"

She didn't respond to this lambasting, but it was obvious, just by looking at her, that his cruel behavior had hurt her. However, he just couldn't help it. There he was, in excruciating pain, and she just wouldn't shut up! She kept talking and talking! He secretly wished that she would just go home.

No words were exchanged for a good minute or two until Patrick finally said, "Hey, listen. I'm sorry for bein' such an arse, but I'm in bits, ya know."

"Do you wanna be alone?"

"Yeah, kind of. I think I'm just gonna go back to bed, and hopefully not wake up again until tomorrow. I just want this day to be over."

After giving him a soft kiss on the cheek, Tara rose and was heading toward the door when he unexpectedly called to her. "Yeah?" she answered.

"Thanks for everything."

She merely smiled and left.

Patrick tried going back to sleep, but he couldn't. He just lay there, the entire day, thinking about his mother. By the time he finally did fall back asleep, it was almost seven that evening, and he still felt horrible.

CHAPTER 31

▼

It was seven-thirty, Tuesday morning, when Patrick's alarm clock began ringing. The moment he opened his eyes, he felt the previous day's discomfort, and although still debilitating, it was definitely better. Unfortunately, the same couldn't be said about his despair.

After dragging himself out of bed for the first time since his inebriation two nights earlier, he headed to the bathroom. And it was there that he at last saw his injury. "Ah, feck off!" he growled as he gently touched the wound. Tara was right. It was pretty bad. He stood there for a moment, examining it, before heading back to his room and searching for the day's outfit, but since the laundry hadn't been done for close to three weeks, the choices were few. Ultimately, he settled on a tan lambswool sweater and an old pair of black Levis that were fraying at the cuffs. With that task completed, he then went and showered, and had just begun shaving when there was a knock at the door. "Yeah?" he answered.

"Are ya gonna be in there much longer?" a voice asked. It was Phil.

"Nah, just give me a few more minutes," he replied. And true to his word, five minutes later Patrick was downstairs making himself a cup of tea. He had just sat down and taken his first sip when Kevin entered the room.

Kevin was off from work this day due to a mid-morning doctor's appointment he had concerning a nagging, old shoulder injury he'd suffered a few years earlier while working his parents' farm. The two men greeted one another as Kevin took the seat directly across from him and asked him how he was doing.

"Grand. And yourself?"

"Good." Kevin then paused, almost as though he wanted to say something but was unsure whether or not to continue.

Patrick picked up on it. "Why, what's up?"

Kevin hesitated for a moment. "Tara told us," he finally said.

"Yeah, well, I kinda figured she would."

"Hey, man, I'm sorry. I totally forgot. Why didn't ya say something?"

"What was I gonna say? 'Hey guys, guess what'?"

"I don't know. I just feel bad, I mean … I'm your friend. I should've remembered."

"Ah, don't worry about it. It's no big deal."

"I think it is."

"Listen, Kev, I'm serious. Don't even worry about it. I know how busy things are for you right now with Joanne and work, and everything else."

"Yeah, well, just the same, my prayers are with you and your family. And if ya need anything, and I mean anything, just let me know, all right?"

"I will. Thanks."

"And you!" Phil exclaimed suddenly as he entered the room and pointed in Patrick's direction.

"Oh God, not another one!"

"Yes, another one! Why didn't ya …"

"Like I told Kev, I appreciate your concern, but it's all right. I'm a big boy."

"But still …"

"But still nothin'! Now are ya almost ready? If ya keep up your blabbering much longer we're gonna be late."

"Just waiting on you, my good man."

"The hell you are!" Patrick shot back jokingly as he got to his feet. After putting on their jackets, the two men then walked up the street to collect Tara. This was a rare occasion: all three were starting at the same time this day, ten. And upon learning this the week before when their schedules first came out, they had made plans to travel together.

Tara was already out on her porch, awaiting them, as they walked up. "Good morning," she said, grinning, as she sauntered down the steps.

"Maybe if you're from Siberia," Phil muttered, referring to the day's frigid temperature, which had to be in the low teens. As they set off for the bus stop, Tara asked Patrick how he was feeling.

"A lot better than yesterday."

"You look a lot better, too. The swelling's gone down quite a bit."

"Why, how bad was it?" he asked, not fully believing it could've looked much worse.

"Oh, Paddy, I'm tellin' ya. You should've seen it. It looked like a golf ball stuck to your head."

"That wasn't a golf ball, Tara," Phil interjected. "It was just his brain tryin' to escape."

"Ha, ha. Funny," Patrick said, snickering, as the bus pulled up and they began boarding. "Just a regular 'ol barrel of laughs, aren't ya?"

"Well, what can I say? I try me best," Phil quipped as they slowly pulled away. They made pretty good time and were at work by nine-forty. After agreeing to meet one another in the cafeteria at the end of their shift, the three then parted ways. Well, no sooner did Patrick put on his headset and log-in, than his phone suddenly beeped.

"Hello, this is Phil Doyle. I'm on Darryl Pompey's team. My …"

"Christ! I can't get rid of you, can I?"

"Paddy, is that you?"

"Of course it's me!"

"Oh God, my prayers go out to ya, lad! I've got a real doozy on the other line!" Phil cried and then proceeded to give Patrick the caller's telephone number and name. While Patrick was pulling up the account, he asked what the problem was.

"Okay, listen to this one. I answer the phone, right, in the same pleasant way that I always do, and this guy starts screaming at me right-off-the-bat. And I mean screamin'! And I can't understand a goddamn thing he's sayin'. So I try calmin' him down, ya know, but your man won't even let me get one word in. Finally, I just told him that I couldn't very well help him if I didn't know why the feck he's callin'. I didn't say it in those exact words, obviously, but … to that effect, ya know. So he goes on ranting and ravin', about this and about that, and then all of a sudden he just stops and you can hear him takin' in this really deep breath and then he says to me, 'I'm not a very happy camper.'

"Well, by this time the initial shock's worn off and I'm on the verge of crackin' up. So in return I say to him, 'Yes, sir, I know what you mean. I went camping once and I didn't enjoy it very much, either.' I know I shouldn't have said it, Paddy, but it was beautiful. You should've heard him!"

"For Christ's sake, Phil! Will ya stop your ramblin' and just get to the point! Why's he callin'?"

"Well, he's on the One-Rate Plus with Five-Cent weekends and he says that he was told by one of our telemarketers that all of his calls would be 10 cents a-minute during the week and 5 cents on weekends. So I said to him, 'Yes, sir, that's correct. Why? Does there seem to be a problem with your billing?' So he tells me to take a look at his current bill; well, actually, his only bill. He's a new customer. And sure enough, they're all calling card calls. So I apologize that he was misinformed and began tellin' him the correct rates. Well, anyways, to make a long story short ..."

"Yes, Phil. Please!"

"All right, all right! Just relax, will ya! For God's sake! Ugh! First him, now you."

"You're right, I'm sorry."

"Well ya should be!"

"Well I am! So just continue, all right."

"Yeah, whatever," Phil scoffed and then paused momentarily before continuing. "Well, he wants all his calls re-rated down to the direct-dialed rates. I told him sorry, but, ah ... no can do. But that I would be happy to put him on the callin' card plan and re-rate 'em all down to twenty-five cents and also give him some free minutes for the inconvenience. Well, anyway, that's when he asked for you. But take a look at the calls, Paddy. I mean, something's fishy about this guy. They're all like two and three hundred minutes long. There's even one on there that's like five-hundred-and-eighty-something minutes! Nah, this guy isn't on the level. He knew how much they'd cost. And ya wanna know something else?"

"What?"

"I guarantee ya he's a saboteur from one of the other carriers. I'm serious."

"Ya think so?"

"I know so!" Phil replied adamantly. "Well ... can I bring him over?"

"Sure, why not."

"Hey, good luck. You're gonna need it."

"Thanks."

"Okay, here we go," Phil warned as he hit the transfer button. "Mr. Harrison, thank you for bein' so patient. I have Patrick on the line, he's a manager. I told him what's goin' on and he's gonna be takin' the call from here. Now you have yourself a wonderful day, sir. And thank you for calling AT&T," he said in the most provoking of tones.

"You punk!" the man shouted, but Phil had already hung up.

Patrick had just greeted him and was about to continue when Mr. Harrison barked, "I just want you to know that it's representatives like that that give your company a bad name!"

And so it was to be that type of day. Each new call brought forth yet another screaming mad customer who felt slighted by the company and who threatened to leave if they didn't have their situation resolved, and done so to their liking. And although that's what being a Customer Service Manager entails, Patrick had never had such a vicious, steady onslaught as he did that day. So by the time six-thirty arrived and he finally logged-off, he felt completely drained, both physically and mentally.

There he was, spending his day in a bright, airy, temperature-controlled environment, sitting down in a soft, ergonomically-designed chair, with a jar full of candies to his left and a Velcro dart-board set to his right, and he was utterly beat. He had never felt this exhausted while working on the farm, and that work was twice as hard. Kneeling, sometimes for hours on end, pulling beets and potatoes from the ground. All the heavy lifting. In retrospect, however, it all seemed like child's play compared to what he was doing now.

So as he lifted himself up from out of his chair and made his way down to the cafeteria, his mind was all a blur. He was bumping into people and he didn't even know it. Tara and Phil were already in the lunchroom, talking with some fellow co-workers, when Patrick stumbled in and sank down heavily in a chair beside them.

"Rough day?" Tara asked, sipping at her can of Diet Coke.

"Yeah, you could say that," Patrick replied dejectedly as he crossed his arms on the table and rested his head upon them. "You know something. I really hate my job."

"Was it that arsehole this mornin'?" Phil questioned.

"It was all the arseholes! All day long! Ya just can't satisfy some people."

"So, what happened with that guy?"

"Not too much. I apologized but told him that when he came over he received a packet in the mail describing the plan and what the rates were. He said he just skimmed over it, but that it still didn't change the fact that he was lied to."

"And?"

"And what?"

"Well, how'd the call end?"

"I don't know, Phil. Christ! It seems so long ago, now. I think he swore at me or something and said that he was just gonna go back to his old company. But like I said, I'm really not too sure, I mean … it's almost as though I spoke with the same guy over and over again. Everyone was complainin' and yellin'. It was just a horrible day."

"And that's why I'm happy just bein' a plain, ol' C.C.A.," Phil asserted as he looked over at Jacob Cohen, one of his teammates, who was now sitting with them. "Sure, we don't get much respect, but we also don't have to deal with that sort of crap—call after call—all day long."

"No shit," Jacob said, shuddering, and then asked Patrick what had happened to his head.

"I fell out of bed and hit my head on the corner of the nightstand," Patrick answered reflexively, for the question had been asked so often throughout the day.

The group spoke for a short while longer, and by the time they finally exited the building, it was close to seven. By seven-thirty they were back in Southie. As they turned onto F Street and approached the girls' house, Tara asked Patrick if he wanted to do something, like catch a movie or just go out for a bite to eat.

"Nah, not tonight. I'm too tired. I think I'm just gonna go home and crash."

"Come on! Just for a little while," Phil implored as he threw his arm around Patrick's neck.

"Yeah, jus' for a little while," reiterated Sandra, who had by this time made her way out onto the porch.

"Nah, Sandra, he's right," Tara affirmed. "He should go home. He had a really rough day. The poor thing's exhausted."

"Oh, I'm sorry. I didn't know."

"Okay, then, um … when ya see Kev, just tell him that I'll be home at around ten or thereabouts, all right?" Phil said as he began walking up the stairs.

"Tell him yourself!" Sandra exclaimed. "He's upstairs right now with Joanne."

"Is he?"

"Yep," she giggled as she began to blush.

Phil looked at her, for a moment, puzzled, before it finally sunk in. "Upstairs? In that sort of way?"

"Yep."

"Oh, thank God! Finally!" he exulted as he threw his arms to the heavens in praise. "Maybe now he won't be so goddamn uptight all the time."

"It's not the first time, Phil."

"Whadya talkin' about? I know Kev. If something already happened, he would've told me."

"Well, maybe you don't know him as well as ya think."

"I'm tellin' ya …"

"Listen, all right! Let's just say that they explored each other a couple of weekends ago and that they've been on the expedition ever since. I'm tellin' ya, Phil. I know it for a fact. I even walked in on 'em once."

"And you're serious?"

"Of course I'm serious! Why would I lie?"

"Great," Phil grumbled as a look of disgust crossed his face. "Then I guess that means he's never gonna change."

Patrick soon left. As he trudged back to the house, he felt both dazed and fatigued.

The clock struck eight the moment he walked through the door. After taking off his jacket, he went to his room, undressed, and climbed into bed; however, to his amazement, he found he wasn't tired. He was positive he would fall asleep the moment he hit the sheets, but apparently he was wrong.

Well, if he wasn't going to go to bed, what would he do? He mulled over the idea of going back over to Tara's, but soon decided against it. She'd be fussing over him the entire time and he didn't want that. The thought of calling home also came to mind, but no, that was out of the question, too. It would be close to one-thirty in the morning and everyone would be sleeping. He soon got out of bed and had just begun pacing back and forth when he felt his lassitude slowly giving way to sadness—the very thing he had hoped wouldn't happen. He had struggled with his emotions for so many months now, and right when he was finally beginning to gain the upper hand, to have all his progress undermined, was something he just wouldn't allow. No, he would stay strong no matter how hard it got, and ultimately, he would win this war once and for all.

This is what Patrick concluded, and to celebrate his reaching this most admirable of resolutions, he decided to go downstairs and have a drink. "Why not? It'll help tire me out," he rationalized out loud. So as he headed down to the kitchen, and took a can of Coor's Light from the refrigerator, he felt sort of triumphant. However, it wasn't long before that changed, and as he finished it, he felt even worse than before. But in keeping true to the illogical, absurd reasoning of the human animal, he opened another. As he sipped at it, he looked up at the clock on the wall and noticed that it was almost quarter to ten. Recalling Phil mention something about returning by ten, and not wanting to be bothered by anyone at that moment, Patrick decided just to head upstairs. But before he did, he walked back over to the fridge and took out four more cans of beer.

A six-pack won't kill me, he reasoned. And besides, he didn't have to be at work until eleven the next morning. As long as he was in bed by twelve, or one at the latest, he'd be fine.

Well, as the evening passed and the number of empty beer cans grew, Patrick fell more and more deeply into thought. And as midnight approached, all the drink was gone. He had reminisced mostly about days gone by since first entering his room, but for the last hour or so, he had just stared blankly at the wall and had taken his gaze from it only when he heard the lads climbing the stairs to go to bed.

He was lost somewhere in his mind and couldn't find his way out. Before he knew it, he was once again thrust into a hell of human suffering, and it was an inferno not even Dante could have imagined!

CHAPTER 32

▼

And so it was.

At first, Patrick tried denying it, but when that failed, he attempted then to mask his anguish. However, he wasn't very successful at that either, and it soon became apparent to everyone around him that he was once again sinking into despair.

Tara and the lads immediately noticed his sudden change of demeanor, but they also knew its underlying cause, so they tried to be as supportive as possible, believing that sooner or later he'd rebound. But when over a month passed, and there still weren't any noticeable signs of improvement, the three decided to convene a private meeting.

"I don't think there's much you can do for someone when they're like this," Phil surmised. "They just have to break out of it on their own."

"But my God, Phil. It's been over a year now! Isn't that long enough?" Tara cried.

"Obviously not," Kevin said, frowning. "It just takes longer for some than others. And then ya have certain ones who never seem to get over it. You know, ya hear about these people grieving over a loved one their entire life. It's sad and all, but ... maybe he's just one of those people. Plus, don't forget. He was pretty close to his mother. I think he feels guilty for not being there with her during her last days."

"Oh, he does. He told me," Tara disclosed, leaning forward in her seat. "But he still shouldn't have to suffer like this. And for so goddamn long. It's just not fair."

"Fairness doesn't have anything to do with it, Tara," Phil exclaimed. "This is life. I mean, screw it. I'm no Freud, but to be honest with ya ... I don't think he's eva gonna come out of it. This is who he is now and we just have to learn to accept it."

"No, we don't, Phil! That's where you're wrong! This is not who he has to be," Tara shot back vehemently. "So, whadya sayin'? The last few months were all just an illusion? No. I don't believe it. He's in there somewhere. We just have to find a way to break him out."

"All right, Tara. We're listening," Kevin interjected. "What do you suggest we do?"

"How about a psychiatrist?"

"A what?" Phil sneered. "Oh, yeah, I'm sure he's really gonna be keen on that. Think about it. Do ya really think he's gonna go to a shrink? I doubt it."

"Well, it's worth a shot. And besides, what do we have to lose? Except maybe Patrick himself."

Kevin sighed. "Maybe she's right. I mean, we've tried everything else. What harm can it do?"

"I'm tellin' ya. He's never gonna go."

"Oh yeah? And how are you so sure, huh? Ya talk about me bein' so negative and close-minded. Take a look at yourself."

"Hey, all right, fine. If that's what ya think's best, so be it. But just don't expect me to be the one to ask him."

"Don't worry, I'll do it," Tara replied abstractedly. She got her opportunity that evening. The lads had been invited over for supper, and just about the time everyone was finishing, Tara motioned for Patrick to follow her.

"What is it?" he questioned as they began making their way up the stairs.

"I just have something I wanna talk to you about."

Soon, they were in her room, sitting on the bed. At first, both were silent. "What's wrong, Paddy?" Tara finally asked.

"Whadya mean?"

"You know what I'm talkin' about."

"No, I don't."

"Yes, ya do. I mean, you never laugh or smile anymore. You're always down. I'm worried about ya."

"Well, ya don't expect me to be happy all the time, do ya?"

"No, of course not. But ya could be once in awhile."

"It's that damn job."

"No, Patrick, it's not the job. It's you. You're sick and you've been sick for a long time now. You need help."

"You're tellin' me!" he snarled, catching her by surprise. "Yeah, Tara, you're right. I am sick. And you have no idea how bad it is."

"I know, Paddy, but …"

"No, Tara, you don't know! You don't even have the slightest feckin' clue!"

"But ya have to be optimistic."

"Optimistic? For what?"

"For yourself!"

"Oh, now I see. For meself," he said sarcastically and then began chuckling. "There's no hope for me, Tara. And the sad thing is … you know it just as well as I do."

"Well, we were thinkin'. Maybe there is something …"

"Is there some magic pill out there that I don't know about? Because if there is, give it to me now. I need it something fierce."

"We were thinkin' that maybe a psychiatrist might help."

"A psychiatrist? What could he do for me?"

"What could he do for ya? Paddy, that's his job. Showing people how to conquer their feelings. Or at least teaching how to cope with them."

"Nah, I don't know."

"Please, just consider it. For me."

Patrick looked down at the floor that moment in complete disgust, shaking his head the entire time, before finally turning back to her and saying, "Yeah, all right, fine. I'll go. But I don't think it'll do any good."

Tara, who was utterly amazed by his response, threw her arms around him. "Oh, Paddy. You don't know how happy you just made me. I promise, everything's gonna be all right."

"Yeah, Tara. Whatever you say," he replied, forcing a smile.

"See! It's already working," she giggled

CHAPTER 33

▼

Over the course of the next few days, what started out simply as Tara's desire to find Patrick a therapist quickly began to take on the dynamics of an all-out, personal crusade as she searched furiously to locate for him the very best doctor available.

She scoured the Yellow Pages and called countless referral hotlines, and in the end, through a host of ardent and spirited endorsement from practically everyone she spoke with, she discovered that the person she should get in touch with was one Franklin E. Wittenour. He worked out of the neighboring town of Milton and was considered the top practitioner of psychiatric medicine in the area.

With her mission now halfway completed, Tara called up Dr. Wittenour's office and an appointment was scheduled for the following Saturday at eleven in the morning. *That was quick*, she thought, as she hung up the phone. And quick it was. But there was a very good explanation: Dr. Wittenour was a native son and had received his entire education within the city confines. A graduate of both Boston College and Harvard's prestigious School of Medicine, he believed he owed a debt to the city that had been so very good to him throughout the years. He also had a policy that quite firmly stated that if help was ever needed, help would be granted. Whenever. Wherever. Since such was the case in this instance, medical assistance would be given promptly.

Patrick wasn't particularly excited upon hearing the 'wonderful news' from Tara, but if there was even the slightest chance that any good could come from it, he had to at least try. And as the day of his appointment drew near, he even found himself growing eager.

Saturday, at last, arrived. At about ten that morning, Patrick left his house and headed up to Broadway, where he caught the Red Line into Milton. In no time at all, he was trampling through the streets, searching for his destination, but he couldn't find it, and this aggravated the hell out of him since he had made a point of it before setting off to memorize both the address and directions that Tara had given him. And now here he was, lost and running late. Finally, he just stopped an elderly man who was passing by on the street and asked for assistance. Much to his chagrin, the man pointed up and said, "You're standing right in front of it."

Patrick thanked him and then turned and hurried in. After glancing briefly at a large brass plaque, located in the lobby, which showed where each office was, he bolted up to the third floor and found the door bearing Dr. Wittenour's name. Breathing a sigh of relief, he entered and walked up to the receptionist's desk to let her know that he had finally arrived. She smiled and handed him a few forms that needed to be filled out, and when completed, she ushered him down a long hallway to the doctor's personal office. Well, no sooner had he taken a seat in one of two large burgundy leather chairs that were situated before an exquisite mahogany desk, than there was a knock on the door and in walked Dr. Franklin E. Wittenour III.

He was quite an imposing man and not the least what Patrick had expected. Towering well over six-feet tall and somewhere in his early fifties, with a head that was completely shaven, he somewhat resembled the actor Patrick Stewart. The main thing that captured Patrick's attention, though, from the very moment that he entered the room, was the subtle yet undeniable sense of warmth and peacefulness he exuded. Patrick immediately liked him. After shaking hands and introducing themselves, the two men sat down and just chatted for awhile until Dr. Wittenour finally got to the matter at hand—the reason for Patrick's visit.

"I don't have any feelings," he answered.

This profound statement quite naturally caught the good doctor off guard. Normally patients weren't so direct; they were hesitant, evasive, ashamed at admitting there even was a problem, but not this man who now sat before him. No, he was asked a question and he stated the answer without delay and without embarrassment, just as Tara had told him to do.

"Be honest with him, Paddy. That's the only way he's gonna be able to help you," she had said to him just that very morning, and that's exactly what he did.

Dr. Wittenour looked at him sagaciously for a moment, then replied, "I think you may be wrong, Patrick."

"No, I'm serious. I don't have any. Or at least not anymore."

"What do you mean when you say, 'Not anymore'?"

"Well," Patrick began, and then continued to describe in detail the events of the past year.

"I wouldn't be so despondent, son. I think there may be hope for you after all," Dr. Wittenour said at the story's completion. "It almost sounds as though you may have what we here in the medical profession call Post-Traumatic Stress Disorder, or it may be something altogether different. But whatever it is I guarantee you one thing: we will unearth the problem, and when we do …"

"So you really think you can help me?"

"Well, it's not going to be easy, and it isn't going to happen overnight, but, yes, I think I can."

"I hope you're right."

The two spent the rest of that meeting going over expectations and just getting to know one another, and before they concluded the session, Patrick agreed to return the following week.

The sun was shining brilliantly as he emerged from the building. It was early April, and as he headed towards the T station, he felt sort of light-hearted. Maybe this was his magic pill after all.

CHAPTER 34

▼

Patrick continued his therapy diligently over the next three months, optimistic at first that it was actually working. After a while, though, he could tell otherwise. He still felt the same way—numb.

By this time, Dr. Wittenour had become rather perplexed by Patrick's lack of progress. They had spoken intimately several times—with talks about his mother and his family back home—and not once had he shown the slightest bit of emotion. He was even eventually put on anti-depressant medication, but that didn't work either. Nevertheless, Dr. Wittenour persevered, with different remedies and different approaches until he ultimately found himself obsessed with the young man and his recovery. Patrick could sense this and tried working with him as much as possible, but when it became evident that he was just wasting both their time, he decided to end treatment.

"Come on, don't give up yet," Dr. Wittenour entreated when first told of the news. "I felt we were finally starting to make some progress. Just give it a little while longer, okay?"

"I'm sorry, but …"

"Hey, Rome wasn't built in a day, you know."

"You're right about that, sir, but wrong about the progress part."

"So you can honestly tell me that you don't feel even the slightest bit better than when you first started?"

"Honestly, sir? No. In fact, I probably feel even worse. But I know you've tried your best to help me and for that I thank you," Patrick replied, reaching out his hand.

"It doesn't look as if I've done a very good job, though, does it?" Dr. Wittenour remarked as he took hold and gave it a feeble shake. "Are you sure you won't reconsider, if only for a few more weeks?"

"Nah, I've made up my mind. But thanks, anyways."

"I don't know what to say, except—I'm sorry."

"Don't be sorry. You tried your best, and that's all anyone can ask."

"Well, if you should ever happen to change your mind, Patrick, just remember, this office is always open to you."

"Thank you." With that, Patrick turned and left. Riding home that day, he felt like the most despicable creature on the face of the planet. His last glimmer of hope was gone. He even contemplated heading over to the Tobin Bridge and just ending it all, but he couldn't do that to his family and friends.

As he got off the train and began trudging back to Southie, the sun's torrid rays beat unrelentingly down upon him and added to his already unbearable wretchedness. All he needed now was to run into Tara. She would ask him why he was home so early and then he'd have to tell her.

No, he would see her tonight, anyways: it was the Fourth of July and the entire gang had made plans to head over to the Esplanade to watch the fireworks. He would break the news to her gently then, if he deemed it the right time. But whatever his course of action, he just didn't want to have to think about it at that moment, not in his current state of mind.

So as he approached the girls' house, he did so with great caution. Surprisingly, though, not a single one was roaming about. A rarity, he thought. He quickly walked past and hurried the rest of the way home. Upon entering the house, however, Patrick was dismayed to find nearly everyone, including Tara, sitting in the front room, drinking beer and talking.

"You're home early," she said, smiling, as she hopped off the chaise and walked over to where he now stood. "Was the appointment cancelled?"

"Getting an early jump on the night's festivities, huh?" Patrick asked, trying to evade the question.

But Tara persisted. "Did you see Dr. Wittenour?"

"Yeah, I saw him."

"Shorter than normal, wasn't it?"

Ah, what's the point, anyway? She's gonna end up finding out sooner or later, he moaned to himself. And besides, with the way that he was now feeling, it really wouldn't faze him however she reacted.

"Patrick? Is everything …"

"I quit, all right!" he barked and then headed for the kitchen. Tara just stood there, motionless, unable to even respond.

Patrick soon emerged with a bottle of Samuel Adams Summer Ale in his hand and a look of intense displeasure on his face. He walked over and sank down beside Kevin on the sofa. His friend just looked at him, but it was Tara who asked him why.

"It just wasn't working, that's why! Now can we just drop it?"

"No, we can't just drop it. I can't believe you. Ya didn't even give it a chance."

"Give it a chance? Whadya talkin' about? I went for three months without missin' a single session. If that's not givin' it a chance, then I don't know what the feck is!"

"But it was finally startin' to work!" she cried, even though she could tell that it wasn't.

"Listen," he growled, "if you wanna air me dirty laundry then get your arse up the feckin' stairs and let's do it in private!"

"Then let's do it!" Tara shot back, glaring, as she turned and began mounting the stairs with authority. Patrick followed quickly on her heels, and when they were in his room, he slammed the door shut with such force that it caused a painting in the hallway to fall from the wall.

"Ooh! Tough guy!"

As he struggled to control his anger, Patrick screamed, "What? What do you want from me, woman? You begged me to go and I went! It just didn't work out! Why can't you just accept it?"

"Because I love you and I wanna see you get better! Is that too much to ask?"

"It's asking more than I can give!"

"Is it?"

"Yes!"

Tara had hoped this moment would never come. "Listen, Patrick. I don't have the strength to go through this again, so let's stop beating around the bush. Is there a chance for us, or is this it?"

He just looked at her.

"Huh?" she asked once more.

"I guess this is it. I'm sorry, but you're right. It's not fair to you."

Tara, who by now had her back to him, murmured, "Don't be sorry. You can't help the way you feel."

Patrick walked over and turned her around. She had tears streaming down her face.

"Please, Tara, don't cry. I'm sorry. I really am. But remember what we agreed upon last New Year's? We'd give it a shot, but I never made any promises. It just hasn't worked out, that's all. I really hoped it would, but … I'm no miracle worker."

"I know."

"You must hate me, huh?"

"No. I told you that same night that I'd never hate you. I love you. And the sad thing is, I think I always will."

This admission crushed him, but he didn't know how to respond, so he just pulled her close and hugged her. "Can we still be friends?" he asked after a few moments.

"Yeah, sure. Why not." She soon wiped the tears from her eyes and left. Everyone was saddened that day when they heard what had happened, especially since it appeared that the two had been on the verge of rekindling their relationship; for it to all end once again was really quite heartbreaking. And to put it mildly, it really screwed up their holiday.

As the months passed, Patrick's condition steadily grew worse. He now became a total recluse, eating and spending all of his free time in his room, and leaving the house only to go to work at a job he despised.

At first, when Kevin and Phil noticed how severe things had actually become, they tried to help him, through a variety of methods, break free from his depression, just as they had done before. This time, however, nothing worked, and they soon gave up on it. It was hopeless, they concluded, so they finally just accepted the fact and learned to live with it. Now, whenever they did run into him, all the friends shared was a simple hello and little else.

CHAPTER 35

▼

It was a frigid, snowy morning in early December when Patrick stepped from the bus and began making his way towards the AT&T building for yet another day of hell. As he walked along, he suddenly heard his name being called. Turning, he saw an old lady scurrying in his direction.

"Are you talkin' to me?" he asked, a puzzled look on his face.

"Of course I am! Don't you remember me?"

"No, why? Should I?"

"Of course you should! It's me, Miss Murphy. Remember, we met at the airport when you first came over. And then a few months later."

"Oh, yeah. Hi, how's it goin'?"

"Fine, fine, thanks. And yourself?"

"All right, I guess."

"That's good," she returned cheerfully and then paused for a moment before saying, "So, will ya take a look at you. All dressed up. I guess you've found work by now, huh?"

"Yeah, I work for AT&T."

"Oh, that's lovely. AT&T's a good company I would think. Do you like it there?"

Patrick, who wasn't in a particularly talkative mood to begin with, retorted, "No, Miss Murphy. I despise my job, if you wanna know the truth. It's horrible. And not to be rude, but … I'm runnin' late so I really do have to get goin'. But it was nice seein' you again, though."

"Oh, I'm sorry. I didn't know I was holdin' you up."

"Yeah, I start work in about two minutes."

"All right, well ... I guess I'll let you get going. I don't want you to be late on account of me," she said, simpering. "But yes, you're right. It was nice seeing you. Hopefully we'll run into each other again soon, when you have a little more time to talk."

"Yeah, hopefully," Patrick answered and had just begun walking away when she unexpectedly called to him once more.

"Yeah?"

"You take care of yourself, all right?"

"Yeah, I will. Thanks." He then turned once again and resumed his march. As he hurried along, he reflected to himself how pretty amazing it was that she had remembered his name after so long a time. His rumination, however, was quickly interrupted by a group of Junior Achievement members who were gathered outside the building, boisterously waiting for their field trip to begin. Without hesitation, and without any pleasantries, Patrick pushed his way through the throng and entered.

CHAPTER 36

▼

Within a few weeks it was winter once more, and with its onset, Patrick and his family resumed a regular phone schedule that his father had initiated after not hearing from his son for close to three months.

Brian tried to let Patrick live his own life and not pester or embarrass him in front of his friends, but three months was just too damn long! So he called him up one evening and they both agreed to keep in touch.

Patrick also flew back home to Loughshinny in March for a week to commemorate the two-year anniversary of his mother's death. The entire time there he concealed his sickness. He laughed and joked with his family, but it was all just a façade. They had absolutely no idea the suffering he was experiencing.

Upon his return, he continued to keep his distance from the lads. They had both hoped that this break from the monotony of everyday life would be good for him, and that he might come back a new man. They were wrong.

CHAPTER 37

▼

It was a gorgeous, sultry evening in late June when Patrick entered his house after an appalling day at the office and found both the lads sitting quietly in the living room. He just nodded to them and began heading towards the stairs when Phil suddenly asked him if he had heard the news.

"About what?" Patrick answered, turning back around.

"About Tara. And how she flew back home yesterday—for good. Just packed up and went."

"Yeah, right."

"No, Patrick, it's true," Kevin confirmed somberly. Patrick looked back and forth at the two men and could tell right away that they weren't joking. Stunned, he just stood there.

"So, are ya happy?" Phil soon asked.

"What?"

"No, no, I just … I just wanted to know how it made you feel, that's all."

"It's none of your goddamn business how it makes me feel!"

"No, ya see, Paddy, that's where you're wrong!" Phil shot back violently as he sprung to his feet. "The only reason Sandra came over to this country was because of Tara and their friendship. And now she's even talkin' about possibly goin' back. So ya see, lad, it is me business!"

"Then ya best mind it!"

"Come on, Phil. Just let it go," Kevin implored as he wedged his way between the two men.

"No, Kev, I'm not gonna just let it go! I'm sick of it! All the bastard eva does is sits in his room and ignores us. And ya wanna know something else, Paddy?"

"Yeah, sure. Why not?" Patrick retorted, inching closer.

"You depress the hell outta me! You know that?"

That was all Patrick needed to hear. In one swift motion he lunged past Kevin and threw a punch that caught Phil square on the nose, knocking him to the ground.

"What the hell are you doin', Paddy?" Kevin screamed.

"The son-of-a-bitch asked for it!"

Phil exploded to his feet upon hearing this, incensed, intent on evening the score, when Kevin, just in the nick of time, caught him in a full Nelson. "Let me go!" Phil cried, trying to break free.

"Yeah, Kev, let him go," Patrick snarled as he took a fighting stance.

"No! You'll end up killin' each other! Now stop it, both of you, or I swear to God, I'll end up doin' it meself!"

All of a sudden, Phil stopped struggling and just glared at Patrick. "You don't care about anyone besides yourself, do ya?" he asked.

"Look who's talkin'! You're the most selfish person I think I've ever met!"

"Oh, really?"

"Yes, really!"

"Yeah, well, I may be selfish but at least I'm not heartless like you. We've busted our arses these past two years tryin' to help ya get over your grief, and this is how you repay me? Nah, no way. I want him out of the house now, Kev. I'm serious."

"Fine, I'll give you your wish. I've been thinkin' about movin', anyways. This jus' gives me even more of a reason."

"Will ya just …"

"No, Kevin! I've been stuck in this goddamn piece of shite ya call a house long enough now! It's a dump and I'm sick of it! I'm getting the hell out!" Patrick bellowed as he turned and began stomping up the stairs. When he was finally out of sight, Phil, who was now completely covered in blood, muttered, "He's gone already. Will ya let me go."

"Only if you promise to stay cool and not go after him."

"Yeah, yeah, all right, I promise. Now come on, let me go."

Kevin loosened his grip; Phil stepped free and immediately began flexing his back.

"You'd better ice that up. It doesn't look too good," Kevin said, a sickened look on his face. He then hesitated. "Stay down here, will ya? I'm gonna go talk to him."

"Why even bother, Kev? He's not worth it."

"Will ya just promise?"

"Whatever."

Drained, Kevin walked over and laboriously began climbing the stairs. He was soon standing outside Patrick's door, which was now closed. He paused for a moment before knocking.

"What?" Patrick shouted.

"It's me, Kev. Can I come in?"

"Do whatever ya want!"

Kevin opened the door only to see Patrick's two suitcases lying on the bed, each nearly halfway full.

"You don't have to leave right this minute, ya know."

"The sooner, the better!"

"Where ya gonna go?"

"I don't know. A hotel, I guess."

"Now just hold up, will ya, for Christ's sake. You can stay here until ya find a place."

"Listen, Kev. I appreciate the concern. You've been nothin' but a friend to me. But Phil's right. I'm cold and heartless, and the sooner I get away from here the better it'll be for all of us."

"That's not true, Paddy! You're a good man who's just goin' through a rough period in your life."

"Call it whatever ya like, but in the end it's all the same, isn't it?"

Kevin sighed. "I don't know."

Both were silent while Patrick finished packing. After zipping up his bags, the two men just looked at each other for a moment before shaking hands and wishing one another well. Patrick then grabbed his suitcases from off the bed and was heading for the door when he suddenly stopped. "Do me a favor?" he asked, looking over his shoulder.

"Yeah, sure."

"When I'm gone, apologize to Phil for me, will ya? I shouldn't have done that."

"Don't worry, I'll tell him."

"Thanks." Without another word, Patrick left. He promptly headed up to Broadway and caught a taxi downtown. It only made sense to get a room near his workplace, and he found one that night at the very first hotel he came to: a moderately priced Howard Johnson's. He stayed for close to a week until he finally rented a one-bedroom apartment at a posh, modernistic high-rise that had just recently opened on the same street as AT&T, only about a half mile away.

Having a new apartment meant that it had to be furnished, and Patrick accomplished this with a single, twin-size mattress (no box spring) that he picked up at a discount bedding store and an inexpensive blue lamp. And that was it. As far as he was concerned, though, this suited him just fine. He didn't do any entertaining, so who was there to impress?

CHAPTER 38

▼

Patrick adapted surprisingly well to his sudden change of environment. It was nice living right in the heart of the city, for it meant that he no longer had to awake so early to get to work, nor did he have to rely on the city's public transportation to get there.

And such was the case as he left his complex one morning. He walked up the street and made it to the AT&T building in less than fifteen minutes. After taking the elevator up to the third floor, Patrick was on his way to the men's room when he suddenly noticed, up ahead in the distance, Phil approaching. It was the first time he had seen him since that fateful day.

At first, Patrick thought about possibly taking an alternate route. But it was too late. Phil had spotted him, also, so he continued on. As the two men's paths crossed, both tried to ignore the other completely; however, neither was very successful, and they each stole a quick glance as they walked past one another.

Patrick had heard the talk for the past week, but now the rumors were finally confirmed: Phil Doyle's nose was broken! Patrick only looked quickly, out of the corner of his eye, but that split-second was time enough. It was swollen and bruised, and the bone even appeared to be protruding from the skin. He felt really bad at that moment. In fact, he had thought about Phil quite a bit since moving out and still couldn't believe that he had actually punched him.

Even more shocking was the realization that Tara had returned to Ireland. Here was this girl—this angel—whom his heart had once ached for so deeply, and who had stood so steadfastly beside him. And now she was gone. What would he do without her? He felt awful but he knew he had caused it, and now he would have to live with it.

CHAPTER 39

▼

The next few months were an up-and-down period for the young man from Loughshinny. The torment that shrouded his every waking moment continued, unabated, but he was also once again promoted, this time to TDL, Team Development Leader. This advancement, which was quite unexpected—probably even more so than any of the others—brought him even more respect and prestige.

Thank God! he thought. No longer would he have to take over all those wretched calls. He was now given his own team of 22 new C.C.A.'s straight out of training and was expected to monitor them and hone their technical and sales skills as needed, to ensure that one day they would be world-class representatives. The best of the best. The elite.

Patrick took on this task with great vigor, and in no time his team was at, or near, the top of the list of every ranking in the building. He was happy with this fact, but it was the only element of his life that brought him any satisfaction.

CHAPTER 40

▼

Patrick was working late one evening, finishing up a sales report that had to be handed in the following day, when he suddenly heard a noise behind him. He glanced over his shoulder only to see both Kevin and Phil standing there, staring down at him.

"Hey, stranger," Kevin said, grinning. "How's it goin'?"

"Good," he replied, getting to his feet. Kevin was right. They did feel like strangers. And albeit Patrick and Phil had sporadically bumped into one another over the course of the last five months, this, in fact, was only the second time Kevin and he had been in each other's presence since the night of the fight; the other encounter came the very next day when he went to collect the last of his belongings.

Not really knowing what to say next, Patrick motioned for the two men to enter the small modular compartment he called an office. Both followed him in and took a seat. At first, all three were silent. "So, to what do I owe this pleasure?" Patrick finally asked.

"We just came by to say so long," Kevin returned.

"So long?"

"Yeah, Paddy. We're goin' back home."

"For how long?"

"Permanently."

"What?" Patrick murmured. "Why?"

"Ah, it's just the right time, ya know. Hey … we did everything we set out to do! Come to America. Have some fun. We had a pretty good run there for a while. We can't complain. Besides, they've been cuttin' back me hours at the bank for the past couple of months, and if ya can believe it, your man here's finally startin' to get a little homesick," Kevin chuckled.

Patrick, who had been up until that point focusing his attention solely on Kevin, now looked over at Phil, who nodded his head in confirmation.

"When's this gonna happen?"

"Tomorrow. We've got a five-thirty flight out of Logan."

Patrick's mind began to drift. First Tara, now them. "What about Sandra and Joanne?" he questioned, finally snapping out of it.

"Everyone's goin' back," Phil answered as he shifted in his seat and crossed his leg. "Like he said, it's just the right time—for all of us. Besides, it just hasn't been the same for the girls since Tara left. Everyone misses her. She was their backbone. Plus, not to mention, everyone wants to be home for Christmas this year. It's been quite awhile, ya know."

"Yeah," Patrick muttered.

A few uncomfortable moments ensued before Kevin finally rose from his seat. "Well, I guess we'd best be goin'," he said. "We still have some packin' to do."

"Some?" Phil exclaimed, springing to his feet. "You know how us Irish are, Paddy. We wait till the last minute to do everything, including," he faltered here briefly, "even lettin' an old friend know that he's still a friend."

Patrick stood upon hearing this.

"I just want you to know that I forgive you, Paddy. I guess in a way I was askin' for it, anyway."

"No, no, Phil. I was wrong."

"We both were. But it's in the past now. So let's just keep it there, all right?"

"Yeah, Phil, whatever ya say. But still, I just want you to know …"

"I know you are, Paddy," Phil acknowledged, placing his hand on Patrick's shoulder and smiling. "I know you are." He then paused. "Well, anyway, like Kev said, we still have a lot of work to do. But hey, if ya come home anytime soon, give me a ring. We'll do something. You've still got my number, right?"

"Yeah."

"That goes for me, too, lad," Kevin seconded.

"Yeah, all right, Kev. Thanks."

After conversing for a short while longer, during which time they shook hands and said their final farewells, the two men turned and left. As Patrick watched them exit the zone, he wondered if he'd ever see them again. He soon left the building and headed across the street to Clancy's Tavern where he remained until almost two that morning.

In fact, Patrick was becoming sort of a regular over at Clancy's. He had always drunk since he was a wee lad—for it was his culture—but this behavior was different. He now changed from beer to hard liquor, and before long, he was there every night of the week drowning his sorrows.

Book 3

CHAPTER 41

▼

As the next few years crept slowly by, Patrick's suffering only intensified. And it became incessant. At least before there had always been breaks—flashed of normalcy, here and there—that had offered him hope. Not anymore. Eventually, the weight of this burden just became too much for him, so he decided to put the demons to rest once and for all, and on what better day to do it than the 10th of March—the five-year anniversary of Moira's death.

It was a cold, dreary Saturday. After arising early, Patrick got dressed in his finest outfit and did something he hadn't done in a long, long time: he went to confession. And even though he no longer believed in God, he figured what the hell, divulge his last five years of sin. So that's exactly what he did. He even shocked the priest with his confession's duration and precision.

With that task out of the way, he returned to his apartment building and paid his rent for the upcoming month. Finally, he headed back up to his room and called home. Patrick had kept in touch over the years, but not as much as Brian would've liked. If he wasn't at work, then he was at the pub, so his father always had a difficult time getting a hold of him. When Brian heard his son's voice on the line, he was thrilled. "Well it's about time you gave your ol' man a ring!" he chortled.

"I know, I know, I'm sorry."

"Relax, Paddy. I'm only slaggin'."

"Yeah, I know you are, Da."

"So, how's it goin'?"

"All right, I guess. And yourself?"

"Good, thanks."

There was a moment or two of silence before Patrick finally asked if Paul or Sinead were around.

"Nah, they're both off gallivanting, God knows where!"

"Oh."

"Why? Is there anything wrong?" Brian questioned. He thought he had caught something in his son's tone, something distressing.

"No, I just … I just wanted to talk with them, ya know. I miss 'em."

"Are you sure everything's all right?"

"Yeah, Da. Everything's grand." Patrick then hesitated. "Well, um … I've gotta get goin'. You tell the kids that I said I love 'em, all right?"

"I will. Don't worry."

"And Dad?"

"Yeah?"

"I love you, too! And don't you eva forget it!"

"Patrick! What the hell's the matter?" Brian now demanded, but his son just said that it must have been homesickness, combined with what day it was.

"Well, why don't ya just take a week off and come home then."

"I'll be back soon. I promise."

"When?"

"Soon. I promise, okay."

"All right, fine. But I'm serious, Paddy, you keep in touch. I mean it! I'm not kiddin'!"

"Okay, Dad. Good-bye."

"All right, bye," Brian grumbled, but Patrick had already hung up. And it was a good thing that he did, for he began crying. It wasn't bad enough to have lost his mother, but the thought of never hearing or seeing his father or the rest of his family ever again was too much to bear. But he just couldn't endure the pain any longer, and no amount of love could've swayed his decision by this point. He was going to end his suffering, and he was going to end it that night. That's all there was to it.

Meanwhile, Brian questioned whether he should call back, but decided against it. No. If there was anything drastically wrong, his son would have told him. He was pretty sure about that, so he just dismissed it and went on with his day.

After regaining his composure, Patrick left his apartment and headed over to Clancy's. It was close to three by the time he walked through the door, and there was only one other person there besides Tom, the bartender, who began laughing the moment he saw him. "How ya feelin'?" he hollered across the room.

"Good. Why?"

"Well, you were pretty lit up there last night."

"I'm feelin' fine now," Patrick shot back, grinning, as he took a seat at the bar. "How about you pouring me a double of that Johnny Walker Black up there."

"Scotch? I thought you were a brandy man."

"Well ya can't live off the same thing day in and day out, now can ya?"

"Isn't that the truth," Tom conceded, reaching for a glass. Patrick stayed at Clancy's till close to ten that night, and as he was leaving, he threw Tom a C-note.

"Hey, don't be foolish."

"I'm not. Show your wife a good time with it, okay? She deserves it bein' married to you."

"Nah, come on ... keep your money."

"Listen, I'm serious. I want you to have it."

"Are you sure?"

"Positive," Patrick answered as he turned and began walking away. "Now behave yourself, lad. I'll be seein' you around."

"Stubborn bastard!"

"You're right about that."

"All right, well—thank you."

Patrick was just about at the door when Tom called over to him.

"Yeah?"

"You take it easy, okay?"

"I always do, Tommy," he exclaimed, reaching for the knob. "Always do."

CHAPTER 42

▼

As Patrick flung open the door and staggered out onto the sidewalk, he was immediately revived by a blast of Arctic air, otherwise known as the Montreal Express. It had made its way down during the past couple of hours and had brought with it freezing, near-zero temperatures and a raw, lashing wind. Patrick paused for a moment, acclimating himself the best he could to the sudden change of environment, before zipping up his jacket and heading down the street.

"Let's do this!" he said aloud.

There was an old, stately-looking gentleman walking by at the time, and by the expression on his face, he must have thought he was about to be the victim of a mugging. Patrick just chuckled at the sight and continued walking to his building. Upon arrival, he boarded the elevator and got off at his floor, the seventh. He would take the stairs up the rest of the way. As Patrick approached his destiny he became invigorated.

No more! No feckin' more! he cried triumphantly to himself as he flung open the large steel door and stepped out onto the roof. The bitter, late-night chill once again stung him to the bone, but now, in a way, it felt good he thought. He hovered there for a moment, taking in a few deep breaths, before walking over to the edge of the roof and looking down. Man, was it a long way to the ground!

Patrick now began second-guessing himself. Was he actually about to take his own life? Could he? It would bring such great suffering to so many people, but was there any other choice? As he pondered these questions, his entire life began to replay in his mind. Faces of family members. Recollections of days long since past. Childhood memories. Then, as quickly as the images began, they ceased and

Patrick was again resolved. No, he wasn't about to go through another day of that hell, and that was that!

"Ya pussy! Just do it and get it over with!" He looked at the ground once again lying so far below. "Did it have to be this way, huh?" he screamed. "Did it?" When there was no response, he knew the time had come.

"I'm sorry," Patrick wept, and then stepped off. He fell a few feet, but then, suddenly, felt a hand tightly clench his shoulder. "Huh?" he gasped, looking up, and was stunned to see the face of old Miss Murphy staring down at him. He closed his eyes for a moment, disoriented, not fully comprehending what was now taking place. But when he reopened them, she was still there. "Let me go, old woman!" he demanded, finally breaking free from his shock.

"Give me your hand, Patrick."

"I said let me go!"

"No. Now give me your hand."

"It's my life! If I want to end it, then let me!"

"It's not your time to die."

"My time? What the hell are ya talkin' about, my time? You don't know anything about me or what I've been goin' through. Now let me go!"

"I can't do that, Patrick. I'm sorry, but that would mean breaking my vow."

"Vow? Vow to who?"

"To your mother."

"My mother's dead!"

"I know that, but when she was still alive she said a prayer for you. It was the night before you came to this country. She prayed that you'd be kept safe."

"How the hell do you know what my mother did?"

"Because I was there."

"What?" He glared at her. "You're mad! Do you hear me? You're mad!" Then suddenly, right before his eyes, a transformation took place, and he found himself looking up at his grandmother.

Patrick then fainted.

When he finally came to, he was lying on his back, staring up groggily at the star-filled heavens. Suddenly, he remembered what he had seen. He shot to his feet and began looking in every direction.

"I'm behind you," a voice said.

Patrick whipped around, and sure enough, there she stood: Veronica Meehan. His grandmother.

"Grandma?" he whimpered as he began walking towards her. "I must be dreaming."

"No, Patrick. It's not a dream."

"Grandma?" he blubbered once again. He was now standing directly in front of her. He reached out, not knowing whether his hand would find something tangible or pass right through, but it found resistance. She was no apparition! Patrick fell to his knees and began crying uncontrollably. "Oh God, Grandma!" he sobbed as he began grabbing blindly at her legs. "I've missed you so much!"

"Everything's gonna be all right," she whispered soothingly, rubbing the top of his head.

"I've missed you so much," he repeated.

"I know you have, Patrick. I've missed you, too."

"What's goin' on?" he exclaimed, struggling to his feet. He looked into her eyes for a moment—eyes which radiated such a profound serenity—then asked, "Are you an angel?"

"Something like that."

"Why are you here? Why now?"

"To help you."

"There's no help for me!"

"God must think there is or I wouldn't be here. And He's never wrong."

"God? Is there really a God?"

"Yes, Patrick, there is. You know that."

"I turned my back on Him a long time ago."

"It's all right. He's forgiven you."

"Why? I'm such a terrible person! I've torn apart so many lives and shattered so many dreams!"

"Look at me!" his grandmother implored. "You've been forgiven! And now it's time for you to go on with your life."

"How can I? Every day is pure misery! I can't feel! I've had no emotions since Ma died. Ma?" he blurted suddenly. "Is she? Have you?" He struggled for the right words.

"Yes, Patrick, I've seen her. Your mother's in Heaven. The doctors were right. She didn't feel any pain. I know, I was there with her when it happened."

"Why, though?"

"It was her time."

"But so young?"

"Yes, but she's at peace now. You can't ask why things happen, Patrick. They just do. There are reasons. To build faith, maybe. If there weren't any tests in life, then there'd be no need for a God."

"I condemned him. I told him I hated him. I failed my test!"

"Yes, in a way you have. But there'll be more opportunities, more tests. He's a forgiving God, and he knows what a good man you are."

"Maybe at one time, but not now. Not anymore."

"You still are, Patrick. Just open your heart and let Him in."

"I've tried so many times, Grandma, but it's never worked!"

"Then try again. Try now! Give me your hand and we'll ask for forgiveness together." They held hands and began to pray. Patrick soon fell deep into petition, as he asked pardon for all his past sins.

When he finally finished, he opened his eyes only to find himself all alone. His grandmother had vanished. Staring out onto the bustling, downtown skyline, Patrick suddenly noticed something: the irrepressible feeling of helplessness and despair that had engulfed him so cruelly for the past five years was gone. He began crying once again, for at that moment he knew that at last the nightmare had ended. Finally, it was done.

CHAPTER 43

▼

It was close to eleven the following Saturday morning when Patrick stepped from the Bus Eiress station. And even though it was pouring, he didn't seem to mind. He was back home and that was all that mattered. His heart was gay and nothing could diminish the joy he now felt as he walked along the streets of ol' Dublin.

He made his way over to Eden Quay and huddled under the awning of a small grocery store, where he awaited the 33-B, the bus that would carry him back home to Loughshinny. After close to half an hour's wait, it finally arrived.

Patrick, who by this time already had the exact change counted and ready, paid his fare and then maneuvered his way up the narrow stairway to the upper level of the double-decker where he found a seat at the very front. As he looked out through the fogged-up window, the bus began to pull away. *The Liffey never looked so charming*, he chuckled to himself. Forty-five minutes passed before he finally stood and pressed the little red stop button. As the bus began to slow, he made his way gingerly down to the lower level.

"Have yourself a good one," Patrick said to the driver, stepping out.

"Aye. And you, too, lad," the man returned pleasantly as he closed the door and drove off.

The rain had let up quite a bit during the ride, and by now it was just a soft drizzle that fell from the sky. After placing both his bags on the ground and stretching his back, Patrick glanced at his watch: twelve-thirty exactly. It was at this time that he looked up and began to survey his surroundings and in the process did a complete 360-degree turn. He smiled to himself when he realized, that in a way, that's how his life had been over the past five years—he had come full-circle. After pondering this insight for a short time, he grabbed his bags and headed off.

Before he knew it, there he was, standing in front of 20 St. Joseph's Avenue, his home. He lingered for a moment, grateful to be back, before heading up the stairs and ringing the bell. After what seemed forever, the door was unlocked.

It was Sinead. She was talking on the phone at the time, completely engrossed in conversation, but when she looked up and finally realized who it was, it slipped from her hand and fell crashing to the floor. "Oh, my God! Paddy!" she screamed.

"Hello, Sinead."

"Oh, my God!" she cried once more as she reached down blindly and picked it up. "I'll have to call ya back, Linda! My brother Patrick's home!"

"Is he? All right, well, tell him I said …"

"I will!" she blurted, hanging up. The two siblings warmly embraced. It had been well over two years since they had seen each other last.

"Step back, woman, and let me take a good look at ya," Patrick said. "It's been a long time."

"I can't believe you're here. I was jus' thinkin' about you this mornin'."

"My God, you're beautiful." Gone was the runny-nosed, freckle-faced child he long remembered, and in her place stood an alluring, elegant 16-year old with porcelain-white skin and blazing-red hair falling halfway down her back. Yes, a fair Colleen, indeed.

"Stop staring, will ya! You're embarrassing me," she said, blushing.

"I'm serious, Sinead. You've turned into a fine-looking woman."

"Well, thanks, but …" she began, but quickly changed the subject. "It's good to see ya, Patrick. Everybody's gonna be so happy."

"And how is everyone?"

"Everyone's grand."

"Good," he nodded contently and then paused. "Dad and Paul. Are they here?"

"No, but they should be anytime now. Daddy went to pick up Paul at Grania's."

"Grania? He's still seein' that one?"

"Aye! And they're pretty serious, too! Talkin' about possibly even getting married."

"Really?"

"Yes, really! But enough about Paul already. Come on in. I'll make us some tea."

Patrick followed her into the kitchen and took a seat at the table as she began filling the pot with water. "And what about you?" he questioned momentarily. "Is there a special someone in your life?"

Sinead turned and flashed him a big grin. "And what business is it of yours if there is?"

"Well, I'm your big brother. I have to look out for ya, protect ya. Let the lad know he better behave himself around ya."

"And what if I don't want him to behave himself?" she giggled.

"Hey, hey, watch it now!"

"I'm only slaggin'! But if ya have to be so nosy, then the answer to your question's 'no.' There's no one right now, but even if there was, you'd be able to protect me real well all the way from Boston."

"Who said anything about Boston?"

"Well that's where ya live, silly!"

"It's where I used to live."

"Whadya talkin' about?"

Patrick smiled. "I'm back home, Sinead. For good."

"Are you serious?" she asked, not knowing whether to believe him or not.

"Aye, it's true. I've been away too long, already. I should've come home a long time ago."

"Ah, Jesus, Paddy! That's wonderful!" she cried as she ran over and hugged him once more. Just then, a key was heard entering the front door's lock. Patrick motioned for his sister to keep quiet and ducked into the living room. Soon, in strolled their father and Paul.

"Ah, just what I like to see. A woman slavin' over a hot stove," Paul quipped as he sat down at the table and reached for the morning's edition of the *Times*. Sinead wasted no time in showing her disapproval by a quick flick of the tongue.

"Now come on, please! Don't you two start! I've got a goddamn splitting headache!" Brian barked uncharacteristically and then fell silent. After a short duration, he looked over his shoulder, first at the tea cups (incorrectly assuming that they were for Paul and himself), and then at his daughter, and said, "That was nice of you, Sinead."

"Oh, don't worry about it!" she answered quickly, grinning away. The two men just stared at her for a moment and then back at each other.

"What?" Brian finally asked.

Upon hearing this, and knowing full well that Sinead was about to burst, Patrick walked in and surprised the hell out of both of them. A festive homecoming ensued.

"Here, sit down, Pat," Brian cried suddenly, pulling out a chair. "And you, too, Sinead. Come sit with your brothers. I'll make the tea." With everyone comfortably situated, he hurried over to the cupboard and made up two more cups. While they were steeping, he rejoined the celebration. A few minutes of blissful laughter was shared among them before he once again sprang to his feet and asked Sinead to come and help him.

"Yeah, sure," she replied, nodding, as she got up and followed him over to the stove. She watched him amusingly for a moment before saying, "Do me a favor?"

"What?"

"Relax, will ya! You're startin' to drive me crazy runnin' around like a chicken with your head cut off!"

"I'm sorry, Sinead. I'm just happy to see Pat, that's all."

"I know, I know," she conceded as they began carrying over the cups. As the four of them sat there, each preparing his tea to his own particular liking, Brian looked at his watch. "So, what time did ya get in?" he asked.

"Flew in last night at about ten."

"Last night?" he muttered, seeming confused. "Why didn't ya call? I would've picked ya up. Where … where the hell'd ya sleep?"

"Ah, I didn't wanna bother ya. I just got a room at the airport hotel."

"Paddy, ya should've called. I was up. That was wasted time. Time we could've all shared together."

"It was only one night, Da. Don't worry about it."

"Only one night? One night's a long time when you're only here for what? A week? Two?"

"A little bit longer."

"Really? Longer than two? I didn't think you got your third until ya put in seven."

There was a brief silence. "I quit my job at AT&T, Da. I'm back for good."

"Are you serious?"

"Aye, of course, I'm serious! Why? Is it so hard to believe? She asked the very same thing," he chuckled, pointing to his sister. "Well, ya didn't expect me to stay over in the States forever, now did ya?"

"I did!" Brian chortled. "I really did!" He was very giddy by this point and acting almost childlike. He sighed contently. "You don't know how happy I am to hear you say that, Pat. Today's a wonderful day. We have to celebrate. Whadya say I call everyone up and we head over to the Yacht Club tonight? How's that sound?"

"Sounds good to me."

"Hey, wait a second," Paul interposed. "I just thought of something. Where ya gonna sleep?"

"I'm gonna sleep in me room. Remember what I told you way back when. Don't get too comfortable."

"No, no, no! I'm a grown man. I'm not gonna be sharin' a room with me brother."

Patrick looked away for a moment. "I guess I can always sleep on the couch."

Unable to keep a straight face any longer, Paul began laughing. "Relax! I'm only slaggin'! It would be my pleasure, brother."

"Okay, then, it's set," Brian exclaimed. "I'll give everyone a ring."

"Yeah, okay, Da. You do that," Patrick said, smiling, as he lifted himself up from out of his chair. "Besides, I've got something to do meself. I'll be back in a little while, though."

After placing his cup in the sink, Patrick walked to where his mother was buried. He said a few short prayers to himself, then spoke aloud: "Hi, Ma. How's it goin'? If you're listenin', I just want you to know that I miss you so very much and that I'm sorry for any pain I may have caused ya. And God knows ... there must have been pain."

He stopped to compose himself.

"I know I haven't done much good with my life over the past few years, but things are different now. But I guess you know that better than anyone, don't ya? Your prayers won't be in vain. I promise. I'll live a good life. A simple one. I'll make you proud." At that moment, a brilliant ray of sunshine broke through the clouds. He smiled at the sign.

"Well, I guess I better get goin'. We're headin' over to the Yacht tonight, and you know how that can be. I'll have a pint for you, though, all right. You know, just for ol' time's sake. And I promise, Ma ... I'll come back soon, I swear. I love you."

As Patrick walked from the graveyard, he felt refreshed. He went home and spoke with his family for a short time before heading up to his room for a nap. At exactly seven p.m., he was awakened by Sinead pounding on his door. "Come on, Paddy! Get your arse up! It's seven o'clock! They're probably already starting to arrive."

"Ugh," he moaned. "Just give me a few more minutes."

"We don't have a few more minutes! Time is of the essence! Now come on, get up!"

"All right, all right! Stop your yellin', will ya? I'm up!"

After lying there motionless for another minute or so, Patrick finally dragged himself out of bed and hopped in the shower, where he lingered for a short time, just letting the hot water rejuvenate his tired, jet-lagged body. By eight, everyone was dressed and ready to go. Brian locked the front door and they walked the short distance to the Yacht Club. Upon entering, however, they were surprised to find only two people in the entire place: Johnny Kelly, the proprietor, bartender, and Brian's childhood friend, and an older, drunken man they had never seen before.

"Hello, John!" Brian said affably as the four of them strolled up and took a seat.

"Well, look what the cat dragged in," the man exclaimed as he leaned over the rich mahogany bar and shook hands with the elder Quinn. "Long time, no see. How's it goin'?"

"Good, thanks." He then paused. "Say, um ... has any of the family been in tonight so far?"

"No, not yet. Why? Should they have been?"

"Yeah, I told everyone to meet us here by eight. Paddy's come home for good. We're supposed to celebrate."

"So you're back for good, eh?"

"Yep."

"Got your fill of the States?"

"Yeah, pretty much, I guess."

"Well, good. Welcome home, lad," he rejoined, smiling warmly, as he reached out his hand once again. Patrick grabbed hold and they exchanged a hearty shake.

"Christ, it's quiet tonight, isn't it?" Brian muttered shortly.

"It'll pick up," John asserted. "It always does."

"Still though, it's rather odd. The place is usually jam-packed by this time." And jam-packed it usually was. For Saturday night was the main night of the Irish week where everyone got out of the house and made merry. And most had usually begun their reveling by this time. And some, such as the old man to their left, who was currently talking to himself, had started much, much earlier. "Well, they said they'd be here and they will. They're probably jus' runnin' a little late, that's all."

"All of 'em?" Paul murmured.

"Yes, all of 'em! Trust me, they'll come! Everyone was ecstatic when they heard," Brian retorted. "Well, there's no rule that says we have to wait for them. Why don't ya pour us four pints of Guinness, John. How's that sound?"

"Make mine a Bud," Paul interjected.

"One always has to be different, huh?" John smirked as he reached for a glass.

"Isn't that the truth," Brian confirmed, shaking his head. "So, how much do we owe ya?" he asked when all of the drinks had been poured.

"They're on the house."

"No, now come on. How much?"

"I told ya! They're on the house! Let's just say they're a wee token to celebrate the occasion."

"All right, well … thanks. But don't expect us to accept anymore wee tokens."

"Don't expect me to offer!" John fired back, causing everyone to smile.

A minute or so passed as they restlessly waited for the heads on their drinks to settle, and when the moment of perfection at last arrived, Brian hoisted his glass in the air. "Cheers!" he proclaimed. Everyone followed suit, and they were just on the verge of touching, when in from the side rushed Moses and the rest of the clan.

The Yacht, in fact, had a back room, and that's where everyone had congregated, quietly awaiting just the right instant to pop out and surprise them. Their timing couldn't have been better! The four glasses shattered violently as they crashed into one another from the sudden burst of excitement.

"Welcome home, lad!" Moses whooped as he picked up his nephew and gave him a big bear hug. "It's good to have ya back!"

"Look what ya made me do," Patrick cried. "I'm soakin' wet!"

"And ya never looked better!"

"Hello, Patrick," a voice suddenly said. It was Catherine. She was just standing there, smiling tearfully. The two tenderly embraced. And before he knew it, Patrick was being bombarded with greetings and hugs from every aunt, uncle, cousin, and friend. Eventually, he even met the fair Grania Plunkett.

In the meantime, though, while this joyous reunion was taking place, Brian was doing the best he could to help John clean up the mess, and it was only after being told for the fourth time that his assistance wasn't necessary that he finally gave it up and joined in on the boisterous gathering. "Bastard!" he chuckled, walking up to his brother and giving him a soft tap on the arm. "And what? You were back there all that time?"

"Aye! We were! We had Shane on the lookout and when he spotted you guys comin' down the road we all hopped in back. 'Very odd. Rather quiet for a Saturday night, isn't it?'" he mimicked.

"Scoundrel."

"Yeah, in more ways than one. But never mind that now. Come on, let's go to the corner," Moses replied, throwing his arm around Brian's neck, and in catching Patrick's eye, motioned for him to follow, too.

He, of course, was referring to the large corner booth near the front door that could easily hold ten, if not more, people. Patrick followed them, and everyone else followed Patrick. Those that couldn't squeeze in either sat at a nearby table or stood.

Moses wasted no time. "So, tell us, Paddy. What ultimately swayed your decision to come home? It was me, wasn't it?" he propounded, earnest in tone. "You said to yourself, 'Me God! How I do miss that man!'"

Patrick didn't respond, but instead just sat there, an amused look on his face.

"That's the real reason, isn't it? Hey, don't be embarrassed to admit it. A lot of other people have felt the very same way," his uncle continued until Patrick just couldn't take it any longer.

"In your dreams, old man!"

"In me dreams, he says," Moses repeated drolly, at last cracking a smile. Then, coming closer, whispered, "No, Patrick. In my dreams ya never left. You know that, don't ya?"

"Yeah, I know."

"Good!" he nodded. "But seriously, what's the reason?"

"I don't know. It was just the right time."

"Well, I guess that's as good a reason as any."

About an hour or so had passed, during which time both the conversation and the Guinness flowed freely, when Patrick suddenly leaned over to his father. "Hey, Da. You wouldn't have any objections to me takin' off for a couple of days, would ya?" he asked.

"Why? Where ya plannin' on goin'?"

"Tipperary."

"Tipperary?" Moses reiterated, overhearing the discourse. "What the hell's in Tipperary?"

"I've jus' got some business there."

Brian was looking at Patrick, also bewildered, when it finally occurred to him what he was talking about. "Oh, right—Tipperary. No, no. I don't have any objections. Why, I think it sounds like a grand idea."

"Thanks, Da."

"What was that?" a voice suddenly shouted from across the room.

"Ah, feck off!" Moses grumbled. "Now look what you've done!"

At that moment, over to their table staggered Michael McGuire. "Did you say Tipperary?" he asked, slurring. He was really drunk and swayed to and fro as he awaited an answer.

Moses gritted his teeth. "Come on, lad! Say no!" he pleaded under his breath.

"Yeah, why?" Patrick inquired.

"No reason," the man rejoined. All was silent for a few moments until Mr. McGuire bellowed, "Come on gang, follow my lead! It's a long way to Tipperary, it's a long way to go!"

This was the exact thing Moses had feared would happen. Michael was a good man. Kind. Friendly. Gentle. However, he had a nickname that the villagers called him when he got like this, "The Singin' Fool." And it wouldn't have been so bad had he actually been able to carry a tune, but that was the thing—he couldn't!

"Come on, Michael. Please don't," Moses implored as nicely as he could. "We're just out havin' a nice, quiet night on the town."

"Nonsense!" Michael retorted, banging his fist on the table. "Come on, Moses! You parted the Red Sea, now be a partner to me!"

"I can't, Michael. I'm startin' to lose me voice," Moses whispered, trying his best to play it off.

"Are you now?" Catherine interjected, a mischievous grin playing over her lips. "Why, ya seemed just fine a few moments ago."

Moses shot her a wicked glare.

"See! It's just your imagination!" Michael confirmed with a nod. "Now come on, Moses Quinn. Stand and join me."

Catherine smirked. "Yeah, Moses, stand and join him."

"Yeah, go for it!" Paul seconded.

"I'll get you back, all of you. I promise," Moses scowled, getting to his feet.

"Okay, on three," Michael instructed as he steadied himself against the wall. "Here we go. One! Two! One! Two! Three! Four! It's a long way to Tipperary, it's a long way to go! It's a long way to Tipperary, to the sweetest girl I know!" The two men began, and it wasn't long before the entire place joined in.

As Patrick stood there, singing and swaying his glass of stout back and forth to the tempo of the song, he suddenly thought of his mother and smiled. And at that moment he knew that everything would be all right, and so too would he.

The End